Fighting at the Table

Cree lunged over the table, taking out the remains of the morning breakfast. "Damn you, Injun!" Cree screamed above the gunfire as Roth's shot drew a long spray of blood from his leg. Another shot sliced off the lobe of Cree's left ear. He screamed, seeing Roth advance on him, and swung the empty shotgun like a club. Roth ducked, grabbing Cree by the throat.

Meanwhile, up on the roof, Sullivan Hart crept forward, toward the sound of panting breath behind a tall stone chimney. A smear of blood marked the path. Hart looked down at it for only a second, then back up at the curl of steaming breath and the tip of the shotgun visible at the chimney's edge. "My God, Raymond," said Hart. "You're bleeding something awful."

"I know it, damn you!" Raymond wailed. "Stay back, you lousy lawdog!" The shotgun barrel poked farther out. Hart flattened against the tin roof as it exploded twice. A weather vane vanished from its pole and sprinkled bits of metal on the street below. "You ain't taking me back, Hart! Not alive!"

"Yes, I am, Raymond," Sullivan Hart said, keeping his voice calmer than he really felt. "You're going back to Fort Smith. The alive part is entirely up to you."

BLOOD MONEY

Ralph Cotton

SIGNET
Published by New American Library, a division of
Penguin Putnam Inc., 375 Hudson Street,
New York, New York 10014, U.S.A.
Penguin Books Ltd, 80 Strand,
London WC2R 0RL, England
Penguin Books Australia Ltd, Ringwood,
Victoria, Australia
Penguin Books Canada Ltd, 10 Alcorn Avenue,
Toronto, Ontario, Canada M4V 3B2
Penguin Books (N.Z.) Ltd, 182–190 Wairau Road,
Auckland 10, New Zealand

Penguin Books Ltd, Registered Offices:
Harmondsworth, Middlesex, England

First published by Signet, an imprint of New American Library,
a division of Penguin Putnam Inc.

First Printing, August 2002
10 9 8 7 6 5 4 3 2 1

Printed in the United States of America

For Mary Lynn . . . of course.

Prologue

On the cobblestone streets of Cleveland, Ohio, all heads turned in sheer wonder at the sight of the two tall, battered Stetson hats. The hats bobbed along above the upturned collars of two long, yellow rain slickers in the early morning mist. The onlookers stared as the two lawmen made their way across the street toward Landau's boardinghouse. The lawman on the right was Twojack Roth, a Cherokee; and the good folks of Cleveland were not accustomed to seeing Indians, except in still-life form, carved in wood and holding a handful of cigars. But Twojack Roth was used to being stared at anytime he strayed very far east of Fort Smith, Arkansas. So he took it all in stride. He kept his dark eyes fixed forward, his right hand held through the open-bottomed pocket of his slicker, keeping the shotgun out of sight and pressed against the length of his thigh. Slightly visible through the open front of his slicker was the tin marshal's badge on his broad chest. This, too, caused people to stare at him. But so be it. Better this than a handful of cigars, he thought.

The two lawmen stepped up onto the curb out front of the Landau Hostel and stopped. Twojack Roth turned to his partner, Sullivan Hart, and asked, "Front or rear?"

"The front," Hart replied, his hand sweeping one side of his rain slicker back, revealing the butt of the big Colt .45 swung low on his hip.

Sullivan Hart might as well have been a cowboy straight off the cover of *Harper's Weekly*. The people of Cleveland stared at him, too, but not until they'd satisfied themselves that the big Indian was real and not some apparition conjured up from out of the gray light of morning. At the sight of Hart's Colt, a gasp went up from the bystanders. Then the gasp turned into the sound of scuffling shoe leather as Twojack Roth swung the shotgun free from beneath his rain slicker and moved around the side of the boardinghouse.

"Somebody get the police!" a woman's frightened voice said among the bystanders. Hart, already knowing he'd have to get these people away from the boardinghouse, took the woman's voice as a good way to get the point across.

"Yes, ma'am, you do that," Hart said, turning toward the remaining faces as they moved farther away. "Tell them two deputy U.S. federal marshals from Judge Charles Isaac Parker's court are here making an arrest. Now everybody stay back. Thank you." As Hart spoke, he raised the Colt from its holster and stepped up the stone steps of the boardinghouse, taking one more quick glance around, hoping the bystanders got the message.

"Judge Parker? The hanging judge?" a voice murmured. Sullivan Hart almost smiled to himself. That ought to do it, he thought. He reached out, turned the doorknob, and slipped inside the foyer of the Landau, his Colt low to his side, but the barrel raised enough for quick action when it came. And it would come; he knew it. Raymond and Cree Doyle were in the Landau. They were wanted in Fort Smith for murder, rape, assault, jailbreak, blowing up a water tank, and many other assorted charges Hart hadn't bothered to read. The murder and rape charges were enough for Sullivan Hart. He and Roth had watched the boardinghouse for the past hour from their position in an alley across the street, back behind an open produce stand. They'd seen the Doyle bothers enter the front door of the Landau only moments ago, one of them wearing a striped cloth railroader's cap, the other carrying a small wooden crate under his arm.

Hart closed the door softly behind himself and crept along a wood-paneled wall to the winding stairwell. Out back, he knew Twojack Roth would be moving in as well. Houses of public use of this size always had a back stairs. Hart moved as quietly as possible up the stairs. At the slightest creak of wood beneath his boots, Hart hugged his footsteps close to the wall to lessen any further telltale sounds. At the top landing, he stopped and looked down the length of the hall. Seeing Roth step into the hall through a small door at the far end, Hart let out a tense breath. So far so good. Then in unison, the two of them converged silently on the third door, the door to the room where they had spotted a glimpse from the street of Cree Doyle's cloth railroader's cap through the window. Twojack Roth hugged his back to the wall beside the door, his shotgun at port arms across his chest. Sullivan Hart stepped back, raising his pistol. Roth braced himself, giving a ready nod. Then Hart raised his boot for a hard kick.

But inside the room, that faint creak of wood on the

stairs had been enough to tip off the Doyles, and as Sullivan Hart and Twojack Roth had moved quietly along the hallway, the two felons had thrown the feather mattress from the bed, jerked up a pair of double-barreled shotguns, a rifle, and a big Smith and Wesson pistol and made ready. Cree had thrown a bandolier of shotgun shells across his shoulder and slipped through a door to the room adjoining theirs. Raymond had stepped out onto a narrow stone ledge outside the window and tested a long metal rain pipe, readying himself for a climb upward to the roof.

When the door to the room burst open and the two lawmen sprang inside, seeing the feather mattress thrown over and a couple of spilled cartridges on the floor, they fanned their guns back and forth on the empty room, then immediately got the picture. Roth turned quickly back to the hall, Sullivan Hart to the open window.

But at the same second as Roth stuck his head out into the hall and saw the double-barrel come out of the door of the adjoining room, Hart heard the downward blast of Raymond Doyle's shotgun and saw the window ledge explode in a spray of splinters and glass. At the door, Roth ducked back just in time. Cree emptied both barrels toward him, the shots ripping the door trim away and leaving a long gash along the hallway wall.

At the sound of gunfire, a woman's scream rose up from the kitchen on the floor below. Roth moved quickly, knowing the double-barrel had spent itself. Hearing the sound of running boots in the hallway, he jumped forward, taking aim on Cree Doyle's back as Cree rounded the staircase, head down, his pistol thrown back and firing wildly. Roth fired twice, the first shot grazing Cree Doyle's shoulder, the second shattering the plaster wall as Cree hurried down the stairs. Now Roth was in pursuit.

At the window, Sullivan Hart had plunged his gunhand out and fired three shots upward. On the street below, the crowd yelled in fright and scurried back and forth like spooked cattle. Hart sprang out onto the ledge and, looking up, saw Raymond Doyle's leg as Raymond rolled over onto the tin roof. Hart grabbed the rain pipe and started to pull himself up as well, but his hand slipped on a smear of blood. He pulled back in time as he saw the shotgun barrel reach down over the edge of the roof. "You sonsabitch!" Raymond Doyle bellowed.

Hart dove through the open window, the blast of buckshot barely missing him. Screams rose from the street. "He's hit!" Hart shouted to himself, coming up to his feet and heading out of the room, searching for a way up to the roof. He caught a glimpse of Roth's yellow rain slicker as Roth disappeared down the stairs, pistol fire exploding upward from the floor below. Hart raced to the small rear door at the other end of the hallway, his eyes on the ceiling as if trying to see through it to the roof above where Raymond Doyle's boots pounded loudly across the tin sheeting. Damn it! Hart had to get up there.

From the large kitchen below, boarders spilled out through the doors and windows at the sound of gunfire ripping down plaster, breaking glass and seeming to cause the entire house to shake on its foundation. As the boarders exited, eggs and gravy sailed through the air behind them, and a small trembling lapdog leapt up onto the center of the wobbling table, its hackles up, its paws spread and dug in. It faced the oncoming surge of man and gunfire, yapping loudly, insistently, until Cree came spilling into the room, firing back down at Roth. The dog retreated quickly as Cree lunged over the table, taking out the remains of morning breakfast. Coffee flew. "Damn you, Injun!" Cree screamed above the gunfire as Roth's shot drew a long spray of blood from his leg. Another shot sliced off the lobe of Cree's left ear. He screamed, seeing Roth advance on him, and swung the empty shotgun like a club. Roth ducked, grabbing Cree by the throat, the lapdog hysterically yapping less than three feet away.

On the roof, Sullivan Hart crept toward the sound of panting breath behind a tall stone chimney. A smear of blood marked a path, and Hart looked down at it for only a second, then back up at the curl of steaming breath and the tip of the shotgun visible at the chimney's edge. "My God, Raymond," said Hart, "you're bleeding something awful."

"I know it, damn you!" Raymond wailed. "Stay back, you lousy lawdog!" The shotgun barrel poked farther out. Hart flattened to the tin roof as it exploded twice. A weather vane vanished from its pole and sprinkled bits of metal on the street below. "You ain't taking me back, Hart! Not alive!"

"Well, yes, I am, Raymond," Sullivan Hart said, keeping his voice more calm than he really felt. "You're going back to Fort Smith. The alive part is entirely up to you." He paused, then asked, "How bad are you hit? I didn't think I hit anything back there."

"You didn't," Raymond Doyle said in pain. "I'm hit bad, but it weren't you did it. I blew my damn toes off firing down at you."

"Oh, Jesus, Raymond." Hart winced. "You better do something quick. You could bleed out up here."

"I told you I ain't going back! Now let's get on with it. I can stand you back all day if I have to."

"Is that the way you want to go out, Raymond? In a strange town? Everybody back home hearing about it later, knowing you blew your own foot off?"

"Not my foot, damn it! Just my toes!"

"Yeah," said Hart, "but by the time the story gets told and retold, you know how that goes."

Raymond sobbed aloud. "Why'd you have to show up here, Hart? Me and Cree was doing good . . . got night jobs at the rail yard. We was going to go straight as ducks. Now look at us!"

"You weren't going straight, Raymond," said Hart. "I saw that crate you brought in a while ago. What's in it? Explosives I bet. You two were up to something, weren't you?"

A silent second passed. "Well, we never said railroading was a career. We was doing it to hold ourselves over. We might have blown up an express car later on, get us some traveling money."

"See?" Hart said. "That's why we had to come after you boys. You're both no good and you know it. Now give up and let's go home. You've run out of string."

"He'll hang us, Parker will," Raymond sobbed.

"Can you blame him, Raymond?" As Hart spoke, he looked around for some better cover, seeing none. "Are you surprised? Haven't you always figured you'd hang some day, the way you two have carried on? Parker will only be doing what you knew was going to be done sooner or later. Be a man about it." The tin roof beneath him had grown wet with sweat from his chest, even in the cool of morning. "Pitch that scattergun out and let's wrap this up. It'll be getting hot up here before long."

"Nope," said Raymond, above the sound of the reloaded shotgun clicking shut. "But you be sure and tell my ma how much I love her. Will you do that for me, Hart? She did the best she could with Cree and me. Will you tell her that her boys are both gone on to heaven?"

"Wait!" said Hart. "Cree's not dead! He gave himself up to Roth. I saw Roth leading him out."

"Well, he can tell Ma for me then," Raymond sobbed. "Either way, she's going to miss me, that poor precious woman. God love her. She'd have done anything not to have this happen."

"Uh . . . Raymond," Hart said, his voice going a bit lower. "I hate to tell you this . . . but it was your ma who told us where you boys were hiding."

"No, it weren't, Hart. I know better than that."

"Sorry, Raymond, but it's the truth. Three weeks back, you mailed her a letter? Sent seven dollars in it? How would I know that if she hadn't told us?"

Another silence passed. "Well, I'll be damned," Raymond said, his sobbing ceased, but his voice flat and dejected. "That scabby old witch jackpotted us? After me sending her money? Pa shoulda choked her to death years ago."

"Too bad, Raymond." Sullivan Hart managed to smile to himself, lifting the brim of his Stetson and wiping a hand across his moistening brow. "Should've sent more than seven dollars, I reckon."

"Well, to hell with her. You sure Cree's still alive, Hart?"

"I'd bet on it, Raymond." Hart fell silent now, letting Raymond talk himself into giving up.

A long moment passed, then Raymond's hand

reached out and dropped the shotgun to the tin roof. "There, it's done, Hart. Come help me out here."

"In a minute, Raymond. First throw out your pistol."

"What pistol?"

"Come on, Raymond."

"Oh, yeah, I forgot."

A pistol arced out and dropped on the roof a few inches in front of Hart. He scraped it up and shoved it down into his waistband. From less than a block away, a police whistle rose up from the street. The sound of horse's hooves clacked loudly above the sound of a paddy wagon bouncing along the cobblestones. Hart let out a breath and stood up slowly. "Step out backwards to me, Raymond," he said. "Keep both hands good and high." As Raymond moved closer, Hart asked him, "What's in the box, Raymond, dynamite?"

"Yep," said Raymond, "real powerful government stuff."

"Government stuff? Where'd you get it?" Hart asked.

"Off of a fellow by the name of Burdine, over in Indian Territory. He never said where he got it . . . not that I asked."

"You're lucky we caught you," said Hart. "You'd have blown your fool head off."

On the street, Twojack Roth stepped down off the curbing, carrying Cree Doyle under his arm. As the police wagon careened to a halt, three uniformed officers jumped down from its running boards. Roth dropped Cree to his feet and steadied him in place with one hand, while his free hand held his yellow rain slicker open, revealing his badge. "Easy, officers, we're lawmen," Roth said.

The officers stopped short three feet back, none of them seeming to know what to do. They looked at one another, then turned for advice to a tall police captain as he stepped down from beside the wagon driver. "Make some room," the captain growled, shoving his way forward as bystanders began to bunch up close to the officers. Before Roth could reply, Sullivan Hart came walking around the side of the boardinghouse, Raymond Doyle's arm looped across his shoulder. Raymond limped along, leaving a dark smear of blood with each step.

"I have a warrant for these men's arrest, Captain," Hart said, a folded document extending forward from his left hand. "We're U.S. Federal Marshals, here to take them back to stand trial for murder."

"Take them back—?" The captain looked confused, caught off-guard by the sight of Hart and Roth. "Back where?"

"To Judge Parker's court in Fort Smith, Captain . . . ?" Hart let his words trail.

"Oh. I'm Dawsey," said the captain. "Captain Leonard Dawsey." Captain Dawsey gave a nod to the officers, letting them know to lower their pistols and billy bats. He turned back to Hart. "Did you say Judge Parker's court? The hanging judge?" As he spoke, he took the offered document from Hart's hand, opened it and read it silently.

"Yes, the hanging judge," Hart said. He leaned Raymond Doyle against the side of the police wagon, took out a pair of handcuffs and cuffed Raymond's hands behind his back.

"Don't forget about my foot," Raymond said.

"I won't, Raymond. We'll get you some medical treatment here in a minute," Hart replied. He turned back to Captain Dawsey. "As you can see, Captain, everything's in order. I'd like to get this man treated. . . . That one, too," he added, nodding toward the long string of blood hanging from Cree's clipped earlobe. "It's been a rough morning. If you'll have your men go inside, they'll find a crate of explosives—dynamite. They best be careful handling it."

"Dynamite . . ." Captain Dawsey just stared at him, not sure what to say next.

A woman in a long white apron pushed her way through the crowd, her hair disheveled, a wild look in her eyes. "Captain, arrest these men! I want them jailed at once!"

"Hold on, Miss Kitty." Captain Dawsey caught her by the shoulder to keep her from pouncing on Sullivan Hart. "These men are evidently lawmen—"

"Look at my house!" she screamed, cutting the captain off. "It's destroyed! Who's going to pay for this!"

"Begging your pardon, ma'am," Hart offered. "We'll see to it that the federal court, Judge Parker's division, pays for any damage and inconvenience we've cause you. We're awfully sorry, ma'am."

"Sorry? You're *sorry*?" Kitty Landau seemed on the verge of cackling hysterically.

"Like I said, ma'am, just figure up the damage and mail the bill to Judge Charles Isaac Parker in Fort Smith. We'll see to it you get taken care of," said Hart. "You have my word on it."

"Your word?" Kitty Landau screeched.

"I'm bleeding worse," Raymond Doyle moaned.

"Come on, Raymond, we'll get you to the hospital," Hart said. He turned to the police wagon, opened the door and helped Raymond inside. Captain Dawsey stood staring as if in disbelief, the officers milling in uncertainty. As Roth moved past Dawsey with Cree Doyle in tow, he swept the arrest warrant from the captain's hand and shoved it down inside his rain slicker. Dawsey stood with his fingers perched as if the warrant was still in his hand.

"What do you say, Captain?" Hart asked, stepping inside the police wagon behind Roth and Cree Doyle. "Can we get these boys patched up? There's a train headed west this afternoon. I need to be on it. Got to be back in Fort Smith for a hanging—the man killed my father and cut his ears off. I've got to be there."

Dawsey gave Hart a dubious glance. "He— he cut his ears off?"

"Yep," said Hart. "You can see why I wouldn't want to miss seeing him hang, I'm sure."

"Uh . . . yeah," Captain Dawsey murmured. Then as if snapping out of a trance, he nodded at the wagon driver, and stepped up onto the running board. "Well," he shouted up at the wagon driver, "you heard the marshal, let's get moving!"

"Captain," Miss Landau shouted, "can they do this?"

Captain Dawsey looked down at her, holding on to his hat as the wagon jolted forward. "Apparently so, Miss Kitty. They just did."

Part 1

Chapter 1

Fort Smith, Arkansas:

Judge Charles Isaac Parker looked up from the document he held between his hands and asked Deputy Dan'l Slater sitting across the desk from him, "Any word yet from that new man? His name escapes me."

"Jake Coak, Your Honor," Slater replied. "No, we've not heard a word since he left two weeks ago." Deputy Slater noted the troubled expression on Parker's face, and nodded at the document in the judge's hands. "Is something wrong, Your Honor? Bad news?"

"No," said Parker, trying to clear up his expression with a deep breath. Judge Parker folded the document absently and put it inside his coat. "Let me know the minute Coak gets back, Deputy. When you see him, tell him to sit tight until I send for him." Parker seemed to consider something for a second, then said, "Refresh my memory, Dan'l. Coak's the one with that cut-down contraption of a rifle, isn't he? Used to be a bounty hunter, among other things?"

"That's right, sir," Slater replied. "He made a good name for himself in a short time bounty hunting, till he got stabbed in the back over in Dodge."

"Yes, yes, I recall his reputation now," Parker said, a bit impatiently, Slater thought.

"Something's wrong, isn't there, Your Honor?" Slater asked again.

"No, nothing's wrong," the judge snapped. "I'm shorthanded here. There are only four deputies in town, and I've enough arrest warrants to reach from here to Texas, end to end. How is he working out, this bounty hunter, Coak?"

"So far, just fine, Your Honor. You had me send him out after Delbert Strom. Coak has taken down some pretty tough hombres, I understand."

"Oh?" Parker drummed his fingertips quietly on his desk. "Then, what exactly is taking him so long on Delbert?"

Deputy Slater shrugged, seeing that nothing he could say was going to settle the creases in the judge's brow. "Maybe the weather, Your Honor?"

"The weather indeed," Judge Parker huffed.

Deputy U.S. Marshal Jake Coak lay atop the mud-slick ridge, keeping a close eye on the cabin eighty feet below him. Beside Coak, his black dog, Buster, lay huddled in the pouring rain. Above them, lightning streaked down through the looming black sky, then vanished. Coak looked at the dog, then back behind himself to where he'd tied his big dapple-gray. The horse stood with its head lowered, long streams of water running down its silvery mane. Coak looked back down at the cabin. Three horses stood bunched together at the hitch rail, soaked and worn. Coak had seen no movement through the window of the cabin for the past hour. He hated to think that the three men inside were sound asleep, taking a little rainy day siesta while he lay up here in this deluge. But that's how it goes with law work, he reminded himself, wiping a wet glove down the front of his drenched riding duster.

Jake Coak knew what to expect, tracking men like Delbert Strom. The idea was to never be in a big hurry, especially in weather like this. He'd only been working for Judge Charles Isaac Parker for two months, but he'd learned a lot the past year and a half bounty hunting on his own. Before that, Jake had served in the army, taught school, hauled freight across Kansas, driven cattle, worked as a gunsmith's apprentice, clerked in a bank, worked for a dentist making false teeth, raised chickens for the navy and worked as a cooper in a barrel factory in Pennsylvania. All this before he'd turned twenty-three.

As he watched the cabin through the heavy rain, Coak tried to work out clearly in his mind how much he would make for taking in Delbert Strom. Delbert was the only man of the three with an outstanding warrant on him. The other two just happened to be riding with Delbert Strom when Coak picked up Delbert's trail. No matter what kind of problem those other two men caused him, Coak wouldn't make a cent for his trouble. Somehow that didn't seem fair.

For arresting Delbert Strom, Coak would make the standard two-dollar arrest fee, plus mileage, which was figured at six cents per mile. It seemed only fair to Coak that should a marshal have to shoot two or three of the wanted felon's friends while attempting to make an arrest, there should be some sort of compensation for it, say . . . a dollar per head? Well, something, he thought, running a hand across his forehead, beneath the dripping brim of his battered Stetson. A lot of things hadn't been made clear to him when he took this job. He wished he'd written a few things down. Fat lot of good that would have done him, he thought.

Let's see . . . He used his gloved fingertips to take a quick tally. He'd traveled eighty miles. At six cents a mile that came to . . . four dollars and sixty— no, four dollars and eighty cents? All right, four dollars and eighty cents plus two dollars for the arrest. Six dollars and eighty cents? That couldn't be right. Coak let out a breath, adding it up again as he scanned the clearing out front of the cabin. Yep, six-eighty. Thunder exploded overhead and rolled off into the distance.

The part he really couldn't understand about the pay was that if he had to kill a man to bring him to justice, he didn't make a thing, only the mileage. That made no sense at all to him. Of course, if that felon should happen to have an outstanding reward still issued somewhere, dead or alive, Judge Parker's court would see to it the arresting officer received it.

That helped some, Coak thought, wishing he'd given all of this a little more thought before taking the job. The fact was he'd been desperate for work, what with the doctor bills and expenses the knifing in Dodge City had cost him. But in the past two months marshaling for Parker—only having met the judge once for about five minutes the day he was sworn in—Coak had only earned a little over a hundred dollars. At this rate he figured he'd have to gather in every wanted man between Fort Smith and El Paso just to keep body and soul together. He ran a hand along the short barrel of his sawed-off rifle, wiping water from it. *Not nearly enough pay . . .*

The dog perked its ears and rose slightly when the cabin door suddenly swung open and the three men walked out to their horses. Coak immediately slid back from the edge of the cliff and listened to them laughing and cursing the weather as they stepped atop the horses and turned them south along the swollen creek bank. As soon as he saw that they were headed upward in his direction, Coak hurried back in a crouch to the dapple-gray, unhitched it and swung upward, nudging the horse forward before he'd completely seated himself. "Let's go, Cyrus," he whispered to the horse. "See if we can turn a profit on this deal before we drown."

In moments, Coak had taken position and sat waiting for them. At the high turn in the south trail where the land flattened above a rise of boulders, Delbert Strom, Lawrence Martin and Kenny Derns drew up sharply at the sight of the single rider sitting mid-trail atop the big dapple-gray. As the three horses backstepped and settled on the muddy path, Jake Coak called out to the men from less than twenty feet away, "Delbert Strom, I have a warrant for your arrest, for armed robbery and the assault of an Indian on a government reservation. Raise your hands and do not move!" As Jake Coak spoke to them, he began counting slowly to himself, *one thousand, two thousand, three thousand, four thousand . . .*

Before the three horses had even settled, Delbert Strom shouted in reply, "Assault on an Indian? If you mean that damned Modoc, he liked to took my damned ear off with a paring knife! Read me that damned warrant! What's it say?"

"What's the difference what it says, you're under arrest," Coak responded. Lightning twisted and curled. *Seven thousand, eight thousand . . .*

"But I was only defending myself, and that robbery was all a misunderstanding, you might call it."

The three men looked Jake Coak up and down in hasty appraisal. Coak was not an imposing figure, nor did his bearing summon up any immediate caution or respect. He was broad shouldered, but with a constant stoop. Out of habit, he always sat a bit low in his saddle, as he did now, his sawed-off rifle across his lap. Coak had an affliction in his left eye that made it seem to gaze off-center. Not much, just enough to give his wide face a flat expression. While his vision was by no means impaired, there was something about his staggered gaze that caused some people not to take him seriously right away—a serious mistake on their part, because Jake Coak was, in spite of his appearance, a very deadly young man.

"You'll have to tell it to the judge, Delbert Strom," Coak called out. "I'm taking you in." *Nine thousand, ten thousand . . .* "You two men, step your horses aside, and do not interfere. I'm a U.S. deputy marshal carrying out my official—"

Jake Coak's words cut short as the first shot from Lawrence Martin's pistol screamed past his shoulder. "Go to hell, lawdog!" Another shot whistled past Jake Coak, this one lifting his Stetson from atop his head. See? They weren't taking him seriously at all. Jake Coak jerked the sawed-off rifle up from across his lap, putting it into play, his actions surprisingly fast for a man of such modest demeanor. *One thousand, two thousand . . .* Something looked unreal, almost out of his control, the way Coak's hand whipped the rifle lever back and forth, round after round exploding from the short barrel.

Two rounds nailed Lawrence Martin in the chest,

sending him backward from his saddle. Another round caught Kenny Derns as Kenny tried to aim his Colt and fire. *Four thousand . . .* Then Coak's rifle fell silent as Derns twisted sidelong out of his saddle and fell to the ground, his pistol going off and grazing Delbert Strom's leg. *Five thousand . . .* Delbert's horse reared as Delbert let out a long scream, his hand going for the holstered pistol on his hip.

"Don't do it, Strom!" Coak shouted, the stub of the rifle braced low against his thigh in both hands, smoke curling upward into the falling rain. "I want you alive!"

But Delbert was too far into his move to stop it. His hand came up cocking the pistol. Coak's rifle bucked again behind the loud explosion. Delbert Strom went down, horse and all in a tangle of limbs, mud and saddle leather.

"Damn it, Strom," Coak said, nudging the dapple-gray forward, the rifle pointing back and forth at the three men on the ground, "I told you not to do it!" He slid from his wet saddle, stooped down beside Delbert Strom and cradled the man into his arms. "How bad is it? Talk to me, Delbert! Do you hear me?" He shook Strom, blood oozing from the deep wound in Delbert's chest.

"I— I'm done for," Strom gasped, rain washing streaks of mud from his face.

"No! No, you're not, Delbert!" Coak demanded. "Don't talk like that! You're going to be all right. Damn, why'd you have to make a move for that pistol? I didn't want to shoot you!"

Delbert swallowed hard, clenching Jake Coak's forearm. He struggled to speak and with much effort managed to say, "Judge Parker's . . . court?"

"Yeah, that's right," said Coak. "Now keep still. You're going to make it."

"You won't . . . get paid if'n I'm dead, will ya?" A trace of a tortured smile moved across his face.

"You'll live," said Coak.

Delbert's glazing eyes went to the sawed-off rifle in Coak's right hand, then up to Coak's face. "I—I heard of you. You're a damned . . . bounty hunter."

"No, I used to be. I'm riding for Parker now. Lay still, I'll get you some water."

"No time," said Delbert. He gripped Coak's arm harder, struggling for words. "Listen . . . to me."

Coak saw the intensity in the dying man's face and leaned in closer.

"I'm . . . one of them."

"One of them? Them what?" Coak asked, already giving up on the two-dollar arrest fee, wondering if there might be some reward on Delbert Strom somewhere.

"*Los— Los Pistoleros*," Delbert gasped. "I'm one." Again a weak smile flickered on his face. "Tell Simms . . . it ain't . . . over yet."

Seeing that Delbert Strom was talking out of his head, Coak dismissed his words. "Well, that's good. Now take it easy, Delbert—"

"No, it's true," Delbert said, tugging at Coak's sleeve for attention. "He . . . thinks it's over? It ain't over."

Coak pried the grasping fingers from his wet forearm as Delbert let out a faint breath and made no effort to draw it back in. "There goes my two dollars," Coak whispered, standing up, looking down at the dead hollow eyes. He studied Delbert's face for a moment, wondering what the man might have been talking about. He'd heard of what had happened a few months back, how a gang called *Los Pistoleros* had been riding rampant across the southwest, how one of the leaders had killed Marshal Coleman Hart and cut his ears off. But that gang had been busted up for good by ole Coleman Hart's son, Sullivan, and his partner, Twojack Roth. The gang leader, J. T. Tuck Priest, was now in Parker's jail awaiting hanging. So what was Delbert Strom talking about? *Tell Simms it ain't over?*

Jake Coak considered it, looking at the other two bodies, walking over to Kenny Derns and kicking the pistol away from Derns's hand, just in case. Before leaving Fort Smith, Coak had seen Deputy Marshal Charlie Simms outside the judge's office, then again later that night at the Red Bull Saloon. The way Coak had heard it, Quick Charlie Simms had played a big part in taking down the leader of *Los Pistoleros*. Delbert Strom had probably only been making mindless death rattles. But still, Coak figured he better mention it to Simms all the same.

"Get back, Buster," Coak said to the dog as Buster moved in close and sniffed one of the dead men's faces. Coak nudged him away with the side of his boot. He dreaded hauling three bodies all the way back to Fort Smith through the rain, just to see if there was any reward money floating around on them. No, sir, he reminded himself, this job didn't pay nearly enough. Not for this kind of work . . .

Chapter 2

The rain hampered Jake Coak and his three-horse string of dead bodies for the next two days. On the third day, once the rain ceased, the land grew sweltering and steamy until by nightfall the sun had baked any remains of moisture from the air. The next day by noon, the ground beneath the dapple-gray's hooves had turned deeply cracked and as hard as iron. Behind the dapple-gray, the bodies began to swell and grow rancid. Coming down a shallow cut-bank the dapple-gray threw a shoe, forcing Coak to walk seven miles before leading his grisly procession into an army encampment, still a full day's ride from Fort Smith.

With his bandanna masking his face to keep out the dust and the smell of death, Coak met two guards at the perimeter of the encampment and followed them in as Buster traipsed off on his own in search of jackrabbit or whatever other creatures might be sifted out of the brushy flatlands.

In the hottest part of the day, an Irish corporal stoked up his smithing hearth and soon hammered out a new shoe for the horse, while Jake Coak sat in the shade of an open-front personnel tent and sipped water from a tin cup. A young captain by the name of

Vertrees sat across from him on a folding army chair and asked him about the sour-smelling bodies on the three horses Coak had tied to a thin cottonwood tree. "The one I was after is a no-account by the name of Delbert Strom," Coak told him. "The other two decided to take a stand with him."

"Then good riddance to them," Captain Vertrees replied. "Our job out here would be twice as easy if we could get rid of the outlaw element."

"I'll do the best I can." Coak smiled. "I was lucky to find you still here, Captain. Saw your encampment here the last time I rode through, but I figured you'd be pulled out by now."

"We did pull out, Marshal," Captain Vertrees said. "I was all set to go on leave. Then that blasted Apache, Victorio, crossed back over the border. This time he's come farther east than anybody expected. He usually stays along the Texas border. The Mexican *Federales* must've pressed him hard lately. He's down to a dozen warriors, but still kicking mean, traveling with no women or children. You were fortunate not to run into him."

"Yep, I reckon I was," said Coak. "I saw no sign of Apache; wouldn't have anyway with the rain."

"I doubt there's any chance of you running into him now, this close to Fort Smith." Vertrees drew on his briar pipe. "But watch your step out there all the same."

"I always watch my step out there," said Coak. "Thanks for the warning though. I can't figure ole Vic coming this far in. It must be his last stand."

"I wouldn't count on that," said the captain, wiping a tired hand across a sheen of sweat on his forehead. "He's got more twists and turns than a rattlesnake."

As the corporal shoed the dapple-gray, two men eased in beneath the tarpaulin overhang. One of them ran his palm along the dapple's rump, and the other looked across the twenty yards' distance to where Vertrees and Coak sat sipping water. "Yep, Henry," said one man to the other, "that's the son of a bitch all right. I'd recognize that sawed-off rifle from a mile away."

"What are you two buzzards doing in here, Davis?" the corporal asked, returning from his dipping trough, holding the new horseshoe with a long pair of steel tongs. "This is for military personnel only."

"Take it easy, Corporal," said Davis Nally, a dark grin spreading across his pockmarked face. "Me and my partner, Henry, like to keep an eye on whoever's coming and going. You never know what you'll run into out here."

"Yeah? Well, for my money the captain should never have let you two border rats into camp. Now get out of here, before I wear you out with a stove iron."

"All right, damn it!" Davis Nally backed away, a hand raised slightly in submission, his partner, Henry, following him. "There's no need to get huffy about it. Let's go, Henry."

Outside the shade of the canvas overhang, Davis Nally grabbed Henry's arm and pulled him behind the cover of an empty supply wagon. He nodded toward Jake Coak and Captain Vertrees, saying in a lowered voice, "That bounty hunter don't know it yet, but he's about to pay me an overdue bill for my uncle Cletis."

"He's the one you told me about? The one what kilt your uncle?" Henry Fletcher asked, craning his neck for a better look at Jake Coak. "He don't look like much to me."

"Oh, but yes, indeed, he is," said Nally. "He's all sand and gristle, but not for much longer. We're going out on the flats to pick up his trail when he finishes up here. Tonight we'll just pay Mister Jake Coak a little visit."

"How do you know he'll be alone?" Henry asked.

"Do you see anybody with him?" Nally gave his partner a bemused look. "Damn it, Henry, he always travels alone. Used to keep a black cur guarding his flanks at all times. Reckon that cur went and got itself killed along the line. We're in luck, Henry." Davis Nally patted the pistol in his belt. "Just pay attention and follow my lead. Pretty soon we'll be the men that killed Jake Coak. I'll have his famous sawed-off rifle to prove it." Davis Nally slipped back along the wagon toward their horses, Henry Fletcher following in a low crouch.

When the dapple-gray was ready and Jake Coak stepped beneath the canvas overhang, pulling on his trail gloves, the corporal rolled down his sleeves, saying, "If you're riding toward the North Fork, watch your back. There's a couple of no-good derelicts named Nally and Fletcher headed out that way a half hour ago. They were eyeing you before they left."

"Much obliged, Corporal. I saw them. Didn't recognize either of them, though." Coak took up the reins to the dapple-gray and rubbed the horse's muzzle with his gloved hand. "Can I pay you something for the shoe?"

"Naw, compliments of the U.S. Army." The big corporal smiled behind a thick handlebar mustache. "But you can do us all a favor and shoot those two buzzards if they cross your trail. We know they're running whiskey, stealing horses and what-not. We just haven't caught them at it."

"We'll see how it goes." Jake Coak nodded. "I'm not about to have them trailing me all the way home." Walking the dapple-gray out from beneath the overhang, he swung up onto his saddle, pulled the bandanna up across his nose, and nudged the horse over to the bodies beneath the cottonwood tree. "Come on, Cyrus," he coaxed the horse under his breath, "I don't like it no more than you do."

In the shimmering afternoon heat, Coak rode out of the encampment and back across the flatlands to the trail leading east toward Fort Smith. A mile out, he stopped the dapple-gray long enough to look around for the Catahoula cur, not seeing so much as a paw print. Ordinarily he would have whistled the dog in, but in light of the corporal's warning, he decided it best to leave the black cur out there, knowing the dog would have a close eye on anything that moved along his path.

Coak spotted only a low skiff of dust on his way toward a low riverbank. It could have been a wind devil, but Coak knew better. That evening, still having seen no sign of Buster, Coak made his camp on the east riverbank, purposefully choosing a stand of willows that afforded thin cover on one side, yet thickened into an impenetrable tangle of whips and branches on the other. No one could slip through and be upon him from the rear without being heard. He hitched the three-horse string of bodies a few yards away, and kept the dapple-gray closer to himself, away from the terrible stench.

At dark, with a low fire licking at the bottom of his small coffeepot, Jake Coak intentionally took the sawed-off rifle from its holster and laid it a full arm's reach from himself, in clear view. Then he settled onto his haunches and sipped hot coffee, with his ear tuned to the slightest sounds around him. When the rustling of willow switches grew more distinct, he sorted the sound out in his mind, determining that this was not going to be an out-and-out ambush. Whatever these two men had in mind, they were going to want to talk about it first. He smiled a half-smile to himself, knowing that this would be their first mistake.

The question was, how did Coak want to play this? Let them get all the way in? Act surprised when he turned and saw them covering him? Yep, that would be it, he thought. He'd already given them the security of thinking his guard was down, leaving the rifle lying there that way, almost out of reach. Let them think they had him cold. Then he'd make his move.

Coak took another sip of his coffee, pretending hard not to hear the footsteps move closer until, at last, one of the men deliberately crushed a twig beneath his boot to get his attention. Jake feigned surprise, turning to the two shadowed faces at the edge of his firelight. He made the gesture of reaching toward the rifle, but then stopped when a voice said, "That wouldn't be a good idea, Pilgrim. Reach for that rifle and I'll cut your arm off at the elbow."

Coak froze, a startled look of surprise on his face, his hand still halfway toward the sawed-off rifle. "Who are you? What do you want?"

Davis Nally stood a foot closer than his partner, Henry, a long Colt hanging loosely in his hand, the barrel only slightly tipped in Coak's direction. "I'll ask the questions here," Nally said. He chuckled low and darkly in his chest. "Henry, it looks like we caught the famous bounty hunter with his mind on other matters."

"You must have me confused with someone else," Coak offered, looking back and forth between the two of them, already beginning to count slowly to himself. "I'm no bounty hunter. I'm a federal marshal with Judge Parker's court. If you men know what's good for you, you'll turn around and—"

"Shut your mouth," Davis Nally snapped, cutting him off. "I know who you are. You're Jake Coak, a bounty-hunting, blood-money sucking bastard."

"Jake Coak? Me?" Coak tried a weak nervous smile. *Three thousand, four thousand . . .* "I've heard of Coak, but—"

"Oh yeah, you're him all right. Don't deny it just because we got the drop on you," said Nally. He nodded at the sawed-off rifle. "I recognize the rifle. You always carry it. You carried it when you killed my uncle Cletis over near Sulfur. You rode a big dapple-gray, and you traveled with a black hound, had brindle legs and a patch of white down its chest." Davis Nally searched around in the darkness as he mentioned the dog. "That fleabag nearly chewed my kneecap off the day you gunned my poor uncle down."

Jake Coak took a deep breath, saying, "All right, I'm Coak. But I don't remember you, Mister."

"Of course, you don't," Nally said. "That damned cur got me before I reached town. He sprang out of nowhere and took me plumb out of my saddle."

"He was quite a dog, sure enough," Coak said. "I hated losing him."

"Oh?" Nally looked around again, searching the darkness. "Well, without him, I reckon you ain't all you was made up to be. Where is he?"

"He's dead," Coak replied. "Indians got him last fall up near Wind River."

"Good, I hope they et that cur for breakfast." Nally seemed satisfied and stopped looking around the campsite. "Now you and me got to settle something betwixt us, for once and for all."

"Go on and shoot him, Davis, quit talking," Henry Fletcher coaxed. "This place is giving me the jitters."

"Hush up, Henry, what's your hurry?" Davis Nally said over his shoulder without taking his eyes off Coak. "It ain't every day a man gets the drop on Jake Coak. I want to watch him sweat before he dies."

"I don't sweat easily." The expression in Jake Coak's eyes changed, whatever fear that might have been there vanishing like a wisp of clouds across a clear deep sky. *Nine thousand, ten thousand . . . one thousand, two thousand . . .* His tone of voice changed, too, turning hard, confident and unyielding. "Now listen good, Davis . . . you, too, Henry. I've been seeing you peckerwoods stir dust ever since I got back on the river trail. I'm on my job and got no time for you idiots fanning me." He raised a finger for emphasis. "Leave your horses where they stand and back away. I'll turn them loose come morning. It's the best deal you'll get here. I killed your uncle for his reward money. But I'll kill you for free in about five seconds." As he spoke, Coak made no reach for the rifle, but he sat the coffee cup down slowly, staring hard at Davis Nally.

Davis Nally looked stunned, but only for a second. A grin grew on his pockmarked face. "He's making a bluff, Henry. Can you see it? He knows we've got him. We caught him out here alone, no witnesses, his rifle out of reach."

"I don't know, Davis," Henry said, sounding shaken.

"Alone?" Coak said. "I lied about the dog." He raised his voice slightly and spoke to the darkness, saying, "Buster, tell these boys hello."

A low growl rose from the black shadows surrounding the campsite. Nally and Fletcher shot quick glances back and forth, trying to pinpoint the sound. "Damn it!" Nally raged, swinging his eyes back to Jake Coak, his pistol coming up, cocked, pointing. But it was too late. From inside Coak's leather vest, a short-barreled, double-action Colt thunderer had appeared as if from out of thin air. All Nally saw was the flash of white light as the first bullet slammed him back a step. Henry Fletcher's pistol never made it waist high. A streak of black shot forward from the shadows like a dark apparition, the Catahoula's jaws catching Fletcher's throat in a full hard grip as it took him backward and down. Coak fired another round into Davis Nally as the man staggered in place, a hand pressed to the gaping hole in his chest. Coak stood up as Nally fell to one knee, then toppled forward facedown in the dirt.

"Stupid peckerwoods," Jake Coak murmured to himself, "they always watch the rifle." Dusting the seat of his trousers, he holstered the pistol up high under his arm in his shoulder harness, walked over past the edge of circling firelight, settled the two spooked horses, and brought them in by their reins. As he looked the horses over, he took the pistol back out of its harness. He punched out the two spent rounds, took two fresh cartridges from his shirt pocket, and examined them both closely before shoving them in the cylinder. Then he snapped the pistol shut with a sidelong toss of his hand, holstered it again and looked down at the Catahoula, who stood shaking himself off beside Henry Fletcher's body.

"Good boy, Buster," Coak whispered, letting a hand drop onto the cur's head, scratching it.

He studied the face of Davis Nally for a second, then said to the dog, "Yeah, I remember him now. Mobeetie, Texas, cattle rustler, one hundred dollars' reward." He looked at the body of Henry Fletcher, then added, "He might even be worth a dollar or two."

He stooped down and took the Catahoula's flews in his hand and looked the dog closely in the eyes. "Buster, we might've just made some money out here after all."

Chapter 3

Coak had traveled even slower the rest of the way to town, leading what had now grown to a five-horse string. Flies swarmed and whined above the blanket-wrapped corpses in a dark spiraling circle, causing the residents of Fort Smith to look on in morbid fascination as Coak sat low, coaxing the tired dapple-gray along the dirt street toward the courthouse. "Guess what?" a small boy called up to him, trotting barefoot alongside Coak's horse, swatting flies. "When I grow up, I'm gonna be a marshal just like you!"

"You do and you might starve to death," Coak replied without looking down.

At the courthouse, Jake Coak signed over custody of the five bodies to Deputy Dan'l Slater, who in turn would submit them to the undertaker for a good face washing and photo plates. Once the photo plates were developed, Slater would compare their dead faces one at a time to wanted posters in a wooden file cabinet. Slater was the oldest of Parker's deputies, and had a keen eye for matching faces to wanted posters. Any reward Slater found on the dead men would be shared equally between himself and Coak—another part of the pay setup that didn't seem quite right to Coak. But what could he say? At least the reward on Davis Nally would be Coak's alone, him having already known about it and not needing Slater to look it up.

"The judge said for me to let him know the minute you got back here," Slater said, swatting flies from around himself, the two of them standing behind the undertaker's office while the undertaker's assistant rolled the bodies down from their saddles.

"What's he want?" Coak asked.

"Danged if I know. But you stay close by. Maybe he'll be sending you back out—give you a chance to make some money."

"I could use it," Coak said. "I'll be staying at the Sunnyside, if you need to find me."

Coak stabled the dapple-gray at the livery barn most frequented by Parker's lawmen and took a room at the Sunnyside, a lodging house only two squares from the courthouse. He fed the dog all the jerked beef left over from the journey; then, after a hot bath and a change of clothes to get rid of the smell of death surrounding him, Coak took an early beef dinner at a nearby restaurant. After eating, he stopped by the Red Bull Saloon for a couple of shots of rye and a cold beer.

Amid the din of the evening drinking crowd, Coak spotted Deputy U.S. Federal Marshal Quick Charlie Simms as Simms hobbled forward supporting himself on a walking cane, one foot heavily wrapped in a plaster cast. Simms seated himself at a poker table in the rear left corner. Coak, deciding this was as good a time as any to tell Simms what the dying outlaw had said about *Los Pistoleros*, made his way through the crowd and leaned down to Simms's side. "Excuse me, Marshal Simms, I need to talk to you for just a second."

"Why certainly, Marshal . . . ?" Simms cut him a sidelong glance as he fanned through his money.

"Jake Coak. I'm still new here," Coak said. "We met a couple of weeks back outside of Parker's courthouse. You might not remember it."

"Of course, I remember," Simms said, taking the stack of poker chips in exchange for cash he slid across the table. "Good to see you again, Marshal Croak. How's the job going?"

Croak . . . ? Jake Coak just looked at him. Simms wasn't listening. "I wanted to tell you about something that happened—"

"Sure thing, Marshal Croak." Simms smiled, cutting him off, "First chance we get, we'll sit down and get acquainted."

"It's not *Croak*, Simms, it's Coak."

"Oh, sorry," said Simms, concentrating on his stack of chips, his back to Coak.

Jake Coak stood there a second longer, watching Simms settle in for the game. Then, without another word, Coak went back to the bar, finished his drink, and left. Back in his room, Coak cleaned and inspected his rifle, thinking darkly about the way Simms had put him off. Finally he dismissed the incident, pulled back the covers on his featherbed, lay down and slept like a dead man until about four-thirty in the morning. That's when Deputy Slater pounded a gloved fist on the door, waking him.

Jake Coak answered the door by warily opening it a crack, one hand out of sight, his thumb across the hammer of the sawed-off rifle. Seeing Deputy Slater, Coak's first thought was of the five dead men he'd turned over to him. "Did you find something out,

Slater?" he asked, rubbing sleep from his eyes with his free hand.

"Find something this soon? Lord no. It'll be two or three days before we get the photo plates." Slater stepped into the darkened room, catching a glimpse of the sawed-off rifle, tossing a nervous glance around the shadowed corners for the dog. "Judge Parker wants to see you and Marshal Simms, pronto, in his office."

"Right now? What time is it?" Coak looked around at the black night outside his half-open window.

"It's early morning." Slater grinned. "I need you to do something for me. Judge Parker said for me to find Simms and tell him the same as I'm telling you. Problem is, if I find Simms at the Red Bull, playing poker, I'll have to tell the judge if he asks me."

"So?" Coak asked.

"The judge laid the law down to Simms just yesterday, either give up the gambling, or turn in his badge. I figure if you go find Simms, I don't have to say where he was. Get it?"

"I get it," said Coak. "Any idea what the judge wants?"

"No, but something's been eating at him for a while. I could tell the other day when he asked about you." Slater looked at the sawed-off rifle in Coak's hand. "That's it, ain't it?"

"Yep, this is it," Coak replied, turning to his trousers draped over a wooden chair.

"I've heard lots about it. I'd like to see you shoot it sometime, Coak." Slater grinned again.

"I don't like shooting it unless I have to," Coak said. "Bullets cost money."

"Aw, come on now. I heard you load your own ammunition," Slater pressed.

"Even if I did, powder and brass ain't free," said Coak, pulling on his trousers, the rifle still in his right hand. "I'll go get Simms and be there in a minute."

Slater nodded, stepping to the door. "I'll tell the judge you're on your way, the both of yas."

"You do that, Slater," Coak said, stifling a yawn.

The poker game was still going on when Coak and Buster walked in through the bat-wing doors of the Red Bull Saloon and took a spot at the corner of the bar. Lantern light glowed in a circling dome above the tired faces of Quick Charlie Simms and the other four players seated around the table. At another table closer to the front door, a drunken cowhand lay facedown in a puddle of spilled whiskey, an overturned bottle near his fingertips. Every other table in the place had been wiped clean, ladderback chairs upside down atop the tables, their stiff legs pointed to the ceiling.

Simms sat with his arms loosely cradled around a pile of poker chips and cash. Coak only shook his head with a tired smile, then turned away from the game as the bartender, Rudy Tuell, came up from a cot behind the bar, rubbing his red-rimmed eyes.

"If that coffee's hot, I'll take a cup," Jake Coak said, nodding at the blue porcelain pot sitting along the wall behind the bar.

"It's still hot enough," Rudy grunted, hooking a clean mug from a stack alongside the pot, "but I'll warn you, it's strong enough to float an anvil. Just the way Roundhouse Eddie says him and his boys like it."

Coak offered a thin, wry smile. "Well, if it's good enough for Roundhouse . . ." He let his words trail with a slight shrug, his right thumb hooked at rest atop the sawed-off rifle standing in the long holster on his hip.

Rudy sat the mug in front of Jake Coak and filled it, catching a glimpse of Buster as the dog slipped over close to Coak's boots and curled down to the floor. "I told you a while back, Mister Ackerman doesn't like that dog being in here. Says he's dangerous."

"He is dangerous," Coak responded, "but only if you cross him."

Rudy shook his head. "Still and all, Mister Ackerman is the owner here."

"But Ackerman's not here right now, Rudy, and my dog is." Coak sipped the coffee and, dismissing the matter, turned a glance toward the poker game. "I need to talk to Simms," he said.

Giving up on the dog, seeing Coak's attention turn to the game, Rudy said to Coak in a lowered voice, "Simms is gonna be hard to talk to right now, but you're welcome to try."

At the table, one of the four other players threw down a handful of cards in disgust, cursing aloud as Quick Charlie Simms spread out his cards and raked more chips and cash into the pile in front of him. Jake Coak had started to walk over to the table, but he stopped and remained at the bar, waiting to see what was about to happen.

"That one's Pete Lamburtis," Rudy offered near Coak's ear. "He's getting more surly every hand. That bunch showed up late last night and horned in on the game. I reckon you know the story on Lamburtis."

"Yeah, I know all about Pete Lamburtis. He's a big gun out of South Texas. Killed a few gunmen, served a couple of years for robbery. I carried a wanted poster on him for a while." Coak sipped his coffee, his gaze moving up and down Lamburtis, taking in the Colt shoved down in the man's waistband. "Simms doesn't mind whose money he takes, does he?" In a chair against the wall, six feet from the game Simms's fiancée, Kate McCorkle, sat slumbering, her chin lowered to her bosom. At the sound of Pete Lamburtis's cursing, she only stirred for a second, lifting her eyes to the game. Then she lowered her face again and adjusted herself back to sleep. On the floor at Kate's feet sat an empty wine bottle and a crushed-out cigar stub.

"Nope," said Rudy. A silence passed, then Rudy added, "If you ask me, Roundhouse Eddie and the other one is no better than Lamburtis. Roundhouse shot a man down once for stepping on his clean boots, the story goes."

Coak chuckled under his breath, unimpressed. "You have to admire a man's dedication to personal appearance, I reckon."

At the table, Quick Charlie Simms shuffled the cards and dealt them out in turn, taking his time, knowing that in the gray hours of morning, suspicion ran high among all-night losers. He'd been keeping an eye on Pete Lamburtis, noting how the man became more and more irritated with each losing hand. Simms knew Lamburtis should have called it a night hours ago. Lamburtis had been making stupid mistakes. But it wasn't up to Simms to tell Pete Lamburtis how to play poker. Simms was there for one thing and one thing only. He'd sat in with the intention of winning as much as he could. And so he had, with little effort. "It's your open," Simms said to his left, to Roundhouse Eddie Jenkins.

"By me," Roundhouse grunted in a tired voice.

Simms turned his gaze to the next man on Roundhouse's left, a swarthy, heavy-set man wearing a patch over one eye. "It's up to you, Macon."

"By me," said Big Joe Macon, turning his good eye to his left, to Pete Lamburtis, who sat directly across from Simms. Lamburtis seemed to have difficulty deciding whether to open or pass. Next to Lamburtis sat the old man, Wiley Sugar. Wiley was the only other real gambler in the game. From the look on Wiley's thin, mustached face, Simms could see the old gambler had no interest in this hand and was ready to go on to the next. Like himself, Wiley Sugar had won some serious money throughout the passing night. Also like himself, Simms could tell the old man was wanting out.

"It's up to you, Pete," Simms said, reminding Lamburtis.

"Not so fast, Simms," Pete Lamburtis growled. "You've kept this game running at your pace all night. What the hell's your big hurry?"

Simms ignored the gruffness of Lamburtis's manner, and cast a glance at Wiley Sugar—just a glance, seeing the old man stifle a yawn with the back of his hand.

"What's that about?" Pete Lamburtis asked Simms, a tight snap to his voice. "Why're you looking at him?"

Simms only stared at Lamburtis, knowing there was no answer that could possibly suit him.

"Yeah, you heard me, Simms," said Lamburtis, rising slowly from his chair. "I've been seeing how you two look at one another all night." He gestured a hand toward the stack of winnings in front of Wiley Sugar. "Think nobody's noticed that you two grifters are the only ones pulling in any pots all night?"

Roundhouse Eddie and Big Joe Macon turned their

eyes upward to Pete Lamburtis, then slowly to Simms. "He's got a point there, Quick Charlie," Roundhouse Eddie murmured, letting his cards fall lightly to the tabletop. "Just how long have you and this old buzzard known one another?"

Simms remained calm. This wasn't the first game he'd seen end on a sour note. Some men couldn't handle the holy game of poker, in spite of having played it their whole lives. This game had been high stakes and no holds barred from the very start. Tempers had a way of flaring and spilling over when men like these saw they'd been bested. They couldn't help it, Simms thought. They had no way of realizing that old Wiley Sugar and he had never met, had never been in a game together. There was no way to explain to the likes of Roundhouse Eddie, Joe Macon and Pete Lamburtis that they had no business sitting at the same table with him and Wiley Sugar. Simms wasn't about to try. Instead, Simms let out a resigned breath as he responded.

"Gentlemen, these are questions you should have asked before we started, if you had concerns." Simms laid the deck down between his hands and kept his palms flat on the table, his way of reminding the others that he was unarmed. "I think perhaps we've all played ourselves out. Let's fold it in. . . . Take it up another time. What do you say?" He looked at each man in turn coolly, unruffled by the way Pete Lamburtis towered above the table, the Colt at Lamburtis's waist appearing larger now than it had all night.

For a silent second, no one answered. Simms shrugged, raking his winnings closer in, picking up a stack of chips and sitting it to one side for the house. "Then, if you will all excuse me . . ."

"You ain't leaving, Simms," Pete Lamburtis said, his hand drifting to the Colt. "I ask a question, I always get an answer, one way or the other."

At the bar, Jake Coak set his coffee mug down without turning his eyes from the game table. At his feet, the dog sensed trouble and formed a low growl in its throat. "Easy, Buster," Coak whispered. A soft tap of Coak's bootheel settled the dog. Coak watched intently.

"I'm unarmed, sir," Simms said. "I never carry a weapon to a poker game, for obvious reasons." His palms went back to the tabletop and flattened in a show of peace.

Roundhouse Eddie spread a crafty smile. "Well now. I expect we could all clear this up by just taking back what we've lost, couldn't we, Quick Charlie? Sort of settle up with no hard feelings? You being unarmed and all." His eyes lifted again to Pete Lamburtis. "Wouldn't that satisfy you, Pete?" His smile widening, Roundhouse Eddie reached a hand over to Quick Charlie's winnings. But he stopped short at the sound of two pistols cocking.

"It wouldn't satisfy me," Kate McCorkle rasped. Her chair squeaked as she leaned forward, her dress up over her knees, her legs spread wide, causing old man Sugar to stifle a gasp. The eyes of Roundhouse, Macon and Lamburtis instinctively at first went to the pale smooth flesh of Kate's bare inner thighs. Only in the split second following did they realize that from beneath her upturned dress had come the pair of big pistols, cocked and ready, out at arm's length, covering them from a distance of six feet away. "Now get your fingers back from that money before I turn them into stubs!"

Simms cleared his throat quietly and said to Wiley Sugar without taking his eyes from the other three men, "You may want to take this opportunity to leave, Mister Sugar. Perhaps we'll meet again somewhere."

Calmly, yet hastily, Wiley Sugar rose up, raking his winnings into his flat-crowned Southern planter's hat. "Indeed, sir, another time," he murmured, moving back from the table. No one seemed to notice Wiley Sugar leave the saloon as the three men's eyes stayed fixed on Simms and McCorkle. As the doors batted back and forth in Sugar's wake, Simms eased his chair back a couple of inches as he spoke.

"Now, it truly is time to call it a night . . . if there are no further objections?" It was not a question at all. Simms stood up, lifted his hat from the empty chair next to him, raked his winnings into it and cradled it under his arm.

"I always figured you for a coward, Simms," said Pete Lamburtis, in a cutting but careful voice. "What kind of man lets a woman take up his fight?"

"Fight?" Simms stepped back a foot from the table, musing. "I didn't come here to fight, sir. I came to play poker, something you should have considered before sitting down with me." He looked around at Kate McCorkle. "Kate. Let the nice gentlemen leave now, if you will, please?"

Roundhouse Eddie and Joe Macon stood up slowly, making an effort to keep their hands away from their pistols. "I ain't believing this," Pete Lamburtis sneered, his eyes still on Kate McCorkle.

"Believe it, Pete," Simms said to him. "She really will empty those pistols into your belly. You ought to take my word for it."

"Simms, only a low snake would allow a woman to

do something like this," Lamburtis added, not ready to turn it loose.

"But she does it so well, don't you think?" Simms replied.

"Why you rotten—" Pete Lamburtis's hand started to tighten around his pistol butt.

"Let it go, Pete," Roundhouse Eddie demanded. "He's not lying. She'll burn a man in half once her bark's on. I've seen her do it."

"Ain't no damn woman gonna stand me down—"

"Pete, damn it!" said Big Joe Macon, cutting Lamburtis off. "She's got you jackpotted cold. We got business to take care of. There'll be another time for Quick Charlie." Macon shifted his stare to Simms. "I'll see to it."

Pete Lamburtis relented, grudgingly, biting his lip as he forced his hand upward and away from the Colt at his waist.

"Leave the chips . . . for my trouble," Kate McCorkle said, seeing Roundhouse Eddie look down at the remains of his stake on the table. "Quick Charlie would have won it all anyway."

Roundhouse bristled, but kept quiet.

Kate stepped forward and jerked her head toward the doors, long ringlets of her dark hair bouncing on her shoulders. "Now skin your ragged asses out of here or I'll start spraying you down on principle."

When the three men had disappeared through the doors and Simms rose up on his walking cane, he and Kate McCorkle walked over to the bar. Jake Coak stopped the slow counting in his mind, reached down and made no show of rehooking the safety strap around his sawed-off rifle. Coak looked at Kate McCorkle, then at Rudy, saying to him in a hushed voice just between the two of them, "And Ackerman thinks *my dog* is dangerous?"

"I heard that . . . Marshal Coak, isn't it?" Simms said, giving a trace of a smile.

"Yep, it's still Coak," Jake answered in a clipped tone.

"And I see you're still here, Marshal Coak." Simms ran his fingers back through a loose strand of hair, laying his hat atop the bar. Gold coins and poker chips jingled.

"No, I left last night and came back," Coak said. "Deputy Slater woke me up, said the judge wants to . . ." Coak's words trailed as he saw Kate McCorkle turn from sight, lift her dress above her knees and tuck the two pistols into hidden places he could only imagine. When she turned back, she saw Jake Coak blush and look away.

Simms chuckled. "Kate, dear, meet one of our new marshals. This is Jack Coak. Marshal Coak, met Kate McCorkle."

"It's *Jake,*" said Coak, correcting Simms. "Howdy, ma'am." Coak tipped his hat brim. Kate smiled, nodding demurely, smoothing down the bodice of her dress.

"Young Marshal Coak used to be a bounty hunter," Simms said, "and quite good at it I understand." Simms's eyes swept down to the sawed-off rifle on Coak's hip, then back to Coak's face. "Shot a lot of holes into some pretty bad *hombres*, eh, Marshal?"

Coak just stared at him.

Rudy sat a bottle of rye and a clean shot glass on the bar. "Thank you, Rudy." As Simms spoke, he pulled the cork, poured the glass full and raised it in a toast toward Kate McCorkle. "Here's to lovely women with six-shooters." Simms tossed back the rye and sat the empty glass down. He lifted the tin marshal's badge from his vest pocket, polished it on his coat sleeve and pinned it on his chest. "Now then, back on duty." He smiled. "Tell me, Marshal Coak, what brings you here at this time of morning?"

"Looking for you," Coak said flatly. "The judge sent Deputy Slater over to my room a half hour ago. Said, find Simms and get over to the chambers as quick as I can."

Simms looked taken aback. "And this was a half hour ago? Why didn't you say something sooner? We both know the judge can't be kept waiting."

"I started to say something, but then the trouble popped up. Figured you wouldn't want me butting in."

"Well, that was courteous of you. . . ." Simms folded the paper money, separated the coins from the chips, and handed the chips to Rudy, for the bartender to cash in.

"Here, I'll help Rudy count it," Kate said, stepping in closer to the bar. "You can meet me here later, and let me know what's going on."

"Good enough." Simms turned to Jake Coak. "Shall we get over there and see what the good judge has on his mind?"

"Lead the way, Simms," said Coak.

On the way to the courthouse, Jake Coak shook his head, saying to Simms, "Pete Lamburtis? Roundhouse Eddie Jenkins? That's some low company, Simms, if you don't mind me saying so."

"Yes, I know. But I wasn't playing them; I was playing Wiley Sugar. They just happen to come in the midst of it."

"So, did you beat him—Sugar, that is?" Coak asked.

Simms said a bit haughtily, "You don't *beat* someone like Wiley Sugar, Marshal Coak. You simply play him for the sheer challenge of it. Did I come out ahead? Yes, of course. Did I beat him in any way? That was not even an issue. I take it you don't play much poker?"

Coak felt the sting of Simms's words and manner toward him, but tried to let it pass. "Not that much," Coak said, "not enough to get me fired."

"Oh, I see you heard about that." Simms shot him a glance. "Parker didn't *fire* me, Coak," Simms said. "He simply gave me an ultimatum."

"Yep, and I see how serious you took it." Coak stared straight ahead.

"The truth is," Simms continued, limping along on his cane, "I have given up gambling. Last night was an exception. Wiley Sugar showing up. I couldn't let the opportunity pass me by." He smiled. "Besides, poker isn't something a man can quit all at once. It could take me years."

"What do you suppose the judge wants with us?" Coak asked, getting away from poker and back to business.

"I have no idea," Simms answered, glancing down, and seeing the dog trot along close to Coak's right boot heel. "But I'd say it's not good news, him sending Deputy Slater looking for us before daylight."

"Slater said the judge was asking about me while I was out in the territory. I've been working for Judge Charles Isaac Parker over two months now," Jake Coak added, "and so far it's never been good news when he sends for me."

"Yes, I know," said Simms. "I'm sure working for Judge Parker is a lot different than it was when you were bounty hunting on your own."

"Yep, it's different all right," Coak replied. "I could actually afford to feed my dog and horse, bounty hunting on my own. I'm lucky they ain't et each other, me working for Parker. How do you other marshals manage?"

"Live modest, Marshal Coak." Simms smiled. "It'll catch up to you sooner or later."

"I don't see how." Coak shook his head. "Six cents a mile, two dollars an arrest, no pay at all if you bring a man in dead. I swear, if there's money to be made here, I can't see it."

Simms looked him up and down as they walked. "You just got back to town yesterday evening, didn't you? You said something about wanting to talk to me last night?"

"Yeah, I wanted to talk to you, but you were too busy," said Coak. "I had to shoot an ole boy named Delbert Strom out in the territory. Before he died, he told me something that's been on my mind ever since. Told me he was a member of *Los Pistoleros*. Said to tell you that they ain't finished yet." He studied Simms's face in the gray light for a reaction. "What do you make of that?"

"Hmmm." Simms seemed to run it through his mind, then toss it away. "I wouldn't let it concern me if I were you, Coak. Men say lots of strange things before they die."

"I know it," said Coak. "I've seen my share of dying men."

"Of course, you have." Simms offered his smile

again. "Didn't I hear that you were a schoolteacher somewhere, or made false teeth or something?"

Jake Coak just stared at him.

They walked on in silence through the first break of gray morning light. At the white picket fence surrounding the courthouse, Simms stopped with his hand on the gate. Looking Coak up and down, he said, "I might as well warn you, Coak, the judge is hard to take this early in the morning. He can be a bit stiff on a new man."

"So?" Coak looked at him.

Simms nodded at the badge on Coak's chest. "So, you might want to shine your badge up some and dust your hat before we meet with the judge. Parker can get real picky if he's in a bad mood. You'll have to learn to waltz around him a little," Simms added, nodding toward the small private entrance off to the right of the main courthouse doors. "I like to see a new man get off on the right foot."

"That's big of you, Simms," Coak said wryly. "What about you? Have you learned to *waltz* your way around the judge?"

"Huh-uh, not me"—Simms smiled, catching the trace of sarcasm in Coak's voice—"Parker knows I'm not a dancing man."

"Then do me a favor from now on," said Coak, stopping in his tracks so abruptly that the sheer force of his action caused Simms to do the same. He looked up at the taller Simms.

"Oh? What's that?" Simms asked, noting the flat expression, the off-center gaze in Coak's dark somber eyes.

"Stop talking down to me every time you open your mouth. I don't tolerate offhanded remarks." He paused only for a second, letting Simms catch the full bit of his words. "I'm new at this job, but I'm trying to make a living here. Don't take me for a fool, and don't be telling me how to handle the judge." Coak hooked his gloved thumb atop the cut-off stock of his rifle. "You see, Simms . . . I don't dance either," he said.

Chapter 4

Outside the door of the judge's chambers, Deputy Dan'l Slater stood with his shotgun at port arms, as if walking guard. "What the tarnation took yas so long?" he asked Jake Coak in a guarded tone, seeing the two marshals step forward. The black shorthaired dog was close behind Coak, causing Slater to take a cautious step to one side.

"We needed a few minutes to get acquainted, Slater," said Simms. As he spoke to Slater, Simms reached a hand down to Buster's head, scratching the dog behind its ears. Coak looked surprised at Buster allowing a stranger's hand on him.

Slater almost gasped, then caught himself, looked at Simms and said, "Simms, I might as well tell you now, Sullivan Hart and Twojack Roth are in there with the judge. Don't go starting no trouble with them."

"Oh?" Simms looked surprised. "I thought Hart and Roth were up in Ohio, bringing back some prisoners?"

"They was," said Slater, "but they're back. If you ask me there's something big in the works. Judge Parker ain't been himself for the past three or four days."

"Then let's see what it is, shall we?" Simms smiled, stepped past Slater and knocked on the door to Parker's office.

Slater leaned in close to Jake Coak, keeping a wary eye on Quick Charlie Simms, saying, "Good luck, Marshal Coak."

Jake Coak only looked at Slater and nodded. Had there been time to answer, and had Jake Coak felt prone do to so before Deputy Slater turned and left him standing there alone behind Simms, Coak would have told Slater straight out that he didn't believe in luck, neither good or bad. Jake Coak only abided what he could connect to his five senses.

"Come in," said Judge Parker's voice on the other side of the door. Jake Coak ran the cuff of his shirt across his badge and followed Simms inside. Buster, the Catahoula, dropped down on his belly outside the judge's chambers as if taking up a guard position. Slater ventured a step closer to the dog, having seen the way Simms had patted him without losing a finger. But as Slater said in a lowered voice, "Good boy," Buster raised his flews in a deep growl, warning Slater.

"Marshals, join us, please," said Judge Parker, standing behind his desk. He gestured toward Sullivan Hart and Twojack Roth, who both stood to one side of the desk, their riding dusters still on and their battered Stetsons in their hands. "Everybody here knows one another, except for our new man, Marshal Coak."

Parker introduced Coak to them, Hart and Roth only nodding their acknowledgment, then turning back to the judge. In the grainy light of morning, Simms noted the drawn, serious expressions on the two deputies' faces. Slater had been right, Simms thought to himself. Something big was in the works.

Parker pointed toward two chairs in front of his desk. Simms and Coak looked at each other, then moved to the chairs and sat down, taking off their hats as they did so. They both looked around at Hart and Roth standing to the side, Simms eyeing the two deputies curiously.

"Marshal Coak," the judge said, "I hope Dan'l Slater didn't awaken you?" As the judge spoke, he gestured a hand toward a pot of fresh coffee sitting on a tray at the corner of his desk.

At four in the morning . . . ? "No, Your Honor, I was awake," Coak replied, noting that the question was not so much a polite apology as it was perhaps an indictment against anyone who wasn't already up and around long before the crack of dawn. Coak ignored the way Simms lifted a brow and smiled at him. Declining the coffee, Coak returned the judge's firm, level gaze. He crossed an ankle to his knee and dropped his hat on his boot toe, getting comfortable. "Deputy Slater had said you would be sending for me."

"Good," said Parker. "I admire a man who takes his work seriously." Coak felt a certain satisfaction, seeing the judge's words as an indictment against Simms as Parker shifted his gaze in Simms's direction. "I trust you were already up as well, Marshal Simms?"

Simms smiled. "You know me, Your Honor."

"Yes, indeed." Parker managed to keep something in check. Whatever was on Parker's mind, Simms decided it must be more important than any problem between the two of them. He studied the judge's eyes closely, settling down to business.

"All right, men, I'll come straight to the point," said

Parker. "Coak, you've only been with me a short while, but I'm certain you know all about the prisoner, J. T. Tuck Priest, whom I sentenced to hang six months ago?"

"Yes, I know about him," Jake Coak replied, "the one who killed Marshal Sullivan Hart's father? He was the leader of *Los Pistoleros,* him and a man back East named Mabrey." Coak passed a sidelong glance to Sullivan Hart and Twojack Roth, then looked back at the judge.

"That's correct," said Parker. "Do you know the whole story on *Los Pistoleros?* How large the gang was? How much trouble Sullivan Hart and Twojack Roth had tracking Tuck Priest down. How, as it turned out, they never caught Priest at all, but rather it was Marshal Simms here who brought him in?"

"I heard some of it, Your Honor," Jake Coak said, "but only heard bits and pieces of all that happened. Nobody has ever told me the whole of it." Coak looked back and forth between Parker and Simms. "I know that Tuck Priest is going to hang for murder in a couple of weeks. I reckon that's the most important thing."

"The marshals here can fill you in on any particulars later," Parker said, cutting Coak off. Coak noticed how Sullivan Hart and Twojack Roth shifted restlessly in place. He also noted how Judge Parker's face had seemed to tighten a bit at the mention of Priest's hanging. Coak settled into his chair, watching the judge's eyes move from him to Simms.

"Marshal Simms," said Parker, "I want to let you know, as I've let Marshals Hart and Roth know, that I've done everything within the power of my office to—"

"I'd like to hear it now, Your Honor, firsthand, from you," Coak cut in. Seeing the expressions on both Parker's and Simm's faces, Coak cleared his throat and added, "That is, if you would, please, Your Honor?"

Hart and Roth seemed to stiffen, turning their attention to Jake Coak. Simms looked Coak up and down as if having just seen something worth attending to. Coak was not to be put off, Simms noted to himself, taking more interest in the strange-looking young man. First Coak had called him down out front, demanding some level of respect. Now Coak had stopped the judge, demanding the same thing. Simms liked that. He watched as Coak and Parker faced one another, curious as to how Parker handled it.

An explosion was apparent behind Parker's eyes, Simms thought. Yet Parker seemed to pull it back, get it under control. After a short tense silence, the judge said to Jake Coak, "All right then, Marshal Coak, perhaps it is important that I bring you up to date on this case first." Parker slid a glance across Simms. Picking up a folded document from atop his desk, Parker tapped it against his palm, as if debating whether or not to pass it over to them. Finally, he only clenched the document and dropped it back on his desk in an air of resolve.

"Marshal Coak," Parker said, "*Los Pistoleros* was, and as it turns out *still is,* the largest criminal organization ever uncovered by any law-enforcement in this nation. At one time the gang had tentacles that reached as far as Washington." He paused for a second as if to let Jake Coak weigh the dark possibilities of such an organization. Then he continued, Jake Coak nodding him on. "Had it not been for Tuck Priest killing Sullivan Hart's father, Marshal Coleman Hart, we would have never heard of *Los Pistoleros*. But as events unfolded, we learned more and more about the gang. Deputies Sullivan Hart and Twojack Roth had a shootout with members of *Los Pistoleros* on the streets of Chicago,* if you can imagine such a thing."

"I heard about it," Coak remarked.

"Yes, I'm sure you have," Parker went on. "Although, I'm sure you had no idea that it was Quick Charlie Simms here who instigated that whole public spectacle."

Simms smiled, lifting his chin a bit.

Coak only glanced at Simms. "No, I didn't, Your Honor. But from what I've heard about Marshal Simms, it doesn't surprise me." He looked Simms up and down now. "No offense, Simms. But I heard you were a wanted man at the time, and that you escaped custody and put Hart and Roth on Priest's trail because Priest had framed you for a bank robbery."

"Yes, that's correct," said Parker, on Simms's behalf. "For all the efforts of my deputies, I have to admit, it was Simms who brought this case to a head. He lead my deputies to Tuck Priest. He turned Priest over to them. Then, when Tuck Priest escaped from my jail, it was Simms who caught up to him and brought him back." Parker paused again for a second, then added, "So no matter what else you hear about Quick Charlie Simms"—Parker's eyes swept across Hart and Roth—"take it from me, he knows how to get a job done. That's why I pinned a badge on him."

"Thank you, Your Honor," Simms said, more serious now, seeing that all this was pointing to something.

*See Book 1, *Hangman's Choice*.

"Now then, Coak," Parker said, "that is pretty much the whole of it. Any questions? If not, I'll continue with why I've called everybody here."

Jake Coak nodded, as if satisfied now that the judge and Simms weren't going to be talking above him, making his mind have to run along behind them to catch up. "I'm new, Your Honor. I felt I ought to hear it firsthand."

"And so you have," said Parker. He picked up the document and pitched it across the top of his desk. Simms leaned forward and took it, after seeing Jake Coak make no attempt to reach for it. "Read it and weep, Marshals." Parker's voice went flat. "It's a sad commentary on what our system of law has fallen to in this country."

"Yes, Your Honor." Simms's eyes darted down the document. Finishing with it, Simms slumped in his chair. Coak saw the expression on Simms's face harden. "Can they *do* this?" Simms's gaze passed from Roth to Hart, then back to Parker as he raised the document slightly as if questioning its content. Then he passed it to Jake Coak.

"They've done it," Sullivan Hart said, his voice low and raspy. Coak took the paper with reluctance, looking it over at arm's length. Simms noted the way Coak's eyes appeared lost as they scanned the words.

"Quite right," Parker said. "Indeed, they *have* done it, Marshal Simms." He nodded at the paper in Coak's hand. "That comes from the highest court in this nation. I must abide by it. Not only has Tuck Priest's hanging sentence been commuted, the jury's verdict against him has been reversed. At midnight last night, Mister J. T. 'Tuck' Priest departed from my jail, a free man." The words seemed to bring about a bitter taste in the judge's mouth. He swallowed tightly and ran a hand down his goatee. "He was accompanied by his attorney, R. Martin Swan," Parker added. "I wasn't there, but I was informed by the captain of my guards that Tuck Priest was laughing aloud."

"I bet he was," said Simms, shaking his head. Beside Simms, Coak passed the document back to him. Simms gave Coak a curious glance, took the folded paper, dropped it onto the desk and gave it a shove back to Parker. The judge stared at it for a second as Simms said to Sullivan Hart, "Sorry, Hart."

Sullivan Hart only nodded and looked away, his brow mantled by dark brooding.

"Fortunately for all concerned," said Parker, "Hart and Roth here were both up in Ohio, transporting a couple of prisoners back here to stand trial for rape and murder. I dare say, if Hart had been here and had knowledge of this, he would have killed Tuck Priest in the street. I couldn't have had that happen, of course."

"Certainly not, sir," said Simms, agreeing with the judge as he gave Hart another glance.

Listening quietly, Jake Coak wondered to himself what would have been so bad about that, Sullivan Hart killing Priest? After all, Priest *had* been convicted for murdering Hart's father. Justice came from more than one direction, Coak thought. Why didn't Sullivan Hart shoot Tuck Priest down in the street in the first place? he asked himself. Get it over with. Save some rope.

"And this all has something to do with why you sent for us, Your Honor?" Coak asked, wanting to get on with it.

"Yes," Parker responded, looking at both of them. "I want the four of you involved in this situation. Tuck

Priest and his men will be out to kill you, Simms. You know that as well as I do. I want you out front on this." He looked at Hart, Roth and Jake Coak. "And I want you three to do whatever it takes to bring this man and his gang down."

"Of course, Your Honor, consider it done," Simms said.

Judge Parker nodded at the cast on Simms's foot, saying, "I realize you are at a disadvantage right now, but you'll have to make do somehow—"

"Excuse me there, sir," said Jake Coak, leaning forward in his chair. "What exactly is this Priest being charged with?"

Parker and Simms stared at him in silence. Coak felt pressed, adding, "I mean, we get paid for arresting a man. What do we arrest him for? Who gets the fee for doing it?"

"As I stated earlier, Marshal Coak," Parker said, "these marshals will fill you in on any particulars—"

"Whoa, Your Honor," Coak said, interrupting him. "Not to cut you short, sir, but I always work alone. If you recall, I told you so when you hired me. You agreed to it."

"Yes, so I did, Marshal Coak," said Parker. "But what I said specifically was that we would try to keep things that way if the situation permitted. This incident with Priest has changed things, for the time being at least. I need your help on this."

Coak stood slightly and shook his head. "With all due respect to everybody here, Judge Parker, why me? There's four other marshals in town right now. Any one of them would be suitable for this job."

Simms managed to stifle a thin smile, enjoying this

exchange. Judge Charles Isaac Parker was not accustomed to having his decisions questioned.

Yet the judge drew in a breath of controlled patience and asked, "How old are you, Marshal Coak, thirty-three, thirty-four?"

"Thirty-four, Your Honor, not that I see what my age has to do with—"

"And you were a bounty hunter for how long before taking on a badge?" Judge Parker asked.

"A couple of years, sir, give or take," Coak responded.

"Before that you were a schoolteacher, I believe? In Nashville?" Parker's gaze turned more piercing as he spoke.

"Yes, Nashville," Coak said. "I left teaching and went north, to serve in the army."

"For the Union," Parker cut in. "In spite of your Southern upbringing and your family's wishes, you chose to fight for the Union."

"It was a matter of personal belief at the time," Coak said. "If I had it to do over, I can't say how it would go."

"Be that as it may, Marshal, you followed your own heart and mind."

"Yes, but I don't see what that has to do with what we're talking about here," Coak said, passing a quick glance at the others, then back to Parker.

Parker went on. "You saw things in the war that for some reason kept you from going back into that classroom. You decided instead to take up a gun and make your living hunting down wanted men for bounty money. Isn't that about the size of it?"

"I made a living at it," Coak said. "I'm not ashamed of what I did." Feeling a bit crowded somehow, he adjusted his position in his chair, his hand resting on the cut-off rifle stock in the long holster on his hip. "They were all killers, felons. Somebody had to bring them in. The regular lawmen weren't all that successful, or they wouldn't have been paying rewards."

Parker raised a finger for emphasis. "Nevertheless, you have shown an aptitude for this kind of work, isn't that correct?"

"Hold it, Your Honor," said Coak, seeing that Parker was painting him into a corner. "There's no point in us going in a circle about this. I work alone, always have, always will. There's no room for discussion on it. I'm not the man for this job. Besides, Simms and I haven't exactly hit it off, and Hart and Roth here don't know me from a load of coal."

Simms looked away in detachment. Hart and Roth shot one another a dubious glance.

Parker sat back with an air of resolve, and at length said, "Very well, I understand. I'm putting together a four-man posse. You were my first pick for this job. But if you don't think you can handle working with these men, I suppose there's little else to be said on the matter."

"Thank you, Judge Parker," Jake Coak said, rising from his chair. "Will that be all?" He looked at the others, seeing the gleam in Simms's eyes. Simms seemed to be getting a kick out of all this.

"Yes, that's all." Judge Parker picked up his pen and lowered his head back over his paperwork. "You can leave your badge with Dan'l Slater on your way out."

Parker's words were so cordial and resolved that Jake Coak didn't catch his meaning until he turned and almost reached for the doorknob. But then he stopped and turned back toward Parker's desk. "Excuse me, Your Honor?" he asked, as if to make sure he'd heard him correctly.

"That's right, you heard me," said Parker. "I can't have a man working for me who won't follow my orders." He glanced up with a short nod, then concentrated on his paperwork, murmuring aloud to Simms, "Too bad . . . I had such high hopes for this one."

"Yes, me, too," Simms replied quietly, "I heard so many good things about that sawed-off rifle."

Sullivan Hart and Twojack Roth nodded slightly in agreement.

"You're firing me?" Jake Coak asked, bemused.

"Yes, exactly," said the judge without looking up.

"Damn"—Coak chuckled in disbelief—"I've never been fired in my life."

"Then today must be a momentous occasion for you. Please close the door behind you."

"All right then, I will." Jake Coak cursed under his breath, turning again to the door. But once again he stopped short of reaching for the knob and turned back to the judge's desk, seeing only the top of Parker's head as Parker bent over with his pen in his hand.

"Can I say something?" Coak asked.

Parker didn't respond.

"I've been with you two months, Your Honor." Jake Coak stepped closer to the desk. "I've been sent out four times with arrest warrants, and all four times I've brought back the men I was after. Every one of them was gunslingers, hardcase murderers—one of them was Ned 'Fireball' Perry. I happen to know that three other marshals avoided going after him because of his reputation with a gun. I brought him back facedown across a saddle for two damned dollars, which come to find out I didn't even get because he was dead. But I didn't complain. Now, all I'm asking is to work alone, the way all your other men do. You're telling me you're going to fire me for that?"

"No, I've already fired you," Judge Parker said, barely glancing up, then turning his face back down again. "All I'm telling you now is to please close the door behind yourself."

When the door closed behind Jake Coak, Simms and Parker sat in silence for a moment, hearing the heavy sound of boots walk away. Then Simms said in a consoling tone, "Don't worry, Your Honor. He'll do just fine . . . once I've had time to work with him."

"He'd better, Simms," said Parker. "If Tuck Priest isn't going to answer for killing Coleman Hart, then, by thunder, I'll see him answer for whatever he does next." Parker's eyes flared like hot steel. "And believe me, Tuck Priest will go afoul of the law. You can count on it." His clenched fist came down on his desk in solid resolve. "When Priest makes a move, I want you deputies there, ready and waiting."

"We'll be there, Your Honor," Sullivan Hart said, stepping forward from his spot for the first time since Simms and Coak had entered the office. "As far as this new man goes, I'd just as soon he not be with us. Roth and I can handle this." His eyes went to the cast on Simms's foot. "Simms has no business on a horse right now anyway."

"Oh? Really?" Simms lifted his chin toward Hart standing over him. "Just because I have a cast on my foot, you think I'm not able to keep up with—"

"That's right, Simms," Hart said. "The fact is, if it hadn't been for you bringing Priest in *alive*, we wouldn't be talking about this right now. I would've brought him in over a saddle." Hart's voice took a bitter turn. "Look at you. Half the time you don't even wear a gun."

"That's true, half the time I don't," Simms said, spreading a devilish grin. "But it's the other half of the time that counts. So don't think that just because we happen to operate a little different that I can't do whatever it takes to—"

"That's enough! Both of you!" Parker demanded, his palm slamming down on the top of his desk. "Is anybody listening to me this morning? I'm putting you men together as a posse, and I'll hear no more dissension. Is that clear?"

Silence fell upon the room like a heavy shroud, until finally Simms cleared his throat and said in a quiet tone, "Sorry, Your Honor. Hart and I always have to clear the air a little before we get down to business."

Twojack Roth had stood back in silence, taking it all in. Now he stepped forward, nudging Sullivan Hart to one side, saying, "Simms is right, Your Honor. Don't worry, we'll all work together on this case."

When the three left the judge's office, Hart turned to Simms outside the closed door. "Any ideas where Priest might be headed?"

Simms only shrugged. "I bet his attorneys would know. But I doubt if they'll be telling us."

A dark gleam came to Sullivan Hart's eyes. "I'd be pleased to go ask them."

Simms smiled. "Well, why don't you do just that while I go talk to Coak, let him know he's still in on this."

Hart turned and walked away. Roth lingered long enough to say to Simms, "Damn it, Simms, you know he's in no mood to be around Priest's attorneys. One cross word and he's apt to kill them."

"Oh," said Quick Charlie Simms in mock surprise, "I hadn't considered that." He hooked a thumb in his vest and leaned slightly on his cane, watching Roth hurry behind his partner.

Chapter 5

"But he fired me, Simms; you heard him do it," said Coak, fuming, standing at the bar of the Red Bull. "What gets me is you're the one he told to stop gambling or turn in your badge! Alls I've done is try to make a living."

Simms brushed a fleck of dust from his coat sleeve. "Well, life does have its irony. The main thing is I straightened everything out for you with Parker. You're not fired."

Jake Coak shot a harsh glare at him. "Simms, what I said still goes. I work alone. Get that in your head."

"I understand, Coak. What you don't realize is that I always work alone myself. We'll all be working alone"—Simms grinned—"only this time we'll all be doing it together."

Coak gripped both hands along the rail of the bar top. "Simms, we're awfully close to having trouble, you and me. I took this job to make myself some money, not to fool around with you and your trifling attitude."

"Easy, Coak," Simms said, chuckling, liking this young man, his serious manner, his straightforwardness. "If we play our cards right on this thing, there *is* some money to be made, a lot more than you're going to make dragging in dead bodies one and two at a time."

"Oh?" That got Coak's attention. "I don't see how." He turned to face Simms.

"Let me call some names off to you, Coak," Simms said. "Denton Howel, Max Sheppard, Joe Cherry? Any of those ring a bell?"

"Yep." Coak rubbed his cheek. "Denton Howel is two thousand dollars on the hoof. Sheppard is worth fifteen hundred. Joe Cherry is worth a thousand, if he's still alive and the opium and cocaine hasn't killed him yet."

"He's alive all right," Simms replied. "So are many others you'd like to draw bounty on." He paused for a second, then added, "They're alive and well, and all of them riding with *Los Pistoleros*. But that's only three men with prices on their heads. There's more, many more. Starting to get the picture?"

Coak frowned, ignoring Simms's question. "How do you know so much about who's riding with the gang?"

"It's my business to know. There are the things I find out playing poker with the likes of Roundhouse Eddie and his rabble."

"Thought you were only playing Wiley Sugar?" said Coak.

"That's true," Simms responded, "but any time I play, there's always more than one game going on. These are men you couldn't beat information out of with a club. But get them around a gaming table, they always let something slip." Simms studied Coak's eyes, seeing if he was going for any of this.

Coak considered it. "If we did this, how deep do we have to cut the reward between the four of us?"

Simms shrugged. "If we do things my way, there's no cut. It's all yours. Hart and Roth aren't in it for the money. You heard what Priest did to Hart's father—killed him and cut his ears off. All Hart wants is to see J. T. Priest pay for it. It's the same with Roth. He and Hart's father were partners. It strictly personal with those two."

"And you?" Coak asked.

Simms shrugged it off. "I'm not in this for the money, either. I can make more money tossing cards any day of the week than I can wearing this badge."

"Then why are you wearing it?" Coak asked.

"Call it a quirk in my extravagant nature." Simms smiled. "The fact is, I won't be wearing this badge much longer. I'm thinking about going into business for myself—Simms & Associates, Detective Agency. Thought I might give old Allen Pinkerton some competition." As he spoke, Simms took a business card from inside his lapel pocket and passed it to Jake Coak. "I've already made up some cards, see?" Simms studied Coak's eyes. "See, right there, it says, 'Simms & Associates, Detective Agency'?"

"Yeah, I see." Jake Coak looked the card over and gave it back to him. Simms saw he had Coak's attention. Taking the card back, he put it in his pocket, then patted his lapel. "So, care to listen to what I have in mind?"

"Shoot," said Coak.

Simms leaned in closer, laying it out for him. "What we need is a man on the inside of *Los Pistoleros*. Last time it was me, playing J. T. Priest along like a big fish. But that'll never happen again. He'll kill me the minute he lays eyes on me. But you can do it, Coak. You're still new enough at marshaling that all you've got to do is convince the gang that you got a raw deal from Parker and quit him. Make them think you've got a mad-on for him, for me, or anybody else riding out of Fort Smith."

Coak thought about it as he listened. "Tell them I refused to work with you and the others, and Parker fired me for it?"

"See?" said Simms, smiling. "You don't even have to make it up. Just make sure from this minute on that no one knows any different except you, me, and Judge Parker himself."

Coak thought about it. "So, what then?" he asked, getting more and more interested.

"Once they take you in, find out where their main stronghold is. I know it's near Sonora, Mexico, but I don't know exactly where. You can bet that's where Priest is headed."

"If you know that, why didn't you mention it in the judge's office?" asked Coak, trying to figure Simms out.

"It must've slipped my mind," Simms replied with a look of sincerity. "But the main thing is, you find out the information we need and get it to me. Sullivan Hart, Twojack Roth and I will join you. We'll take *Los Pistoleros* down for good." Simms let it sink in for a second as he tipped his drink up and finished it. "You get the bounty money on every man there. . . . Of course we have to get them back across the border, but we'll work that out when the time comes."

"We really *could* be talking about a lot of money," Coak said as if thinking out loud. "All I have to do is get to Sonora as quick as I can, hook up with the right gunmen and let them take me in."

"There you are," Simms said, seeing it was a done deal. "How fast can you get there?"

Coak tipped his hat brim upward, coming to a decision. "With spare horses, I can be there before Priest clears the road dust out of his mouth."

Simms relaxed an elbow on the bar and gestured to the bartender for another round. "That's the kind of talk I like to hear. *Partner*," he said.

After a moment of discussing their plans, Jake Coak left the saloon, tipping his hat to Kate McCorkle as she stepped inside, the two of them passing one another through the bat-wing doors. Kate watched him step down onto the dirt street, then turned to Simms, who stood smiling at the bar. "What are you up to, Charlie?" she asked warily.

"Why nothing, Kate," Simms responded. "I'm just trying to figure the best way to go about carrying out the judge's orders."

"Yeah, what orders?" She cocked her head slightly, not yet having heard about J. T. Priest's release from custody.

Simms's expression turned serious. "Brace yourself, Kate. You're not going to like this any more than I do." He raised a hand, summoned the bartender and had him bring Kate a tall mug of beer.

When he'd told her the whole story, Kate McCorkle studied the mug in her hands and shook her head slowly. "And now the four of you are going to be going after them, you with your busted ankle?"

"Well, that's what the judge would like to see happen," said Simms. "But it's not quite what I have in mind. I've convinced Marshal Coak to ride down to

Sonora and take up with some of Priest's men. Then Hart, Roth and myself will ride in and close this thing for good."

"You mean you trust this Jake Coak enough to send him ahead?" Kate asked. "That doesn't sound like you, Charlie. Does Hart and Roth know you're doing this?"

"No, they don't. I'll tell them about it later. But it doesn't matter. I've got a good hunch about this man Coak. I believe he can handle J. T. Priest, *Los Pistoleros* and anything they throw at him. I think he's an interesting man, our young bounty hunter." Simms stared past her, out the bat-wing doors as if following Coak with his eyes. "He isn't able to read, you know?" Simms murmured.

"How do you know that? Did he tell you?"

"Yes, in a roundabout way." Simms took the business card from his pocket and handed it to her. "I suspected it in the judge's office when Coak looked confused at the court order. Just to make sure, I handed him this card, told him it was a card for Simms & Associates Detective Agency."

Kate read the card aloud, "Devers, Lyons, and Swan, Attorneys-at-law?" She shook her head and handed the card back to Simms. "You should be ashamed of yourself." She grinned.

"It pays to know about the man you're going to be working with," Simms said. "Jake Coak's a serious young man who won't let anything stop him."

"Oh, and you've decided all this just because he can't read?" Kate gave him a curious look. "I've known plenty of people who can't read. I didn't see where it made them anything extraordinary."

"Oh, really?" Simms finished his drink and set his

glass down on the bar. "How many of them did you know ever taught school?"

"He can't read . . . and he was a schoolteacher?" Kate asked in a surprised tone.

"Yep, among other things. Shows real enterprise, don't you think?" Simms stepped back from the bar, supporting himself on his cane, and took the business card from her hand. "But you misunderstood me, Kate. I never said he *can't* read. I said he *isn't able* to. That's much worse." Simms tapped a fingertip to his cheek. "He has a problem with his eye, you may have noticed. I'm sure he knows how to read and write as well as you and I. The problem is, I suspect when he tries to focus on words, they appear all jumbled up. So, yes, I do think it's extraordinary that a man can overcome something like that."

"Can anything be done to correct it?" Kate asked in a sympathetic tone.

"So far there's no cure," said Simms. "Some people live with it their whole lives, others . . . well, I hate to say it, but if it keeps getting worse, they often go blind."

"That's horrible," Kate whispered. "Do you suppose his eyes affect anything else?" Kate asked. "Say, his aim, his ability to fire that sawed-off rifle?"

"No, but I think he must prepare himself before doing any serious shooting," Simms replied. "One young man I knew as a child had a trick he used. He counted numbers in his mind. Somehow keeping a rhythm going helped him focus."

"You think Coak does the same thing?" Kate asked.

"Who knows?" Quick Charlie Simms shrugged, putting the conversation aside. "He must have some technique worked out for himself. He's still alive after all. Now, if you'll excuse me, I need to meet Hart and Roth and get on Priest's trail. Hart wanted to talk to Priest's attorneys before we head out, see if he can get a lead on Priest."

"Hart ought to know better than that," said Kate. "Priest's attorneys won't give him the time of day."

"Oh, I don't know," said Simms. "Sullivan Hart can be very persuasive when he has a mind to."

In the livery barn behind the courthouse, Deputy Dan'l Slater walked in as Jake Coak drew the cinch taut on his dapple-gray's saddle and dropped the stirrup. "I understand Parker fired you?" said Slater, resting a hand on the dapple's rump. On the straw floor near Coak's feet, the Catahoula rose slowly, its eyes pinned on Slater, causing the deputy to stop short.

Jake Coak just stared at Slater for a second, then said in a gruff tone, "News travels fast around here." He jerked back and forth on his saddle horn and ran a gloved hand along the dapple's neck.

"I hated hearing it," Slater said, letting out a breath to show his remorse.

"Yeah, well, I ain't too broken up over it." Coak went about his business attending his horse. "One thing stops, another thing starts, I reckon."

"Going back to bounty hunting, are you?" Slater looked him up and down, taking note of the sawed-off rifle.

"Nope, I've had my fill of making a living with a gun. If a man's going to risk his life, he ought to make sure he's making the best dollar he can from it."

"You're talking outlaw talk, ain't ya?" Slater asked, narrowing his gaze on Coak.

"If I was, do you think I'd tell you, Deputy?" Coak

stepped away from the dapple-gray to where he'd hitched three of the horses he'd brought the bodies in on. He led them forward, looking them over.

When Coak tied the horses behind his big dapple-gray, Slater rested a hand on the rump of a wiry roan, saying, "Three spares? Looks like wherever you're headed, it's going to require some hard traveling."

Coak brushed Slater's hand aside, politely but firmly. "These horses are my ticket across the territory, if you must know."

Slater took a step back, but was unruffled by the gesture. "No need to be testy with me. I just came down to see you off."

Coak stared at him again, seeing the deputy was only passing the time of day. "I appreciate that. How well do you know this Quick Charlie Simms?"

"As well as I ever want to, I reckon," Slater said, raking his fingers through his long white beard. "He nearly drove Sullivan Hart and Twojack Roth crazy, trying to figure out what he was up to. Simms is a gamesman. You have to watch his every move. He doesn't even carry a gun, you know. Says a man should be slick enough to never have to shoot his way out of a tight spot."

"Yeah, I heard that about him," said Coak. "I also saw that young woman in action. I reckon with her around, a man need not worry."

"Kate's got the temper of a wildcat," said Slater. "You don't want to cross her."

"I'll do my best not to," Coak said wryly. He turned and walked to his loaded saddlebags hanging from a row of wooden pegs. Slater stepped in beside him as Coak opened the bags, took out a tin of gunpowder and a bag of lead and empty brass cartridges. Coak emptied the bag onto a flattened bale of hay, took stock of his supplies, then put them away.

"So, you really do load your own ammunition," said Slater, watching him shake the pint tin of gunpowder enough to gauge its contents.

"Yep, I always do. I trust nobody's skill like I do my own." Coak stuffed the tin down into his saddlebags, then carried the bags to the dapple-gray and laid them across its back, behind his saddle. He said as he tied the bags into place, "I figure there's been men that died because somebody somewhere didn't have their mind on business the day they loaded his cartridges. When I load my own, all I'm thinking about is that it's these babies' job to keep me alive. I like knowing they're standing ready."

"Makes sense, I suppose," Slater said. He watched Coak check the dapple-gray over carefully. "I heard a man say that he once saw you swing that hip rifle faster than two fellers facing you could draw their pistols."

"You heard that, huh?" Coak continued checking his horse. "Well, a man can hear most anything out here, if he listens close enough."

"Then it ain't true?" Slater asked.

"Oh, it's true enough. But it ain't something I go around telling. The less a person knows about what I can or can't do, the more advantage I have if push comes to shove between us. Once a man shows his hand, he has no hand left to show." He offered Slater a slight smile. "Now, if you'll excuse me, I want to put as much distance between me and the hanging judge as I can. I've wasted two months of my life in this place."

"I understand," said Slater. "But don't be too hard

on the judge. Parker has to make the law work out here, one way or the other."

"Well," said Coak, taking his sawed-off rifle from its long holster and checking it as he spoke, "I'd expect you to say something like that, being the judge's right-hand man." He stepped over to the dapple-gray with his short rifle in his hand, picked up its reins and led it out into the midmorning sunlight, Slater following him. When he spun the reins around a rail in the corral, he walked a few feet away from the horse, then turned to face Slater. "If you've got something to do, go ahead. I need to check my rifle before I ride out into Indian Territory."

Slater grinned. "I got nowhere I've got to be right now."

"I don't like doing this in front of people," Coak said. "I already told you why."

Slater shrugged, offering a thin smile. "I never saw a thing."

Jake Coak considered it for a second, looking around the large empty corral until he spotted an old out-of-use jail wagon sitting twenty yards away. Then he said, "All right, cover your ears, these are overloads."

"Overloads?" Slater's smile widened. "I never heard of such a thing as an overlo—" His words were cut short beneath the booming explosions as Jake Coak walked sideways back toward the dapple-gray. Each step Coak took, the butt of the sawed-off rifle bucked against his hip, his hand levering round after round in what sounded like one long roll of angry thunder. Splinters and dust showered upward from the wheels of the old jail wagon as spoke after spoke vanished from its hub.

Ten thousand . . . On the tenth shot, Jake Coak stopped less than a foot from the dapple-gray's side. Smoke billowed around him as he looked closely at the horse's eyes. The big dapple-gray stood as if frozen in place, except for a twitch of its shoulder muscle. Coak patted the dapple's shoulder with his free hand. "Good boy, Cyrus," he said. Twenty yards away, the jail wagon lay on its side in the dirt, the spokes of both right wheels lying in splinters. Deputy Slater stared at it in awe. Jake Coak rolled the short rifle into its holster. He took ten fresh loads from his cartridge belt and inspected each one in turn. "Don't forget, Slater, you never saw a thing," he said over his shoulder.

"Lord God!" Slater gasped, rounding a finger into his ear as he stepped closer, looking down at the smoke still curling up from the holstered rifle barrel. "You could have warned a feller first. I'm near deaf!"

"I did warn you first," said Coak. "You just weren't paying attention."

"I will from now on. How many rounds does that fire-bucket carry?" Slater asked.

"Fifteen," said Coak, still checking his fresh cartridges. "I make it a practice never to fire over ten at a time unless I have to. The barrel gets hot." He looked at Slater and added with a clipped smile. "Besides, you never know, the men you just shot might have angry kinfolks hanging around."

"See there," said Slater, "it's no wonder the judge wanted you to work with Simms. You've got the most weaponry of anybody here."

Coak looked at him. "Then the judge shouldn't have fired me."

"I bet he'd give you another chance if you talked to him real respectful like," Slater said.

"You think so, huh? Just go dragging in there with my hat in my hand? No thanks, Deputy." Jake Coak turned away and grumbled something under his breath as he swung up atop the dapple-gray and straightened it toward the corral gate, leading his three-horse string behind him. At the gate, he stopped long enough to unlatch it and swing it open without leaving his saddle. "Go on ahead, Buster," he said down to the dog. Buster sprang forward in a low fast trot. Then Jake Coak nudged the dapple-gray forward into a cantor along the dirt street, leaving Dan'l Slater standing in the empty corral.

By the time Simms arrived at the brick building that housed the offices of Devers, Lyons, and Swan, Esqs., a crowd had gathered out front in the dirt street. Upon nearing the scene, Simms saw the crowd part as Lyle Devers staggered backward through it, Sullivan Hart stalking forward, his fists drawn tight. Devers tried to speak as he caught his balance and raised his fists into a guard position. But Sullivan Hart shot a hard right to Devers's nose, sending the dazed attorney staggering in a short circle before he fell facedown in the dirt. Simms winced, but managed a faint smile as he stepped forward.

"Hold it, Hart," Simms shouted, stepping in between the two of them, holding a raised hand toward Hart to keep him back. On the ground, Lyle Devers rolled over onto his back and started to rise up, but Simms planted the point of his cane on Devers's chest and pinned him down. "Stay down, you idiot," he whispered, leaning close to the attorney's bloody face. "Tell him what he wants to know. Priest is headed for Sonora, isn't he?"

"I— I don't know," Devers gasped, running a hand across his swollen jaw. "Swan went with him . . . to collect our fee."

"There, you see how easy that was?" Simms glared at him, speaking in a harsh whisper. He jerked a handkerchief from his pocket and pitched it down into Devers's face. Then, turning to Sullivan Hart, who stood ten feet away ready to spring forward again, Simms called out, "He said Priest is headed for Sonora."

Devers started to protest, but Simms jammed the cane harder into his chest. "Lie still."

"He didn't tell you that, Simms," Hart said, stepping closer.

"Yes, he did," said Simms. "He said young Swan went with Priest to collect their legal fees." Simms looked down at the attorney's battered face. "Isn't that true, Devers?"

Devers wiped the blood from his flattened nose, considered it for a second, then said in a relenting voice, "That's right, Hart, they're headed for Sonora." He raised up slightly, the tip of Simms's cane now allowing him to. "This isn't over between us, Hart," he said. "You can consider yourself sued!"

Simms poked him back down with his cane. "You don't know when to shut up, do you, Devers?"

Sullivan Hart started forward once again, but this time Twojack Roth stepped out from the crowd, caught his arm and stopped him. "Come on, Hart, you got what you came here for. Let's get moving."

"Simms is lying," Hart said, just between the two of them. "Devers never told him that."

"Can't you see what Simms did?" Roth whispered. "He knew Priest was headed for Sonora all along. He just played it this way to get you to beat the hell out of

Devers. You know how Quick Charlie is. He's playing with all of us."

"Yeah?" Hart blew out a breath. "Well, this time I'm glad he is." He straightened his hat and riding duster as Simms stepped toward him, limping on his cane. Behind Simms, Devers crawled a few feet away before rising to his feet and slinking off toward his office.

"Feel better now?" Simms asked.

"A little," said Hart. "If you're all through fooling around, we best get under way. Did you straighten things out with Jake Coak?"

"Yep, Coak's with us one hundred percent."

Hart and Roth both looked around the street. "Then where is he?" asked Roth.

"Oh, he's already headed out," Simms said matter-of-factly.

Hart gave Roth a puzzled look, then asked Simms, "Headed out to where?"

"Why, to Sonora, of course." Simms smiled and limped past them toward the livery barn. "I figure Priest went as far as he could by train or stagecoach, especially if he had that young attorney with him. Priest likes to travel in comfort as far as he can. He figures we'll be on his trail so he'll be bound to set a few traps for us along the way. We'll just have to be ready for them."

"How does Coak play into this?" Roth asked.

"Jake Coak is headed out straight across Indian Territory," said Simms. "With any luck at all he'll be getting to Sonora around the same time as Priest. Coak is going to work his way into *Los Pistoleros* and lead us to their hiding place. It pays to have a man on the inside."

Hart and Roth looked at one another, surprised.

"You came up with all this since we left Parker's office this morning?" Hart asked.

Simms tapped a finger to his forehead. "Makes sense, don't you think?" He limped farther on ahead of them. "Let's get moving. I want to slip out of town without Kate. She's got no business in this. If things go the way I've got them planned, we'll be fighting *Los Pistoleros* down below the border. Things are going to get a little ugly, and I don't want Kate involved."

"You think of everything, don't you, Quick Charlie?" Roth said to him.

"I certainly try to," Simms responded, sounding a bit smug. "It pays to look ahead."

"Yeah? Well, one day you're going to slip up," Sullivan Hart called out behind him. "You're going to outsmart yourself! Mark my words."

But Simms limped on down the street, not seeming to hear. His mind was on J. T. Priest and *Los Pistoleros*.

Chapter 6

J. T. "Tuck" Priest looked out the window of the stagecoach, watching the land roll past through a rise of dust from the large wheels. Beside him, R. Martin Swan, attorney-at-law, sat with his brown bowler hat lowered on his brow, dozing in the noon heat with his tie loosened and his leather satchel cradled on his knees. Across from the two of them, a couple of young cowhands slept off their hangovers on the way back to Texas. In the cramped quarters, the cowhand directly across from Tuck Priest sat with his dirty boot crossed onto his knee. Twice in the past few minutes, Priest had to shove the boot away to keep it from rubbing dirt on his new pin-stripe trousers. Now as the boot once again encroached toward him, Priest stared hard at the slumbering face of the young drover. "Hey, you, cowboy, wake up," Priest said, kicking the boot away from his trouser leg for the third time. The young cowhand only let out a long snore and rolled his head sideways onto his other shoulder. But hearing Priest's voice, R. Martin Swan raised his face and lifted his hat brim.

"Yes, sir, excuse me?" said Swan, rubbing his eyes

as he responded to what he thought was Priest speaking to him.

"I wasn't talking to you," Priest growled. "I was talking to this crude peckerwood." He nodded at the dirty boot, then jerked his chin toward the snoring cowboy.

"Oh, I see." R. Martin Swan straightened in his seat all the same and clutched the satchel as if it might have tried to slip away from him in his sleep. He drew his own knees away from the sole of the dirty boot. "Perhaps we should have the driver pull over for a moment, get ourselves better situated—"

"Do you happen to have a gun in that pile of paperwork?" Priest asked, cutting him off with a harsh glare.

"No, of course not." Swan chuckled at what he took to be Priest's way of making a joke about the situation. But Priest only glared at him in disgust, then shook his head and gazed out the window again. Across from R. Martin Swan, the other cowhand had heard the conversation and, raising his flat-crowned hat from his forehead, he looked back and forth from Priest to Swan, then said to the young attorney, "What did he say about a gun?"

Swan felt his stomach tighten up. "Why, nothing, nothing at all."

Priest only turned from the window long enough to shoot the cowhand a hate-filled glance, then he looked back out the window, toward a fresh rise of dust moving upward along a distant ridge line.

"Yeah he did. I heard him," said the cowhand, keeping a cold stare on Swan as he nudged his sleeping buddy in the ribs. "Hey, Casey, wake up. You've got an old boy wanting to shoot you for rubbing your boots on him."

"Do what?" a sleepy voice grumbled.

"Oh my." R. Martin Swan gulped down a dry swallow in his throat and slipped a tense sidelong glance at Tuck Priest, wondering at what point Priest was going to turn around and straighten this thing out before it got out of hand. But Priest was occupied now with the distant scenery. "I'm afraid you must have misinterpreted Mister Priest's words. He was simply using a wry form of humor to express what he obviously felt was a—"

"The hell's he saying, Bell?" the other cowhand asked, rubbing sleep from his eyes as he interrupted Swan.

"I don't know," said Bell, his gaze still fixed on Swan, "but fat boy there was asking him if he had a gun. Seems you got some dust on his trousers."

"Fat boy?" Priest turned from the window to face them. The rise of dust was growing closer now, a thin dark line of men on horseback leading the dust toward the rolling stage. "You don't know who you're talking to, do you, cowboy?" Priest's eyes glistened with fury.

"I'll bet I'm fixin' to find out," said Bell, his right hand drifting down to the range Colt on his hip.

"You damn sure are," Priest hissed, coming forward a bit until R. Martin Swan raised a forearm, blocking him.

"Gentlemen, please!" Swan leaned forward between them, Bell leaning close from one direction, Priest from the other. Swan said quickly to Bell, "My client— that is, Mister Priest here is unarmed! We're all a little testy from this heat! But surely we can calm down and act like rational men!"

"What heat?" Bell sneered.

"Hold it," Casey cut in, pulling Bell back by his shirt sleeve. "This is all my fault." His eyes cut to Priest. "Mister, if I rubbed my boot against you, I apologize. Hell, I was asleep. I didn't do it on purpose."

"Priest, did you say?" Bell asked Swan as he looked Tuck Priest up and down. "You don't mean J. T. Priest? The man I was just reading about in the newspaper? The man who was supposed to hang for murder? The leader of some big outlaw gang?" His expression changed. "You mean, you're him?" he asked Priest.

"Yeah, I'm him," Priest growled, smoothing a hand down his vest as he settled a bit, still glaring hard into Bell's eyes. "I'm J. T. Priest . . . but my friends all call me *fat boy*," he added in a venomous tone.

Bell blushed, looking worried. "Hell, I meant no harm, Mister Priest," he said, his whole demeanor relenting, his hand coming up away from his pistol. "Me and Casey here have been drunk for three days. If we've done something wrong, we truly didn't intend to." He started to say something more, but his words trailed away beneath the squeaking sound of the stage brakes as the coach began lurching to a sharp halt. J. T. Priest only glared at him. Outside, the sound of horses' hooves closed in a circle, surrounding the stage. Swan and the two cowboys craned their necks, trying to look out the windows, but J. T. Priest only sat silent, still staring at Bell.

"Boys, we're not carrying any payload," said the voice of the stage driver.

"Who asked you?" a gruff voice responded. Two pistol shots exploded. R. Martin Swan ducked and flinched. The coach's horses milled nervously in place as the driver's body hit the ground with a heavy thud.

"Oh Lord," said Casey, seeing nine gunmen circling in close around the small stagecoach. He pulled his face back from the window, his eyes going first to his friend Bell, then to J. T. Priest. "We're done for, ain't we?"

Priest only offered a slight smile, sitting back, folding his hands in his lap. Beside him, R. Martin Swan sat wide-eyed, his mouth agape. "Mister Priest! I can't be a party to a robbery! As your attorney, I have to advise you that this is a reckless way to begin your freedom—"

"Shut up, Swan," said Priest. "You heard the driver. There's no payload on here—just some friends of mine come calling."

"You in there, Tuck?" a voice asked from atop a dusty red roan as the horse moved up close to the coach's window.

"I'm here, Macklinberg," Priest replied through the window, his eyes still on the two cowboys. He smiled. "Give us a minute to say good-bye." He looked first at Swan, then back at Bell and Casey. "If I let yas go, it's going to be a long hot walk back to town, don't you think?"

"Hell, we don't mind," said Casey.

"No, sir, not one bit," Bell added hastily. "We're ready to go right now."

Priest nodded and held out his palms toward them. "I didn't think you would mind. Now both of yas give me those range Colts, butts first."

Bell and Casey lifted their pistols and handed them over, a sickly look on their faces. A long streak of sweat ran down Bell's weathered cheek and dripped from the edge of his mustache.

"Mister Priest," Swan cut in, "I think you need to

seriously consider the consequences of what you're doing here! Do you realize what lengths we've just gone through, keeping you off of Judge Parker's gallows? This is completely insane!"

Priest turned to him, a strange, tight grin on his face. "Swan, you must be the finest, most brilliant attorney I've ever seen. I owe you my life, and that's the God honest fact. But if you don't shut your mouth, I'll put a bullet in it."

R. Martin Swan cringed back in his seat.

The two cowboys sat staring wide-eyed. "Now then, boys," Priest said, "there's a grifter back in Fort Smith named Quick Charlie Simms. Either of you know him?"

"Quick Charlie Simms? Why, hell yes," said Bell, eager to please. "Everybody knows Quick Charlie. We played poker with him a few nights back."

"All right now, listen close," Priest said, letting them see the pistols move back and forth on them as he spoke. "I want you to walk back to the relay station, find yourselves a way back to Fort Smith, and give Simms a little message for me. Would you mind doing that?"

"Not at all, Mister Priest, sir," Casey said in an anxious voice, "we'd be pleased to do it."

Outside the stagecoach, Rance Macklinberg and the others grew restless waiting in the heat. Finally Macklinberg leaned down in his saddle and poked his head inside the coach's window. "Are you all through saying good-bye?" he asked, looking at the sweat-streaked faces of the two cowboys, then at Priest and Swan. "It ain't getting no cooler out here waiting for you."

Priest chuckled, hefting both pistols in his hands, checking them out. Then he swung the door open and motioned the two cowboys out. No sooner had their boots touched the dirt than the two cowboys moved away and headed back along the trail in a trot. "Damn, it's a beautiful day!" Priest exclaimed, following them and shoving the pistols down into his waistband. He took in a deep breath of hot dusty air, reached a hand back inside and pulled Swan out of the coach. "Come on, lawyer," he said, "don't make me start thinking it'd be easier to kill you than it would be to pay your fee."

Swan steadied himself against the side of the coach. "Mister Priest, this is not what we agreed to. I'm simply to accompany you to Texas, collect the legal fees for my partners and myself and return to Fort Smith!"

"And so you will, Swan," said Priest. "First I've got to collect the money to pay those fees." Priest looked around at the nine horsemen gathered around the stagecoach, then up at Rance Macklinberg, who sat atop his roan, holding the reins to a big black gelding. "I expect you boys are all eager to get to making some money?"

"You got it, Boss." Macklinberg pitched the black gelding's reins down to Priest. "If you don't mind me asking, J. T., why don't you shoot this peckerwood? He's just going to get in our way wherever we go." As Macklinberg spoke, Priest swung up atop the black gelding.

"I'll take care of our brilliant young attorney here." Priest looked down at Swan, smiling at the startled look on the young lawyer's face, then back to Macklinberg as he reached down, snatched Swan up by the shoulder and hauled him up behind his saddle. "He looks like he could use a few days of fresh air and sunshine, wouldn't you say? There's a ranch down the other side of Mobeetie I want him to see."

Macklinberg only grinned. "Anything you say, Boss," watching Swan squirm behind Priest's saddle, adjusting himself.

Priest turned to one of the horsemen nearest to him and Macklinberg, saying, "Clayton, you and your brother Earl set fire to this rig. I don't' want nothing left but a pile of ashes." He nudged his horse away from the stagecoach with Rance Macklinberg close by his side. "Where's your manners, Mack? Introduce me to these new men."

"Sure, J. T." Macklinberg nodded at each man in turn, saying their names aloud. "Dean Spence, Harry Turpin, Clarence Ames, Huey Moss, Leonard Hergo, Dick Witt."

"Damn good to see you boys," said Priest. "As of now, you're all riding with *Los Pistoleros*. Be proud of it."

The men nodded their greetings in return.

"What about those cowboys, Boss?" Macklinberg asked. "Why didn't we kill them?"

"They're doing me a favor," said Priest, dismissing the subject. "Did you send the word out to anybody who's even ridden with *Los Pistoleros*? I want every gun behind me from now on. I've lost a lot and it's time I take back what's mine."

"The word's out, J. T., just like you asked," said Macklinberg. "We'll be gathering strength as we go."

"Good work, Mack." Priest grinned, looking around at the others, judging them, getting a feel for his strength. "Parker will have his deputies trailing me by now. We'll leave some men waiting for them along the way." He raised his voice for all the men to hear. "I'll pay one thousand dollars a head to anybody who takes down Sullivan Hart or Twojack Roth."

"Don't you want to take care of Quick Charlie Simms first, Boss?" a voice asked from amid the horsemen.

"Nope," said Priest. "I've got plans for Simms. First of all, I want to make a stop at that ranch I was talking about on our way to the border," he said, "get ourselves up some money, gather our forces. Then I want to find myself a woman . . . hell, make that three or four women, all at once." He nudged the black gelding forward, the rest of the riders gathering around him. "As soon as I get myself filled up on the things I've been missing the most, we'll take care of Quick Charlie Simms. Any idea what I'm going to do that snake?"

"Oh yes," said Rance Macklinberg, "I got some notions, after all he did to you . . . to this whole gang, for that matter."

"Good, then I don't need to explain," said Priest. "As soon as Simms shows his face, I'm paying two thousand dollars to any member of *Los Pistoleros* who brings me his head in a gunnysack."

A murmur stirred through the gunmen. "You heard me right, boys," Priest added, raising his voice. "*Two thousand dollars*, just to be able to look into his eyes and know they ain't looking back at me."

"I figure you're right about Hart and Roth coming after you, Boss. But how do you know Simms will show up?" Macklinberg asked.

"Oh, he'll be coming, I can promise you that. I happen to have the one thing that Simms cares about more than life itself, Mack. I have Kate McCorkle." Priest nudged his horse forward.

"You do?" Rance Macklinberg grinned, booting his horse forward beside J. T. Priest, looking around as if Kate McCorkle might be there.

"Oh yes, indeed, I do," said Priest. "She's on her way to Sonora right now. I've learned that the only way to deal with a gamesman like Simms is to think ahead of him, get the first punch in while he's not expecting it." Priest jerked his head back toward the two cowboys as they disappeared over a rise. "I just sent them to tell him, if he ever wants to see Kate alive in one piece, he'll have come to Sonora, *alone*, and face what's waiting there for him."

Kate McCorkle had already thrown a few things together for the road, taking her personal items from the large trunk she usually kept them in and stuffing them down into a pair of worn saddlebags. If Charlie Simms had any notion of leaving her behind while he traipsed out across Indian Territory, he better think again, she said to herself, tossing the saddlebags onto the large featherbed. Earlier, when she'd gone back to the saloon to meet Simms, Rudy the bartender had told her Simms, Hart and Roth had left town over two hours ago. Well, she wouldn't stand for it. Kate would not be left behind, even if it was for her own good. She could handle herself. Simms ought to know that by now.

An evening breeze stirred through the open window as she stepped out of her dress, letting it fall to the floor, then walked into the small adjoining dressing room. She took her riding clothes down from the shelf and began putting them on, first unstrapping her hideaway holsters and laying her pistols on a stool beside her.

She put on her riding skirt and her cotton blouse,

first taking the time to adjust the straight razor in its leather case up under her arm, held there by a soft cotton harness. Then she slipped into her riding vest. She had pulled on her boots when a slight scuffling sound from the bedroom drew her attention. Instinctively, her hand went for one of the pistols, but then froze as the outline of the three men filled the doorway.

"Don't try it, McCorkle," said the raspy voice of Roundhouse Eddie, his Colt cocking in his hand. On either side of him stood Pete Lamburtis and Big Joe Macon, each with their pistols drawn and aimed at her.

Kate McCorkle let her hand ease back from her guns, but stayed tensed, looking for some move to make, but seeing none. "So, I take it this isn't a social call?" she asked, looking from one to the other, weighing her odds. "If you came looking for Charlie, he's not here. He rode out on the afternoon stage, headed south, for New Orleans. Sorry to disappoint you—"

"Shut up, McCorkle," said Pete Lamburtis, "we know you're lying." He stepped, forward grabbing her roughly and swinging her around, turning her back to him as he yanked out a long length of rawhide. He snatched her wrists and pulled them behind her, binding them quickly. "We're one step ahead of you two snakes," he added, leaning in so close to her ear that she could feel and smell his hot whiskey breath. "We'd find Simms easy enough if we wanted him. But we don't want him. We came here for you." Behind him, the other two chuckled under their breaths. "That little episode last night over the card game," Lamburtis added, hugging her back against his chest, his hand coming up to squeeze her face, "it was all a setup. We just needed to feel everybody out—see which one of yas was the real gun handler. Now we're taking you for a little ride with us."

"Where— where to?" Kate managed to ask, cutting her eyes back over her shoulder to him.

"Never mind where," said Lamburtis, spinning her around, shoving her to Big Joe Macon. "You'll see when we get there. An old friend of yours sent us here; said he wants to see you real bad."

"Yeah," said Big Joe Macon, grabbing Kate around her waist, raising her onto her tiptoes against his chest. "J. T. Priest sent us for you. But I don't reckon he'd mind if I smell your hair a little on the way."

"Smell this, you son of a bitch!" Kate McCorkle's boot came up behind her, hard, burying the edge of its heel in Big Joe's crotch. Big Joe jackknifed forward with a loud gasp, letting her go as he clutched himself with both hands.

"Get her, Pete!" Roundhouse Eddie demanded, shoving Big Joe to one side, making a grab for Kate McCorkle as she lunged toward the door. Lamburtis sprang forward, throwing an arm around Kate's throat and pulling her back, her bound wrists struggling against the rawhide straps.

"She's not getting away," Lamburtis said with a short laugh, seeing Big Joe Macon's blue, gasping face. Lamburtis tightened his grip on Kate McCorkle, mindful of her boot heel as he dragged her back to where Roundhouse Eddie stood helping Big Joe straighten up. "Damn, lady," Lamburtis remarked, "you nearly put Big Joe on his knees. Try that with me and I'll pistol whip you all the way to Mexico."

"Shut up, Pete," Roundhouse Eddie snapped. "She don't need to know where we're going." He jerked the dusty bandanna from around his neck and pitched it to Lamburtis. "Gag her and let's get moving."

Mexico, huh? Kate looked back and forth at their faces as Lamburtis raised the bandanna toward her mouth. Mexico could only mean one place, she thought. Sonora. She jerked her face to one side, bypassing the dusty bandanna. "Simms will kill you, all three of you! You pigs! If he doesn't, I will! I swear to—"

Lamburtis muffled her words with the dusty bandanna.

Roundhouse Eddie stepped forward, giving her a nasty grin. "I don't think you're in a position to make any threats. And as far as Simms goes, we already seen him hide behind your skirt tails." He looked at Lamburtis standing behind her and added with a dark chuckle, "It would almost be worth giving up what we're getting paid just to shoot her and Simms ourselves, wouldn't it? After the way they treated us?"

"Not for me, Eddie," Lamburtis said, still clutching Kate tight against his chest. "I'm in it for the money. Keep that in mind, both of you from here on." He looked at Big Joe Macon as Big Joe limped over to the open window with one hand pressed low on his aching belly.

"Don't worry, I'll keep it in mind," said Roundhouse Eddie Jenkins, giving Lamburtis a firm look, then turning back to Big Joe Macon. "Damn, Big Joe, are you able to ride?"

"I'm . . . all right . . . here," Big Joe said in a tight strained voice, "but keep . . . her away from me . . . or I'll kill her."

"Yeah," said Roundhouse with a slight chuckle, "we won't let her too near you from now on. Wouldn't want you hurting her." He reached inside his shirt, pulled out a wrinkled envelope and pitched it on the featherbed. "I'd love to see Simms's face when he reads that." Kate just looked at him, not about to tell him that Simms had already left town. Roundhouse turned and followed Big Joe Macon out the open window, Lamburtis staying back with Kate McCorkle until the other two checked out the street below.

Lamburtis moved forward to the window with Kate pressed against him. He whispered, "You be a good girl now, don't cause any commotion on the way to the horses."

But Kate had already made up her mind. She wasn't about to raise a fuss right now. Simms and the other two deputies were out there somewhere on the same trail perhaps, or at least headed in the same direction. She'd have to play it safe, bide her time and wait. She only nodded in agreement with Pete Lamburtis as they moved through the open window, across the balcony, and down the wooden stairs to where the horses stood waiting.

Chapter 7

At dawn, Jake Coak had already traveled past the army encampment to his right and onward toward the north fork of the Red. Guiding the dapple-gray beneath rock ledges and along soft dirt, he kept its hooves and the hooves of the three horses behind him from going across stone where the sound would carry. Silence was now the difference between life and death if Victorio's warriors were nearby. And they were—he'd come upon a set of unshod tracks less than a quarter of a mile from his campsite. All he could do now was to try to sidestep them, weave past them somehow.

The tracks had belonged to one lone scout, Coak figured. If that scout was any good, he'd have picked up Coak's trail by now. Coak stopped the dapple-gray for a second beside a thin runoff of water and listened intently for any sound on the air. *If he was any good?* Who was he kidding? They were all good, these Mescaleros. This land was as much a part of their being as their blood and heartbeat. He was the outsider here, and he'd best remember that single fact, if nothing else. He coaxed the horse forward, leading the other three upward into a narrow crevice of rock. From a more narrow crevice above him, Buster swept down silently and sat on the ground a few feet away, the dog's full attention giving to probing the air with its raised muzzle. "Talk to me, Buster," Coak whispered, watching the way the dog tensed slightly to the right, toward the path they'd just abandoned.

The dog rose and moved forward a few slow cautious steps, then stopped, its hackles raised, but no sound of a growl leaving its throat. Good dog, Coak said to himself, stepping down slowly from the dapple-gray to avoid any creaking of saddle leather. He eased a hand down to his boot and lifted the long bowie knife from his boot well. Then he moved upward, taking to the smaller crevice the dog had used, until he was a few feet above the horses. He inched forward into a slice of sunlight and looked down from atop his boulder perch. Beneath him, less than twenty feet down, he watched the thin young warrior stoop in front of his horse and touch his bony fingers to Jake's fresh hoofprints, reading them as if they were words on a printed page.

Coak inched close to the edge of the boulder, ready to make the long leap, knowing it was too high, and knowing that the least slipup would leave him lying dead in the morning sun. He held his breath and waited, watching as the warrior stood up and took a step closer toward the narrow rock crevice. Feeling the scout's eyes move upward along the rocks, Coak ducked back to keep from being seen. He's checking everything out, Coak thought, playing it safe.

In a second, he inched forward again, this time seeing the young warrior take a step back, still watching the entrance to the rock crevice. Sweat ran freely down Coak's forehead. After a moment, the warrior swung up onto his horse and backed it away from the rock crevice a few feet before turning it and giving it his heels.

When the warrior was out of sight on the meandering rocky path, Coak let out a tense breath and moved back and down quickly. The other Mescaleros had to be close by. That was all that had kept the scout from venturing into the crevice where the three horses stood back behind the dog. Whatever awaited the lone warrior inside the crevice was not worth the risk, not when all he had to do was go summon the others. Coak knew this, and knowing it made him act fast.

Coak led the horses deeper back onto the upward path through the crevice. At the top of the path where the land reopened onto a rocky ledge, he swung atop the dapple-gray and drew his rifle from his holster. Looking down, he spotted a half dozen warriors as they raced forward, the scout leading the others back to where he'd followed Coak's tracks. *All right, here goes . . .*

Coak raised the rifle and fired shot after shot as the warriors' horses rounded closer in. Rock and dirt sprayed upward at their horses' hooves, sending the animals backward, bunching them up onto themselves. Then, as the warriors righted their spooked horses, Jake sat tall and still in his saddle, purposefully skylining himself, holding up the reins to the three-horse string.

As the warriors looked up, their horses stepping nervously back and forth in place, Coak dropped the reins to the three spare horses, backed the dapple-gray and slapped a hand on the horses' rumps, sending them back down the crevice path. "All right, Victorio," he said aloud, "these horses are free. Anything else is going to cost you plenty."

Coak sat for a moment in full view, his rifle propped on his thigh, letting the warriors get the idea. He wanted to show no fear, just good reasoning. As the three horses broke free of the crevice and into the waiting hands of the young scout and another warrior, Coak saw the eyes of the lead warrior look at him and offer a sharp nod. Then Coak backed the dapple-gray slowly, taking his time. Only when he knew he was out of sight did he turn the horse and look down at the Catahoula.

"Let's get out of here, Buster," he said to the dog, "before they change their minds." Batting his boots to the gray's sides, he raced forward along the higher trail, not stopping until he was sure he'd put a mile or more between himself and the Mescaleros. He swung the horse a full circle, looking back, checking his trail. When the horse slid to a full halt, Jake Coak called down to the dog, "Get on up, Buster," and he looped out an arm and caught the dog across his lap as it sprang upward to him.

The Catahoula was wet and mud streaked, white froth swinging from its open flews. Coak slung a long string of drool from his gloved hand. "Damn, boy, you best learn to pace yourself," he said. Then he straightened the dapple-gray forward. "Gid-up, Cyrus," he said, and looked southwest toward Mexico. "Quick Charlie, you better be right about all this," he said to the white blazing sky, again batting his heels to the dapple-gray.

Throughout the rest of the day he rode without incident, yet carefully choosing the cover of brush, dry washes and shadowed ledges. He knew if Simms,

Hart and Roth came along this same trail, which they no doubt would, the Mescaleros would be waiting for them. But there was nothing he could do about that. If the army hadn't found Victorio's band and chased them southwest, the deputies would have their hands full. In the late afternoon, Coak spotted a long rise of dust two miles to his left and swung toward it. As he'd suspected, it was Captain Vertrees and his cavalry.

Lying in wait above a rocky ledge just to test the skill of Vertrees's scout, Coak stood up slowly and waved his rifle back and forth as the single rider moved forward within ten yards without showing any sign of having known Coak was there. But when the scout saw Coak and nudged his horse toward him, Coak noted no surprise on the bearded, dust-covered face as the man stepped his horse quarterwise the last few feet. The scout stopped, saying up to Coak who stood on the ledge above him, "We're seeing a lot of you these days, Deputy. Did you run into trouble and have to turn back?"

"No, nothing of the sort," said Jake Coak. "I've already been to Fort Smith and back." He moved down from his lofty position with his sawed-off rifle in his hand, his horse following close behind him.

"You're lucky you didn't run into Victorio," said the scout, looking him up and down. "We've got him on the run, but he's still got some fight in him."

"I did run into him and his men earlier," said Coak. "I passed along three horses to them, then lit out. Keep on the way you're headed and I expect you'll be tangling with them come morning."

"We figured as much," said the scout. "I'm Sam Griebs. I've been riding point all day. Captain Vertrees hoped that seeing our dust might draw Victorio into a fight, but I mighta known better. Victorio didn't get as old as he is by falling for any tricks the army can come up with." Griebs let out a tired breath, slumping a bit in his saddle. "I don't expect you'll be wanting to travel with us? Give yourself some protection in case Victorio's got some stragglers back that way?"

"No, but much obliged," said Coak. "I've got to push forward. Parker's got me trailing some men all the way across Texas. Seen anything back that way I ought to know about?" He nodded southwest.

Griebs thought about it for a second, then said, "There's four horsemen about ten miles back, headed toward the Red. They took care not to be approached. Don't know what they're up to, but you might want to ride wide of them."

"Thanks, I'll do that, if I can," said Jake Coak. As he spoke, he adjusted the cinch on his saddle and stepped atop the big dapple-gray. "There's three deputies back there, coming this way. Should be about ten hours behind me by now. I bet they'd appreciate you keeping Victorio off their backs."

"We'll keep an eye out for them," said Griebs. "You'd do well to let them catch up to you, wouldn't you? Stay close to the pack, take some safety in numbers?"

Coak smiled, tipping his hat brim an inch. "I might say the same to you. But I expect we're alike in that regard. The only person I like watching my back is me."

"I understand." Griebs spit a stream of tobacco juice, wiped his hand across his mouth and grinned. "I had an ole teamster tell me he once saw you snuff out a row of candles with that rifle of yours. Is that the truth?"

"Snuff out candles?" Coak turned his horse as he replied, "Now why would I do a fool thing like that?"

"That's what I wondered," said Griebs, his grin widening, turning his horse as well. "Just thought I'd ask." The two men parted in opposite directions, the dog waiting until the scout was twenty yards away before coming down a snaking path from the rock ledge and moving forward onto Coak's trail.

Late evening shadows stretched long across the floor of a sandy rock basin by the time Coak caught sight of four fresh sets of shod hoofprints that had broken sharply left out of his path. He slowed the dapple-gray and sidestepped it past the darkened shadows of a deep crevice, already counting steadily in his mind as he called out in a calm voice, "Who goes in there?" *Two thousand . . . three thousand . . .*

Without even checking to see, Coak knew the dog had dropped off behind him and by now would be circling, getting behind whoever waited. Coak levered his rifle one-handed, searching the shadows. "Best tell me something. I hate guessing games."

"Hold down," said a voice. "We're coming out."

Still, Coak counted to himself, watching the four horsemen file out and stop their horses abreast along the stony path. "We heard your horse and decided we better drop to the side," the voice continued. "Can't be too careful out here."

"That's a fact, Mister." Coak counted silently, sizing them up. They had the look of long trails and bad whiskey. Each wore a tied-down Colt, and each man kept a hand near his gun butt as if on instinct. The one doing the talking saw the way it had to look, the four of them spread abreast in what could easily be considered a fighting position. He nudged his sweat-streaked dun forward a step, letting his right hand move up from his pistol to tip his hat brim. Jake Coak stopped counting and returned the gesture warily.

"We're headed to Texas from New Orleans," said the man. "I'm Lewis Prior. These are my partners, Bob Herns, Tommy Kendall, and Bo Romans."

Coak looked at the faces of the other three men, comparing them to old wanted posters he'd carried over the past year. He couldn't say one way or the other about Bob Herns, as the man's face did not look familiar to him. But the others he recognized right away. On Lewis Prior's right, a stocky man stared at him. The man's name was not Tommy Kendall, at least not according to Pinkerton's Detective Agency. His name was Orville Meins, a gunman and train robber out of Kansas. Next to Meins sat a tall thin man with a pockmarked face and a long crooked nose. Prior had called him "Bo Romans," but Coak recognized him as Harvey Kettle, also known as Hooknose Snell and Black Bo.

"You took the long way, didn't you?" Coak asked.

"What's that?" Prior glanced around, then said, "Oh, from New Orleans? Yeah, I suppose we did at that." Then he straightened back toward Jake Coak, saying, "You look familiar. Have we run into one another before, say . . . Texas? Maybe Abilene?" Prior deliberately kept himself from looking at the sawed-off rifle in Coak's gloved hand.

Coak saw that Prior had recognized him, and he thought about it for only a second before deciding to take his chances, saying, "Yep, we've met before. I nearly bagged you for a reward back last year. You just happened to get out of my gunsights while I blew the hell out of your ole buddy, Morris Neworth. I'm Coak . . . Jake Coak."

The men tensed as one. Coak sat calm, but with his hand ready on his rifle, his mind starting to count silently again. "That was back before I quit bounty hunting." He offered a tight smile. "No hard feelings, I hope?"

"By God," said Prior, "I thought that was you." He chuckled under his breath. The men seemed taken aback by Coak's disarming honesty. Prior cocked his head slightly, as if having to consider Coak's question. Then he said, a bit grudgingly at first, "I did have to leave town in a hurry. Lost a fine pair of boots."

"We all lose stuff along the way," Coak said flatly, still waiting for an answer.

"Yep, we do," said Prior. He paused just long enough to make a good show of not giving in too easily. "Well . . . since it was ole Morris and not me you blew all to hell, I reckon I've got no hard feelings." He shrugged. "A man has to make his living some way. Can't say I was all that broken up over Morris Neworth."

"Good," said Coak. "Seems everywhere I go, I run into somebody I used to hunt for a living. I get tired of having to excuse myself." He let his hand visibly relax on his rifle stock.

"How long ago did you quit bounty hunting?" asked Lewis Prior.

"A few months back," said Coak, deciding to play it all above board, and see where it would take him with these men. "Went to work for Judge Parker. Turned out that wasn't worth fooling with. I'm looking around now, seeing what's left to get into, you might say."

"You shouldn't have any trouble finding something," said Prior, nodding at the sawed-off rifle. "I seen how you can spray that thing around when you want to."

"Yeah," said Black Bo Romans. "You dogged me and some pals of mine for over a week, coming out of Denton last year."

Coak noted the bitterness in his tone, and came back quickly, saying, "I know you thought I was on your tail, Hooknose, but you were wrong. You never was worth over two hundred and fifty dollars, facing up or down. You were just spooked on snakehead whiskey."

A muffled laugh came from the one Prior had called Tommy Kendall. Bo Romans threw a harsh stare at Kendall, silencing him. Then he looked back at Coak. "Nobody calls me Hooknose anymore. I never did like it. It's plain ole Bo Romans from now on."

"So be it, Bo Romans," Coak said. He turned his eyes to Tommy Kendall. "What about you? Does anybody still call you Orville Meins, or is that out of fashion?"

Now Bo Romans let out a short laugh as Orville Meins's face reddened. "I'll be damned," said Romans. "Even his mama forgot his name was ever Orville! How'd you come by it, Coak?"

"An old Pinkerton poster," Coak replied. "You'd be surprised what a man can learn from riding bounty."

"I bet," said Prior, cutting in, getting interested in maybe talking to Coak some, seeing what else he knew that a man might find helpful should he need to steer clear of the law, or at least find out how much the law knew about him. "Don't suppose you've heard any dirt on me that I ought to know about, have you?" Prior asked.

Coak looked around at the others, taking his time, putting Lewis Prior off. "You wouldn't have any whiskey, coffee, or anything fit to drink would you?"

"We might." Lewis Prior grinned.

"I ain't drinking with no lawdog," said Bob Herns, who'd been sitting quietly, observing Coak and the others.

"You won't be drinking with one now," said Coak with a snap to his voice. "I told you I was out of the law business. If I wasn't, we wouldn't have been talking this long"—his tone turned colder, his hand tightening again on the rifle stock—"you'd already be dead, Bob Herns."

"You sound awfully cocksure of yourself," Herns responded, not giving an inch.

"Hush up, Bob," said Lewis Prior, chuckling. "Can't a man change his ways? Hell, I had an uncle once been a preacher his whole life, took to drinking and chasing whores. Winded up dead of the clap in a St. Louis sanitarium. Said he never regretted a minute of it. You can't always judge a man straight up." He looked back at Jake Coak. "Coffee, huh? Yeah, we got some. No whiskey, though."

"Coffee will do for me," said Coak. "I've been ducking Apache all day; haven't had a chance to stop." He backed his dapple-gray a step and lowered his rifle barrel. The dog was somewhere in the shadows on the rocks above them, but Coak knew he'd stay back out of sight unless he signaled him in. Things were under control here—for now at least.

"Yeah, us, too," said Lewis Prior. "Hadn't figured on Mescaleros being around here." He swung down from his saddle and stretched his back. "Where you headed, Coak, if you don't mind saying?"

"Beats me," Coak replied, stepping down, holstering the sawed-off rifle, but keeping it loose in the leather. "Like I said, I'm looking."

"Yeah?" Prior moved closer, the others stepping down and joining him. "We're meeting up with some ole boys here sometime tomorrow, if they ain't got themselves shot. We're headed for the border. Ride along with us as far you need to. I'd like to hear more about what you learnt bounty hunting."

"I thought you might." Coak smiled. "I'll gather some brush for a fire. We'll bank it low . . . keep the Mescaleros out of our hair." He shot a quick glance at Bob Herns, seeing the angry look on his face. "Whatever you're thinking, Herns, either put it out of your mind or put it into play. I can't stand drinking coffee with somebody bad-eyeing me."

Before Herns could respond, Lewis Prior cut in sharply, "What the hell is the matter with you, Herns? All Coak here ever did was kill men for money—tell us you ain't done the same thing at some time or another."

"You really don't remember me, do you?" said Herns to Coak, his eyes still riveted coldly on him.

Jake Coak looked him up and down again, just to be sure. "No, I reckon I don't."

Herns continued, saying, "It was 1861. That one-room schoolhouse? Somebody stole the bell off the post out front? Sound familiar?"

"Yep, it does." Recognition came slowly as Coak studied Bob Herns's face closer. "Well, I'll be, you're Henry Herns. My worst ole student . . ."

"That's me, all right, Bob Henry Herns. You don't

know how many nights I've laid awake hoping I'd meet up with you again. My pa took a layer of hide off my back with a razor strap over you accusing me of stealing that damned bell. I owe you something for that."

Coak leveled his gaze, getting ready. "You did steal it, didn't you?"

"That ain't the point," said Herns. "You had no proof." His hand slid down near his holstered pistol.

"No proof?" Coak gave him a look of disbelief. "Hell, Henry, your neighbors heard you ringing it a half mile away. Said half the menfolks left the fields an hour early, thinking it was dinner time."

"That don't matter," said Herns. "I've waited half my life to kill you, Coak—"

"Whoa, whoa, whoa," Prior said, cutting in with a bemused look on his face. "Let's stop it right here, boys!" He cut a glance at Jake Coak, seeing Coak was ready for whatever came next. "I've seen men on the vengeance trail for lots of reasons, but damned if I've ever seen it over stealing a schoolhouse bell! Herns, you better calm yourself. You fire that pistol and bring a mess of Apache down our shirts, you and I are going to have a serious problem."

Herns relented grudgingly, his eyes still fixed on Jake Coak, but his hand coming up an inch away from his pistol butt. "All right, Prior, I'm off the prod for now. But mind what I'm saying, Coak, you and I are going to finish this thing, first chance I get."

Coak didn't answer. Instead, he stood firm, staring at Bob Herns until Herns finally stepped sidelong and turned away from him.

"Damn it all, Coak," said Lewis Prior, a slight chuckle in his voice, "you taught school?"

"Yeah, some, back before the war," Coak said.

"And now you've got former students wanting to kill you?" Lewis Prior shook his head. "That's the damndest thing I ever heard of."

"Me, too." Jake Coak offered a trace of a smile. "That's the first one I ever ran into . . . but for all I know there might be others."

Sullivan Hart, Twojack Roth and Quick Charlie Simms had only stopped at the relay station long enough to water their horses and ask the old hostler if two men fitting the description of J. T. Priest and R. Martin Swan had been on one of the stages coming through from Fort Smith. But before the hostler had finished answering them, the two cowboys, Bell and Casey, came walking out the door of the relay shack, Casey shoving his shirttail down into his trousers. "Barnes, did you tell them what happened?" Bell asked.

"No, but I was just fixin' to," the old hostler said, turning to them, then back to the deputies. "They was on the stage all right, day before yesterday. They threw these boys off, and sent them back here on foot."

"That's right," said Casey. "We can't swear to it, but it looked like they might have burned the stage after we left. We saw smoke."

"You didn't go back to check?" Roth asked, looking down at the two cowboys.

"Hell no," Bell said. "We was lucky we didn't get a bullet in the back as it was. The only reason we figure they didn't kill us was because they wanted us to deliver a message to you." He pointed up at Simms. "I hate to tell you Quick Charlie . . . but Priest is holding your woman hostage. Said if you want to see her alive again, you'll have to come face him in Sonora."

"But—" Quick Charlie Simms's words failed him. He had started to say it was impossible, Priest's holding Kate McCorkle hostage. Yet as he put it together in his mind, he realized that while he'd been figuring a way to outfox J. T. Priest, he'd allowed himself to be taken in by him. Of course, Priest hadn't taken Kate hostage himself. But, as Simms felt the low sick feeling down deep in his stomach, he knew that J. T. Priest had sent somebody to snatch Kate right from under his nose. "Jesus," Simms whispered.

Sullivan Hart sidled his horse close to Simms, saying in a consoling voice, "Don't jump to conclusions, Simms. This could all be a bluff on Priest's part."

"No . . . it's the truth," Simms said, sounding as if half the life had gone out of him. "He pulled it off some way, or he wouldn't be saying it. Damn it! I've been a fool. The first thing I should have expected was something like this."

Roth and Hart looked at each other for a second. Then Roth said to Simms, "Go on back to Fort Smith. We'll stay on his trail. For all he knows you never got the message. He can't hold you to something you didn't know about."

"Sure he will," said Simms, contemplating it. "Don't you see? He gets his revenge whether I show or not. He's had plenty of time to sit and think this out in his cell. If he kills Kate because I don't show up, he knows I'll have to live with that the rest of my life—and he's right. If I show up, he'll kill me and her, too. Either way, he wins."

Hart looked away toward the southwest, in the direction of the distant trail where Simms had sent Jake Coak. "Whoever he had take her, they didn't come this way or we'd have seen some sign of them along the trail." He looked at Twojack Roth. "Have you seen anybody behind us?"

Twojack shook his head. "No, there's nobody back there—no dust, nothing. Anybody riding for Priest wouldn't risk riding our trail, not with Kate McCorkle in tow."

Hart looked back at Simms. "You want to cut down? Maybe catch up with Coak? Watch the trail along the way?"

Simms considered it for a moment. "No . . . if whoever has Kate is on the same trail as Coak, he'll see them. I'm going on the way we're headed. I'll have to figure out my move along the way." He looked down at the two cowboys. "Did they have any spare horses?"

"No," said Casey, seeing what Simms was trying to calculate in his mind. "They can't travel any faster than you three can. Fact is, they'll be traveling slower. J. T. Priest was riding double with some puny-looking dude who called himself an attorney. Riding double will slow them down by half in this heat, across this rocky land."

"Then come on," Simms said to Hart and Roth. "We can push hard, close in on them." He started to gig his horse forward, but Hart caught the animal by the reins, holding it back.

"Take it easy, Simms," Hart said. "This is no time to go killing our horses. Let's stop here and water down. If Barnes will let us have some extra horses, we'll ride straight through the night."

"You can have ev'ry horse on the place if it'll help," said the old hostler. "Come on, I'll help you cut out the three best ones."

As Simms bolted on ahead to the corral beside the

relay shack, Roth said to Hart, "This is taking a bad turn. Kate McCorkle is Simms's only weakness. If she's in trouble, we'll have to watch him, make sure he doesn't lose his head and do something stupid."

Hart nodded in agreement. "I just wonder what Coak is doing along the other trail. Think there's any chance of him running into whoever has Kate?"

"The odds are long against it," said Twojack Roth, nudging his horse forward. "But who knows? Maybe Coak'll get lucky on us."

Chapter 8

Jake Coak spent the night with Lewis Prior and the others camped beneath the rising rock crevices. No sooner had the coffee boiled than they'd killed the small fire and drank and talked in the thin light of a quarter moon. Coak let Prior and the others see him keeping an eye on Bob Herns as he told Lewis Prior and Bo Romans about the bad deal he'd gotten from Judge Parker, and how Parker had fired him for some trivial matter. As Coak talked about it, Lewis Prior had only nodded, weighing his words. "I always said Parker was a no-good bastard," Prior offered as if in condolence. "I reckon you just had to learn it the hard way. Damn shame, a man can't even trust a federal judge for a fair shake. Makes you wonder what this country's coming to."

"Ain't that the truth," Bo Romans added. Coak looked at them, wondering how much of this they were believing.

When it came time to turn in for the night, Coak spread his blanket at the base of the rock crevice, knowing that Buster lay somewhere up there watching, listening. Yet, even with the dog guarding his back, Coak allowed himself to only fall into a half-sleep, keeping his senses tuned toward the dark camp and any sound in the night.

Near dawn, he heard the voices of Lewis Prior and Bo Romans, speaking barely above a whisper. "Maybe Bob Herns is right," Coak heard Bo Romans say in the stillness. "We don't know what Coak has in mind."

"You worry too much," Prior replied. "Can't you see the man is packing a mad-on at Judge Parker? If I had a dollar for every man Parker's fired, I'd be fatter than a coon in a cornfield. Half of Parker's deputies are just outlaws in the making any damn way. Besides, there's no price on any of our heads. If Coak's back to bounty hunting, he knows he's struck a dry well here. What's the worst that can happen? There's four of us . . . three more coming tomorrow. If he ain't on the level, we'll find out. If he really is looking for something to get into . . . there ain't a better man to have on our side."

Bo Romans said, "Did you know that about him, that he used to be a schoolteacher?"

"Nope, I didn't know it." A brief silence passed, then Prior added, "I might not have been so friendly if I had. But it makes no difference; he's still a good man with a gun."

"Herns said he remembered Coak used to carry a cur pup around in a gunnysack. Said by the time that pup was three months old you couldn't get near Coak without it trying to take your leg off."

"So?"

"So nothing. But I also heard he traveled with a big cur down in Texas. That dog was as bad as he was about throwing down on a fellow."

"Did you see any dog, Bo?" Prior asked, sounding a bit testy.

"No, I didn't."

"Then hush, damn it. You're starting to sound like an old woman. We've got some big days ahead of us. We can use good gunmen."

Bo Romans looked over at where Jake Coak lay rolled up in his blanket, his hat pulled low over his face. "He ain't losing no sleep over Herns's wanting to kill him, that's for sure."

"Yeah," Prior said. "I like that kind of nerve in a man."

At first light, Coak stood up, holstered his rifle, which he'd kept against his chest, shook out his blanket and rolled it. A small fire stood slanted in the morning wind beneath the blackened coffeepot.

"You're not one of them late sleepers are you, Coak?" Lewis Prior asked, stooping down and raising the pot with his shirt sleeve pulled down and wrapped around the hot handle.

Coak didn't answer. Instead, he tied his blanket roll, batted it against the edge of a rock crevice, then walked over and joined the others around the flames. Picking up his tin coffee cup from where he'd left it turned down on a rock, Coak rounded a finger in its handle and squatted down near the flames.

Lewis Prior reached out with the coffeepot and spoke as he filled Coak's cup. "Me and the boys were just talking, wondering if you might be interested in making some money."

Coak just looked up at him.

"Because if you are, it might be a lucky thing, us running into one another out here."

"I'm listening," said Coak. He blew on the coffee and took a small sip, testing it. He looked from one to the other of the men, then back at Lewis Prior.

"We've got some things in the works, Coak, if you

don't mind using that rifle of yours, and maybe having to pull a mask over your nose."

"Outlawry," Coak said in a flat tone, not wanting to sound too eager.

Lewis Prior grinned, stooping down close beside him. "Well, that's one word for it. I prefer calling myself a long rider. Think you could stand the pace?"

"I can stand whatever pace I'm put to," said Coak. "How much money are we talking about? Who do I have to answer to?"

"Money-wise, I'd have to say the sky is the limit. As far as who you'd answer to . . . well, that would be me, for the time being."

"For the time being?" Coak asked. "You mean you're in charge now, but might get shot any day?"

"No." Prior laughed, looking around at the others, then back at Coak. "I mean, I'm in charge of this here bunch. But once we get where we're headed, we'll be hooking up with . . . a bigger bunch. We make our moves, then we all break up, go our own way until we get together again. It's the only way to go these days."

Coak liked what he was hearing. Could he be this lucky? Simms wanted him to get inside *Los Pistoleros*. From what Jake Coak had just heard, he had a feeling he was talking to some of them right now. "I can't argue that," Coak said. "It's the way the James-Youngers have been doing it for years."

"Ha! The James-Youngers are small potatoes to what we're talking about," Prior said. "The bunch I'm talking about is bigger than some armies."

"Yeah, who are they?" Coak gave him a skeptical look.

"Not so fast," said Prior. "Let's go one step at a time.

If you want to ride with us, check things out, you'll see what I mean. Fair enough?"

"Fair enough," Coak said. "I don't want to jump into something I can't jump out of, if you know what I mean." He jerked his head toward Bob Herns, who sat a few yards away sipping coffee with a sullen look on his face. "What about him? Am I going to have to kill that bell-stealing peckerwood if I ride with you?"

"That's hard to say." Prior spread a grin. "Is it something you'd have qualms doing?"

"Not at all," Jake Coak said, seeing that Lewis Prior was testing him. "I'll hammer him right now!" He sat his cup down, stood up, drew his rifle and swung it toward Bob Herns, his thumb cocking it, moving just slow enough to give Prior a chance to stop him.

"Easy, Coak!" Prior raised a hand toward him. Bo Romans ducked aside. Bob Herns's face turned stark white as he took a dive across the ground and rolled into cover behind a rock. Prior saw Herns's pistol above the edge of the rock. "Don't shoot, Bob!" he yelled at Herns. "It was all a misunderstanding! Coak didn't mean nothing by it!"

"Like hell he didn't!" Herns shouted. "Step out of the way, Prior! I'll kill that sonofabitch!"

"Now look what you've done, Coak," said Prior, chuckling under his breath. "He's so fired up now, you'll likely *have* to kill him!"

"Then let me get it done," said Coak.

"No, not now!" Prior almost put a hand on Coak's arm, but caught himself. "We don't want no gunshots going off right now. Settle down." He turned his gaze toward Herns behind the rock. "Bob, holster that pistol and act like you've got some sense! There ain't going to be no shooting this morning. Do you understand me?"

For a moment, Herns said nothing. Finally, he spoke in a resolved tone, saying, "I'll hold off for now if he will. But I ain't going to be thrown down on without defending myself."

"All right," Prior called out to him, "now let's all simmer down here. Coak is going to be riding with us. I can't keep getting between the two of—"

"Who says this man is going to be riding with us?" said a voice from the edge of camp, cutting Prior off.

The men all turned at the same time, and looked up at the face of Roundhouse Eddie Jenkins, who sat atop his horse with his rifle cradled toward them. Coak looked past Roundhouse at Pete Lamburtis, then past Lamburtis at Big Joe Macon. Behind Big Joe, Coak caught sight of a woman, her head bowed, her arms drawn behind her back.

"Jesus, Roundhouse!" Prior exclaimed, caught off-guard. "Let a body know when you come riding in like that! We might have shot before we saw who it was!"

"Yeah, so might have we," said Roundhouse, nudging his horse past Prior, closer to Jake Coak, staring down at him. "I just saw this man back in Fort Smith three days ago, wearing a badge." His rifle tip honed onto Coak's chest. "Now he's riding with us? I don't think so."

Coak only stared up at him, glad he'd decided to tell Prior and the others he'd been riding for Parker's court. Now he wasn't going to explain anything else. If he'd played it right the night before, Prior would be the one doing the explaining. "Who's in charge, Prior," Coak said in a lowered voice, "you or him?"

Prior hesitated for a second, then stepped forward, speaking up to Roundhouse Eddie Jenkins. "Draw your rifle back, Jenkins. Coak rides with us if I say he does. Yeah, I expect if you saw him in Fort Smith, he was wearing a badge. But he told me last night that he dropped it on Parker's desk—the judge fired him. Don't come in here telling me what to do. This here's my gang."

"Pete," Roundhouse Eddie called back over his shoulder, "did you hear anything about a deputy getting fired?"

Pete Lamburtis stepped his horse closer, looking down at Jake Coak. "Yeah, I did . . . but I didn't hear who it was. That old deputy was talking about it at the bar the night we left."

"It was me," said Coak, glad that he hadn't let Dan'l Slater in on what he was up to before leaving Fort Smith. "I wouldn't bow and curtsy for the judge, so he yanked my badge. That's all I've got to say to you about it."

Pete Lamburtis looked at Eddie Jenkins. "He was in the saloon the other morning when Simms and us were playing poker."

"Yeah, I saw him." Roundhouse Eddie raised his rifle tip from Coak's chest. "Who do you suppose he would've backed if the lead started flying?"

Before Pete Lamburtis could answer, Coak cut in. "If I backed anybody, it would have been Quick Charlie Simms," Coak said. "Let's face it, you were in the wrong. Simms cleaned your clocks at poker, and you couldn't stand it. Any other questions?" *One thousand . . . two thousand . . .*

A tense silence loomed. Then Roundhouse Eddie smiled and let out a short, hollow laugh. "Hear that, Pete? He thinks Simms skinned us."

Jake Coak stopped counting to himself.

"Yeah, I heard." Pete Lamburtis turned half around

in his saddle and said to Big Joe Macon, "Bring her up here, Joe. . . . Show this man who got skinned in the long run."

Coak was stunned for a second at the sight of Kate McCorkle as Big Joe Macon led her horse forward and swung it to a halt in front of Coak and Lewis Prior. Kate sat slumped in her saddle, half-conscious. "Miss McCorkle?" Jake Coak stepped forward, looking up at her as if in disbelief. She stirred at the sound of his voice, but only looked at him, nodding slowly before dropping her face as she swayed in the saddle.

Coak reached up and pulled her down into his arms, speaking to Roundhouse Eddie as he wiped a strand of damp hair back from Kate's forehead and saw the cut above her swollen left eye. "What kind of low cowardly snakes would treat a woman this way? How long has she been riding with her arms tied back?" He kneeled down with her across his knee, pulled up a knife from his boot well and sliced the rawhide strips pinning her wrists behind her back.

Roundhouse Eddie grinned, ignoring Coak's insult. "She's got worse treatment than that coming to her when J. T. Priest gets ahold of her. But if you're no longer a part of Judge Parker and his bunch, what's it to you?"

"What's it to me?" Coak held Kate to his chest. "I wouldn't see a dog treated this way, let alone a woman!"

"She's not just a woman, Coak," said Pete Lamburtis. "She's Quick Charlie Simms's woman. J. T. Priest is going to hold on to her to get Simms to come to him." Lamburtis looked around at the others and winked. "Of course, that doesn't mean we can't all get to be real good friends between here and where we're going.

You'd like to know where that is, I reckon." Lamburtis eyed Coak closely.

"I don't give a damn where we're headed or how long it takes to get there." Coak stood up, holding Kate against him. "But if anybody touches this woman, I'll kill them where they stand." He looked around at the others as well and saw the smiles fade from their faces. Even as he eyed them, he reminded himself that if there had been any doubts who Lewis Prior and his boys were riding for, those doubts were now removed. He was on the right track to J. T. Priest—if he could play it out without getting himself killed over Kate McCorkle.

"Don't worry, Coak," said Lewis Prior. "I hadn't planned on her arriving in this kind of shape. I won't stand for any more harm coming to her. Take her over by the fire, give her some water and clean her up." He looked up at Roundhouse Eddie as Coak carried Kate McCorkle away. "You had no cause to rough her up."

"You should've seen what she did to Big Joe," Pete Lamburtis said. "She nearly kicked his balls up into his belly. She acted all right until we got out of Fort Smith. Then every time we'd stop to give her water and let her attend to herself, she'd go wilder than a mountain cat!"

"Still, I don't like this kind of business," said Lewis Prior. He looked over at Jake Coak by the fire, then back at Roundhouse Eddie, Lamburtis and Big Joe Macon. "I ride the long trail for money, not for beating up women. And another thing"—he pointed his finger for emphasis—"I don't like being called upon to act out revenge for J. T. Priest, or for anybody else."

"Then you better turn your boys around and head a different direction, Prior," said Lamburtis. "Priest is going to kill Quick Charlie Simms if it's the last thing he does. He'll use that woman or anybody else he has to. That's just where things stand with him." Lamburtis grinned. "But, let's be honest about it. Riding with *Los Pistoleros*, you'll make ten times what you're used to making, robbing them little hole-in-the-wall banks like you've been doing."

Prior considered it for a second, then relented a bit. "Well, maybe things will go a little better once Priest gets his killing done."

"Yeah, I expect they will," said Roundhouse Eddie. He and Pete Lamburtis looked at each other and laughed.

But Big Joe Macon jerked his head toward Coak and Kate McCorkle and asked Lewis Prior, "What's the story on you bringing that bounty hunter in? You really think you can trust him? Wasn't a week ago he was riding for the hanging judge."

"Trust ain't got nothing to do with it—I never trusted my own ma," said Prior. "As far as riding for the judge, half the outlaws I know were lawmen at one time or another. Priest put the word out, said gather all the guns we could find. That man right over there is one shooting sonsabitch. If you don't thinks so, you walk right over there, take his rifle and chase him out of here."

"Don't tell me that," Big Joe Macon grumbled. "I might just do it."

"Yeah, you might," Prior responded with a sarcastic snap, "but I ain't counting on it."

Near the low fire, Jake Coak wet his bandanna with water from his canteen. Carefully, he touched the tip of it to the swollen cut on Kate McCorkle's head. She looked up at him, her head in his lap, and said in a groggy voice, "I . . . fought them off. . . ." Her words ran out of breath.

"I expect you did, Miss McCorkle. Now lie still," said Coak.

"They didn't . . . I didn't let them—"

"Sssh, you take it easy," said Coak, cutting her off.

Kate relaxed for a second, but then raised her head and looked all around. "Where . . . are we?" Her voice was still weak, but growing stronger. She rubbed her elbows to loosen the stiffness in them.

"We're headed for the Red," said Coak, keeping his voice lowered to a whisper. "From there we'll cross Texas to the boarder. Sounds like we'll be meeting up with J. T. Priest and the rest of his gang."

Kate offered a weak smile. "You . . . didn't waste much time, did you?"

"I got lucky," Coak said in a wry tone, cutting a glance around the band of outlaws.

"Where's your dog?"

"He's around. He won't come out unless he has to. Buster don't like people. But he'll come if I get in trouble."

Kate looked into Coak's off-center gaze, noting how his eyes gave him a dark, serious look, but at the same time making him look uncertain, or even simple-minded. "How do you know he will?"

"Because I carried him home in my coat pocket nine miles through the snow the day his mama shunned him out of the litter." Coak smiled. "Don't worry about Buster. He was the runt, but he's made up for it."

"Then, what's our plan? Are we going to make a run for it?" Kate's puffy gaze moved across the camp.

"No, not now, Miss McCorkle. We'd likely catch a

bullet in the back. Besides, this is where Simms wanted me, wasn't it? In the midst of Priest's gang?"

Kate laid a hand on Coak's forearm, stopping him from wiping the bandanna across her forehead. "Listen to me. Charlie and the other two deputies aren't behind us. They took the coach trail."

"Oh . . ." Coak tried not to let her see his surprise. "I suppose Simms figured it would give me more time to get inside *Los Pistoleros* that way."

Kate let out a weak breath. "Do yourself a favor, don't try to figure out what Charlie has in mind. Until we see otherwise, don't count on anybody but yourself . . . nobody else is on our side."

"I always count it that way, Miss McCorkle," Coak said, a bit bemused that she might even think he relied on anybody but himself. He gently touched the wet bandanna to her forehead again. "But we've got an ally here if things get out of hand. So don't worry, we'll be all right."

Kate glanced around at the men standing a few yards away, talking among themselves. "An ally? Who?"

"See that man over there?" Coak made a glancing gesture toward Bob Herns. "He used to be a student of mine when I taught school."

"Jesus," said Kate, seeing the angry look on Bob Herns's face as Herns stood staring coldly at Coak from twenty yard away. "He looks like he wants to kill you."

"That's what he told me." Coak chuckled, inspecting the cut above her eye. "But he didn't mean it. He's working undercover for somebody—Pinkerton's probably."

"How—? How do you know that?" She looked surprised, seeing something in Jake Coak that she hadn't noticed before, a conning, a mind at work like the ticking of a clock.

"A couple of things he said when I first got here last night. He figured he'd better feel me out, see if I'm still working for the law, or really throwing in with this bunch. He ain't sure yet, but he's waiting to hear back from me."

Kate stared at him, the off-center gaze looking deep, knowing and in command. "What did he say that led you to think this?"

Coak grinned. "Said he wants to kill me because I once blamed him for stealing the schoolhouse bell." His voice lowered even more. "He knows that school was too poor to ever afford a bell."

Kate shot a glance over at Herns, then looked back into Coak's eyes. "That's pretty thin ice, Coak. . . . I wouldn't step out on it."

"I will though," Coak said. "I've got faith in him." He finished with the cut above her eye, wringing out his bandanna and straightening her up from his lap. "You see, Miss McCorkle, not meaning to brag, but I was a good schoolteacher." He sat back from her and slung the damp bandanna around his neck. "I didn't teach school very long, but I can promise you this, no student of mine ever turned out to be an outlaw."

Kate McCorkle only stared at him for a second, trying to understand this man, with his strange eyes and his odd way of looking at things. Other than what she'd hard of him and his sawed-off rifle, there was little about him to instill confidence. Yet now she'd seen something, perhaps the very thing that Quick Charlie had told her about. This *was* the kind of man you wanted on your side in a tight spot. She looked around once again at the camp, the hardened faces, the holstered guns surrounding her. Then she looked back at Jake Coak and saw by the look on his face that he was waiting, needing to hear something from her, something to let him know where they stood with one another.

"Well, Miss McCorkle? What do you think?" He stood up and reached his hand down to her, helping her to her feet.

Miss McCorkle . . . ? She nodded, rising up beside him, feeling the strength come back to her legs, to her mind. In a resolved voice she said, "I think from now on you should call me Kate."

"Thank you, Kate," Coak said, turning her loose, letting her stand on her own when she gestured his hand away from her arm. At the horses, the men were saddling up, getting ready to move out. Stepping toward them, Jake Coak cast a sidelong glance at Bob Herns, then whispered near Kate's ear, "First thing we've got to do is let this man know we're on the same side. I can't get close enough to talk to him without it looking suspicious. Think you can do that for us?"

"You've got it, Jake," she whispered. "If he's with us, I'll find out."

"He's with us, I'm sure of it."

"I hope you're right," Kate said as they moved forward toward the horses. "If you're wrong, I'll have to kill him."

"Kill him? How?" Coak was taken aback by her words.

But Kate offered no reply. The straight razor up under her arm was going to be her own little secret.

Chapter 9

They pushed hard toward the banks of the Red, stopping at noon only long enough to water the horses. Roundhouse Eddie and Pete Lamburtis had insisted that Kate McCorkle ride double with Jake Coak on his big dapple-gray. Coak saw their logic. If he and Kate decided to make a run for it, they wouldn't get far with two of them on the same horse. By midafternoon, when the sun bore down in its fiery intensity, they stopped once again, this time in the shaded edge of a long dry creekbed. When Kate McCorkle started to walk off among a stretch of brush to relieve herself, Pete Lamburtis stepped in front of her, blocking her path. "Where do you think you're going?" he growled.

"Where do you *think* I think I'm going?" Kate snapped in defiance, sidestepping him until he caught her by her forearm.

"Turn her loose, Lamburtis!" Coak shouted, stepping away from the side of his dapple-gray. His hand came up with the sawed-off rifle, too quick for anyone to respond. "She's been in the saddle all day!"

Lamburtis let go of Kate's arm, but did so slowly, not wanting to appear rattled by the rifle in Coak's hand. "She goes anywhere, I go with her." He thumbed himself on the chest with his right hand. Coak noted it was his way of showing he wasn't about to make a move for his pistol.

"You ain't going nowhere with her alone, Lamburtis," Coak hissed. "Not without going through me."

"Is that a fact?" Lamburtis shoved Kate to one side. Now he had to take a stand or risk looking bad to the others.

"Hold it," Bob Herns cut in. "I'll go about watching her." He looked at Pete Lamburtis, adding, "If it's all right with you. I don't want nobody shooting Jake Coak before I get a crack at him."

Pete Lamburtis gave Herns a puzzled look, and stood watching him as Herns reached out and shoved Kate McCorkle forward. "Go on, lady, and don't take all day."

Lamburtis looked back at Coak, then at Lewis Prior as Coak holstered his rifle. "What's that all about?" he asked Prior.

Lewis Prior let out a breath, seeing things simmer down between Lamburtis and Coak. "It's the damnedest thing every Pete. Herns there has a grudge against Coak that goes all the way back to his school days. Coak was a schoolteacher . . . seems he got Herns in some trouble over stealing a bell."

Pete Lamburtis stood looking back and forth between Prior and Coak with a curious smile. Then he looked at Roundhouse Eddie, shook his head and laughed. "Damn, what kind of gang have we got here?"

Jake Coak stepped back to his dapple-gray and checked its hooves, glancing around into the distance for Buster, but not seeing him. He'd caught sight of the dog's tail above a sandy rise earlier in the day, but hadn't seen him since. But he wasn't concerned. Buster knew how to take care of himself. The dog was close by; Coak knew it.

When Kate McCorkle stepped out from the brush smoothing down the front of her riding skirt, she kept her head lowered and spoke to Bob Herns in a guarded tone. In the flat of her right hand she concealed the razor, just in case.

"Coak tells me you were one of his best students. Said there's no way you'd be thrown in with the likes of this bunch."

"Really?" Herns looked relieved, but still cautious. "I don't know what else he's told you, but I've spent the last three months getting close to Lewis Prior—hoping it would take me where I want to go."

"To *Los Pistoleros*?" Kate whispered.

"Maybe," said Herns. "Let's go. They're looking this way."

On the walk back to the others, Herns whispered, "I've heard of you. You used to be J. T. Priest's woman. He got you out of jail in Colorado."*

Kate stared straight ahead, slipping the razor down into her skirt pocket, not offering anything about Priest or the time she'd spent with him. Instead, she weighed her words, then said, "I'm going to tell Coak you're not nearly as hot on killing him as you appear to be."

"Thanks, ma'am, you do that," Herns whispered. "We've all got a lot at stake. Let's try to sit tight until we reach Sonora."

When they had returned to the spot where the others readied their horses, Herns gave Kate a shove as the rest of the men looked on. He gave Coak a cold stare, then walked away, seeing Lamburtis and Roundhouse Eddie swing up into their saddles.

When Kate stepped over to Jake Coak's dapple-gray, Coak mounted and pulled her up behind him. Nudging the horse forward, he asked quietly over his shoulder, "What'd he have to say?"

"He played it close. Didn't say anything that would get him in a spot. But I think you're right . . . he's a lawman."

Coak smiled, gazing ahead.

"He said we all need to sit tight until we get to Sonora."

"That says it all," said Coak. They rode forward, past Roundhouse Eddie, Pete Lamburtis and Big Joe Macon, the three men lagging back to guard them from the rear.

"Can you picture what J. T. Priest is going to do to Prior if he's wrong about Jake Coak?" Lamburtis asked Macon and Roundhouse Eddie Jenkins, chuckling under his breath.

Roundhouse Eddie Jenkins spat and ran a hand across his parched lips. "But imagine how pleased Priest is going to be if Coak is on the up and up. He's a hell of a gunman, there's no denying that."

"I know," said Pete Lamburtis, his smile fading quickly. "That's why he ain't laying dead back there."

From the distance of a hundred yards, Buster rose up from his spot beneath a scrub juniper and, at the sight of the party moving forward single file, he loped forward, pacing himself at an easy trot.

J. T. Priest led the horsemen through the rail fence surrounding the long front yard of the Burdine spread, and stopped his horse for a moment to raise his hat and wipe sweat from his brow. Beside him, R. Martin Swan sat nervously atop a sorrel mule they'd taken from a small goatherder the day before. Swan had a hard time adjusting to the stiff gait of the animal beneath him. He knew that J. T. Priest's putting him aboard the mule was a gesture of humiliation. Swan was starting to wonder if he would ever get away from these men alive. The night before, when they'd come upon the goatherder, Swan had seen firsthand the ugliness, the insane violence that lay boiling just beneath the surface of J. T. Priest and his men. As an attorney, Swan had not allowed himself to see Priest as anything more than a client in need of his service. Last night, the reality of what he was dealing with struck him with the force of a lightning bolt.

Priest had ordered Macklinberg and the others to slaughter the herdsman's favorite goat and roast it over a crackling fire before the man's eyes. When the old herdsman pleaded in resistance, J. T. Priest shot every animal he owned, except for the mule Swan was riding. Come morning, as they'd ridden out from amid the bodies of the animals, Swan had seen the charred body of the herdsman lying dead in the smoldering ashes of the fire. R. Martin Swan dared not look at the body. Instead, he stared straight ahead, as if by not acknowledging the atrocity, he could somehow make it go away. This was not the same J. T. Priest he had represented in a court of law. This man was a bloodlusting monster struck from Swan's darkest nightmare.

"Boys," Priest called over his shoulder to Macklinberg and the rest of the riders, "this is Vincent and Sergio's spread. Let's make ourselves at home, but be sure we leave this place the way we found it—no burning, no pillaging." J. T. Priest smiled, looking first at R. Martin Swan, then back at the others. "In other words, everybody tidy up after themselves, the way your ma raised you to do."

Dark laughter rose from the men as they sidled their horses loosely abreast and rode the last hundred yards toward a large house constructed of adobe and sun-bleached frame. "Ole Vince and Sergio have done well for themselves," Macklinberg commented, gazing at the sprawl of cattle in the distance to his right.

"Yep, makes you proud for them, don't it?" said Priest. "I always get a warm feeling knowing a couple of former *Pistoleros* have made good." Beside him, R. Martin Swan rode forward pensively on the mule. "You can rest easy now, Swan," Priest added, "you're about to get your fees paid."

Ten yards from the house, Swan saw four men step out onto the front porch and spread out, each carrying a rifle, each taking positions behind the thick posting timbers. Swan looked at J. T. Priest's face, but saw no sign of alarm or even surprise as they moved slowly forward.

Two more men stepped out of the house, one a tall, slender Mexican, the other a barrel-chested man with a long red beard. Swan watched them step forward side by side, their right hands hooked in their pistol belts.

"Sergio! Vincent!" Priest called in a cheerful voice, stopping twenty feet back from them. "My goodness, boys, looks like you're expecting rustlers. It's only me!"

"*Sí,* we recognized it was you, Tuck," said Sergio, with a flatness to his voice that offered no harshness, but very little welcome. "What are you doing out of jail? We heard you were going to hang."

"I know," said Priest, raising his hat brim. "Wasn't that a terrible thing? But thanks to R. Martin Swan here, I'm back in the saddle, prime as ever." He looked around at the men stationed behind the thick posts. "If you saw it was me, what's these boys doing all cocked and ready? Ain't I welcome here?"

"We are ranchers now," said Sergio. "We have nothing more to do with—"

"You'll have to excuse Sergio," said Vincent Burdine, cutting his partner off. "He don't get off the place enough—makes him testy as hell." Vincent Burdine took a step forward, wanting to keep things in check. "The fact is we have had trouble with rustlers of late." He cocked his head a bit to one side, eyeing J. T. Priest, giving him a message. "You'd be surprised how many of them are ole boys we knew back when we rode the long-rider trail. Reckon they figure we owe them something . . . ?" He let his words trail, then added, "Of course we always knew you didn't feel that way. Step down, Tuck, you and your men water your horses. While you do it, I'll have the cook prepare something and bag it for yas . . . something for the road?"

"Vincent, you're all heart." J. T. Priest chuckled, swinging down from his saddle. But Vincent and Sergio noted that the rest of the men stayed atop their horses, some of them stepping their horses into a loose half-circle as if looking the place over, then coming to a stop in a wider, closer position to the men behind the posts. Swan sat still, looking around nervously. "The fact is, we can't stay that long," Priest continued, "and you know me, I never was much of a greasy-bagger.

No . . . I just hadn't heard anything from yas, no letter or nothing while I sat there in that jail. Said to myself, you know, as soon as I get out of here, I better go check on the Burdine spread, make sure everybody's all right." He grinned. "So here I am."

"We sent no money because we thought you had plenty," Sergio said in a tight tone. "You and Mabrey had everything, a private Pullman car, stocks and investments—"

"That was true at first." Priest raised a wagging finger, stopping him. "But after ole Mabrey disappeared and I started running from the law, you just can't imagine how quick the wealth went dry on me." He swung a hand back toward R. Martin Swan, still atop his mule. "Why, this poor brilliant lad hasn't even been paid for getting me off Parker's hanging scaffold."

"That's too bad, Tuck," said Vincent Burdine, seeing where things were headed, hoping to bring this to a halt. "We'd be glad to help you out, for ole times sakes. How much do you need, a thousand, two thousand?"

J. T. Priest looked down at the ground, shaking his head slowly for a moment. "Your generosity overwhelms me." Then he raised his face with a dark grin, a fiery gleam in his eye, and nodded at the house. "I bet you've still got that big, steel railroad safe in there, don't you? The one the newspapers in New York said could never be broken into?"

"So what if we do?" Seeing there was no stopping it, Vincent Burdine's hand slid from his belt to his pistol butt.

J. T. Priest laughed. "Hell, Vince, you already know the answer to that."

"Wait!" Sergio cried out. "We are the only ones who know the combination!"

But it was too late; the firing commenced.

Vincent Burdine was the first to fall. A shot from Rance Macklinberg's rifle hit him from the side at the same time as Priest's drawn pistols slammed two shots into his chest. On the porch, chunks of bleached pine exploded into splinters as men fell beneath a bloody mist. J. T. Priest turned his pistols to Sergio, grinning as a bullet whistled past his head. Priest fired low, at Sergio's legs, the first shot shattering the slender Mexican's kneecap, the next one slicing through his thigh. Sergio's feet flew out from under him. He managed another shot as Priest sprang forward. But the bullet went wild, clipping the tip of the sorrel mule's ear, causing the animal to bolt. Swan sailed backward from atop the animal and hit the dirt.

On the porch, two of the riflemen lay dead, another hunkered down into a ball with his hands raised, his elbows tucked in to protect his face as shards of pine lashed at him. The fourth rifleman had flung his weapon away and made a run for it. Halfway between the house and the barn, Rance Macklinberg took his time, giving the running man hope, then dropped him as the man's hand reached out for the barn door. "I love it when they think they've gotten away," Macklinberg said to anyone listening.

J. T. Priest kicked Sergio's pistol across the dirt and clamped a boot down on his neck, pinning his face to the ground. "There, now, that didn't take much. You boys got rusty I expect, living the good life."

Sergio's voice hissed up at him, "You better kill me, Tuck, or by all the saints, I swear—"

"Don't start babbling on me, Sergio!" Priest reached

down with one of his pistols and shot him in the calf of his left leg. Sergio howled, bucked and twisted in pain. "I can't kill you yet. You just said you and Vincent are the only ones knows the safe's combination."

"I will never tell you the combination," Sergio rasped, his hands slick with blood, trying to clamp around his leg.

"Sure you will, *Ser-gi-o.*" Priest laughed, shoving both pistols down into his waist belt. "You never was that tough. Mack, come get this fool. Stop the bleeding. Sounds like he's got a long day ahead of him."

The fall from the mule had knocked the breath out of R. Martin Swan. He was still struggling when J. T. Priest stepped over, reached down and pulled him to his feet. "Come on, Swanny-boy, pull yourself together. Let's go inside, have some hot beef and biscuits. Soon as Mack gets Sergio settled down, we'll see how hard it's going to be to collect what I owe you."

Swan struggled to get his breath and find words "I— that is, we . . . my law partners and I, don't want the fee. Forget the money—"

"Nonsense, lad!" Priest dusted Swan's back, reached down, picked up his bowler hat and jammed it down on his head. "Come on, you'll like this. It'll make you appreciate a hard-earned dollar."

Priest pulled Swan along behind him, saying to the men who had stepped down from their saddles and led their horses to a water trough, "Get this mess cleaned up out here before we leave, boys. Remember what I told you—leave this place looking like we found it."

Inside the large house, J. T. Priest pulled the cringing Mexican woman from beneath a covered table and shoved her through the house toward the kitchen.

"You better get some food whipped up here. Just consider us houseguests for the time being. I know ole Burdine would have wanted it this way." R. Martin Swan stood back, shaken, as Macklinberg and two of the men, Spence and Ames, dragged Sergio across the stone floor into the long kitchen. The Mexican woman whined in fright, but set about her task, taking food from the pantry with trembling hands. J. T. Priest stepped over to the kitchen wall and slung open a wide door to reveal the tall, steel railroad safe.

"I knew that baby was still here," Priest whispered, running a hand along the thick door of the safe until he came upon the large double-combination dials, each of them recessed deep into the safe's thick belly of steel. He looked at it and took a deep breath. "Well, let's get to work, Mack. Swanny-boy here needs his fees paid."

R. Martin Swan stood in silent awe, looking at the huge impenetrable safe. "This is the one I read about years ago? The one that was made special for—"

"Yep, that's it," said Priest, cutting him off. "Everybody wondered where it disappeared to." He patted the big wall of seamless steel. "It took six mules just to haul it here on a construction wagon. Vincent Burdine found the man who designed it living in Bath, England. You don't want to know how old Vincent got the combination from *him*."

Swan swallowed the tight knot in this throat, knowing it would do no good to protest what was about to happen to Sergio Jejoles.

Macklinberg slid a heavy high-backed Spanish chair to the center of the room, jerked Sergio up by his shoulders and slung him into it.

"It does not matter what you do to me. . . . I will never tell you the combination."

"I almost hope that's true, Sergio," said Macklinberg, tightening the leather glove on his right fist.

"You hit and I'll talk, Mack," said Spence.

"Sounds good to me." Rance Macklinberg crouched down in front of Sergio while the two men stood behind the chair, bracing it. Macklinberg hit him twice, two well-placed punches straight to the bridge of Sergio's nose. Blood flew.

"Ouch!" said Spence, wincing with a short laugh as Sergio's nose flattened with the sound of small bones crunching. "Now I even felt that myself. You sure you don't want to give Mack here the combination? I sure would if I were you." Spence leaned around close to Sergio's battered face with a dark grin.

Spence grabbed Sergio's hair and jerked his face up. "Now listen to me, you little—"

A gob of blood and phlegm flew from Sergio's lips into Spence's face. Macklinberg and Ames laughed aloud. But J. T. Priest only stood back staring, impatient, ready to get on with things. Swan's knees quivered weakly beneath him. He tried to look away, not wanting to acknowledge the grisly scene taking place before his eyes.

"Why, you dirty—" Spence wiped his hands across his face, stepping back. He raised a boot and aimed a sharp kick to Sergio's chest. But Sergio managed to turn sideways in the chair enough to deflect the full impact. Still he struggled to catch his breath.

J. T. Priest stepped away from the safe and in between Spence and Sergio. "Hold it, damn it! He can't talk with his ribs caved in, you idiot!" He looked at Rance Macklinberg. "Mack, you handle the persuasion part, personally. Keep him alive until he tells us something."

"Sure thing, J. T." Macklinberg readjusted his bloody glove, tightening it across his knuckles.

Priest darted a glance at the Mexican cook, who stood cringing in place. "How's that grub coming along?" She seemed to snap out of a trance, murmuring a prayer under her breath as she busied herself with biscuit flour, spilling a long stream of it to the blood-splattered floor.

Macklinberg crouched and readied himself, taking his time, straightening Sergio up in the chair. Grinning, he said, "I just want you to know, Serg, ole buddy, this is going to hurt you a lot worse than it does me. . . ."

Priest walked about the kitchen, looking things over as R. Martin Swan hid his face and tried to shut out the sounds of the hard, repeated punches above the gut-wrenching groans of Sergio Jejoles.

Priest fingered through the drawer of a small table, took out a black cigar from a wooden box, struck a sulphur match to it, and puffed it into a red fiery glow. "Maybe this will help," he said, turning back to Macklinberg and the others.

Sergio managed with all his waning strength to raise his swollen, bloody face toward Priest. "I . . . will die before . . . I tell you anything."

"Oh? I just find it hard to believe that." As Priest stepped closer, Clayton and Earl Hubbs came hurrying through the house, carrying a dusty, wooden crate between them.

"Boss!" Clayton Hubbs shouted, the two of them stumbling into the kitchen. "Take a look at this! It's Agrade dynamite—the big stuff! The kind they use to move mountains!"

"Jesus, be careful!" shouted J. T. Priest, seeing the symbol for explosives on the side of the crate. Then his words fell hushed as the Hubbs brothers laid the crate down on the big wooden table. Priest ran a hand across the top of the dusty crate where some nails had been pulled loose. "Where'd you find this?"

"In a little shed beside the barn," Earl Hubbs said, panting in his excitement. "We figured you want to see it right away!"

"Right you were," said J. T. Priest. He turned to Sergio. "Looks like you and ole Vince Burdine weren't nearly as out of the robbing business as you let on. What's this for?"

Sergio slumped in the big chair. "We kept it . . . just in case."

"Just in case what?" J. T. Priest asked, carefully holding the cigar back as he raised a large stick of dynamite from the crate and inspected it. "In case you wanted to blow yourselves a dam from here to El Paso?"

"In case . . . the cattle business did not work out," Sergio said through swollen lips.

Priest and the others laughed. "See? Nobody ever really quits the outlaw trail once they've been on it," Priest said, winding down to a chuckle. He looked down at Sergio. "Tell the truth. This is part of that big government shipment that got stolen last fall, isn't it?"

Sergio only nodded and dropped his head.

"I thought so," said Priest. "It's been showing up everywhere. I even heard about it in jail." He moved close to Sergio, wagging the stick of dynamite in his face. "There was also over a half million dollars taken in that robbery. You and Burdine were in on that, weren't yas?"

Sergio stiffened, looking down and shaking his head.

"Mack, punch him," said Priest, stepping to the side.

"No, wait," said Sergio quickly, before Macklinberg got into position. "It is true . . . we did it. It was the last time though, I swear it. We . . . only needed money . . . to hold us over till spring."

"Hell, Sergio," said Priest, "I don't care *why* you did it." He patted Sergio's slumped shoulder, "All I care about now is *where's the damn money!* Is it in that safe?"

"No, it is not here. It is with my brother, in *Mejico*."

"Now, bullshit!" Priest sneered. "I know where your brother lives down there. There ain't a way in the world you and Burdine would have left that kind of cash with him. Paco is a bigger thief than any of us."

"Then think . . . what you will, Tuck," Sergio said with resolve. "I will not tell you the combination . . . so you might as well kill me."

"Well"—Priest shrugged, drawing one of his pistols—"whatever you think's best." Even Rance Macklinberg and the Hubbs brothers stood stunned with the ease with which J. T. Priest fired a bullet through Sergio's temple. The chair fell over onto its side with the impact of the bullet in Sergio's body. A stream of blood rose through the air like a spinning red ribbon. The cook screamed loud and long. R. Martin Swan felt the warm blood whip against the side of his face. Priest shoved the smoking pistol back down into his waistband and shrugged again. "I don't want to argue about it."

"Damn, J. T., why?" whispered Rance Macklinberg

in a puzzled tone. "Now we'll never know the combination."

"Pay attention, Mack," Priest said, wagging the stick of dynamite. "We don't need to fool with him all day. I'll blow the door off that sucker." He nodded toward the safe. "I'm betting that government robbery money is right inside there."

Macklinberg looked the big safe up and down. "But I always heard this safe can't be blown, J. T."

"They only said that to keep people from trying, Mack." Priest broadened his chest. "I've never seen a safe that I can't crack like a duck egg."

Macklinberg looked all around the room, then at the large stick of dynamite in Priest's hand. "I don't know, J. T., you've been out of circulation for a while. This stuff is more powerful that it used to be."

"Give me some room, boys," said Priest, waving them back. "Let me show you how it's done."

Chapter 10

The earth had stopped quaking long before the shower of splintered boards and debris pelted down from the sky like heavy rain. From his spot behind the small shed, J. T. Priest had seen the sorrel mule roll by in a blast of dust and a tangle of shattered window frame and shredded curtains. The mule scrambled to its hooves, braying and shaking itself off, standing on wobbly legs. Shards of glass stabbed the ground like sharp icicles as J. T. Priest rose up from his huddled position, dusting his shoulders.

"Lord God!" Rance Macklinberg cried out, his voice loud, yet sounding muffled in his throbbing ears. He looked at the spot where the kitchen had stood, and flinched as a table leg fell to the ground in front of him. "J. T., it's gone!"

"Yeah, I see it, damn it!" J. T. growled, stepping forward, seeing the hull of the front part of the house still standing, dust and smoke billowing from the doorway and blown-out windows. "They don't build nothing like they used to."

"No, J. T.," Rance Macklinberg exclaimed. "I mean the *safe* . . . it's *gone!*"

"Well, I'll be damned," said Priest, stepping forward, fanning the air. "Where is it?" Behind him came Macklinberg, the Hubbs brothers, Swan and the others. R. Martin Swan rounded a finger in his ear, trying to get his hearing corrected.

"You don't suppose—?" Macklinberg shot a glance upward, ducking back a step.

"No, *hell*, no," said J. T. Priest. "It was too heavy to be lifted that far. Everybody spread out; look around for it! Damn it, do I have to do everything myself?"

Harry Turpin and Dean Spence hurried off to the left, looking all around the flat sandy soil now strewn with debris. Dean Spence looked around and saw Dick Witt, Huey Moss and Clarence Ames scurrying in the other direction.

"This is crazy," Spence said in a lowered voice. "J. T. better show me more than this or I'm putting my knees in the wind. He damned near blew us all to hell."

"I know it," said Turpin. "I barely made it behind the water trough before that blast went off. Now he's yelling like we all caused this? Huh-uh, I wasn't raised to be talked down to."

"I wish you'd look back there," said Spence, nodding toward Leonard Hergo, who hadn't gone off in search of the safe, but rather had sat down on a chunk of broken kitchen table and crossed a boot over his knee. "Ole Leonard ain't exactly giving it his all is he?"

"I don't blame him," said Turpin. "Leonard said he didn't lose the safe, he wasn't going to look for it. And if I was J. T., I wouldn't get too bossy with him. Leonard's not been what you'd call an outlaw till now . . . but he will shoot a man for very little reason if he's crowded, and that's a stone-cold fact."

"Reckon Leonard is as put out by all this as we are?" Spence asked, going back to the search.

"I don't know. Go ask him if you want to," Turpin replied. "But Leonard doesn't like things getting on his nerves, if you know what I mean—he won't tolerate a whole lot of foolery."

"Here it is, Boss! We found it," Clayton Hubbs called out, he and his brother, Earl, waving their arms. At their feet the big safe lay upside down, one corner of its top jammed three feet into the ground.

"Look at those two," Spence said to Turpin. "Hadn't been for their dumb asses taking that dynamite to him, this wouldn't have happened. They been all over Priest like he's their long-lost daddy." He spat. "Makes me sick."

"You ever rode with any of these men before?" Turpin asked.

"Naw, just Macklinberg," said Spence. "Him and me robbed our share of trains back in Kansas."

"Did he use dynamite that way?" Turpin jerked his head toward the charred remnants of the house.

"Ha, ain't nobody but a damn fool ever used dynamite that way," Spence scoffed. "But Macklinberg's all right. I ran into him a few weeks back. He said *Los Pistoleros* was taking in men. . . . I jumped at it. Now that I've seen this J. T. Priest up close, I ain't at all impressed, and neither is Hergo."

"Neither am I," Turpin murmured, almost to himself.

The men gathered around the upturned safe and stared as J. T. Priest kicked it with his boot toe and cursed upon seeing the door was still soundly intact. "Damn it to hell! Somebody get a rope!"

"A *rope*?" Leonard Hergo said in an incredulous

tone. He had moved in with the others and stood with his arms crossed, a cigarette between his gloved fingers. "There ain't a big enough rope in the state of Kansas to heft that big sonuvabitch." He shook his head. The other men only milled in place.

J. T. Priest gave Hergo a hard stare as he spoke to the others. "All right then, three ropes, a dozen ropes! Damn it!" He flailed his arms wildly. "Can somebody do what the hell I tell them?"

Leonard Hergo had led his horse behind him. He turned, stepped over to the saddle horn, took down his coiled rope, walked back over and pitched it on the ground at J. T.'s feet. He spat and nodded at the rope. "There you are . . . now pluck her out of there."

The men stood in tense silence. Priest looked Leonard Hergo up and down, his right hand resting on one of the pistols in his belt. "What's your name—Hergo, right?"

"Yep," said Hergo, flipping the cigarette butt away with his right hand.

"What's stuck in your craw, Hergo?" J. T. asked, his voice dropping low and level. Failing in his attempt to blow open the safe had made J. T. Priest look bad in front of the men and he knew it.

"Nothing," said Hergo, "I just don't like being damn near lifted out of my boots because somebody doesn't know what the hell they're doing."

"Whoa now," said Macklinberg, stepping in and picking the rope up from the ground. "We're all a little shook loose right now. So, let's get back together. Clayton, Earl . . . come on, let's get some ropes around this sucker, get it up from there."

"Everybody stand tight," said Priest. Still staring at

Hergo, he said, "You're saying I don't know how to blow a safe?"

"Do I *need* to?" Hergo nodded at the big safe stuck upside down in the ground.

J. T. Priest's jaw tightened, so did his hand around his pistol butt. But he saw no fear in Hergo's dark eyes, only confidence and determination. A tense second passed, then J. T.'s firm lips curled slightly in a faint smile. His hand loosened on the pistol butt. His smile turned into a quiet chuckle, then a short laugh. "By God, that is one contrary safe, I have to admit. I've never seen one like it before." He turned to the others, laughing aloud now. "Have any of you, boys?" The men laughed with him, letting the tension pass.

"See what I meant awhile ago?" Harry Turpin whispered to Dean Spence. "Leonard'll speak his mind every time."

"All right, boys," J. T. Priest called out, "that's enough kidding around for one day. Let's get some ropes around this sucker and drag it up. We've got more dynamite."

Leonard Hergo turned and led his horse back toward the hull of the house. As the men walked to their horses to get their ropes, J. T. Priest turned to Rance Macklinberg and nodded at Hergo. "Where'd you find that smart-mouthed bastard?"

"El Paso. Why? You want to get rid of him?" Macklinberg asked, raising his rifle slightly, his thumb going across the hammer.

"No, let it go," said Priest. "I got something for him to do, something that'll suit him just fine. I figured on leaving a couple of men here to bushwhack the marshals. Hergo will be one of them."

Macklinberg looked around at the blown-out house.

"But the element of surprise is gone now, J. T. The marshals will see something's wrong here from a mile away. They'll be ready for an ambush."

"Then Hergo and the others will just have to make out the best they can, won't they?" said Priest. "Now let's blow that safe and get going. We're wasting time here."

Sullivan Hart, Twojack Roth and Quick Charlie Simms had picked up the tracks of J. T. Priest and his men's horses at the burnt stagecoach. "Well," Roth had said, looking down at the ashes and bent-steel remains of the old Studebaker stagecoach, "if we needed a reason to be on Priest's trail, we've got it now."

From there they had pushed almost nonstop throughout the night, only getting down from their horses long enough to swap saddles to the spare mounts they'd brought along from the relay station. By dawn, they'd reached the outskirts of Mobettie, Texas.

"I know where they'll stop first," said Simms, reining his horse down as a silver thread of sunlight mantled the horizon behind them. "Vincent Burdine and Sergio Jejoles have a spread four miles out along the old Comanche trail." He nodded down at the hoofprints veering off to their right. "Burdine and Jejoles are supposed to have gone straight a few years back, but I never believed it."

Hart looked at Roth. "Burdine? That's the name Raymond Doyle gave me . . . said that's where he got the boxful of government dynamite."

Roth gazed out along the hoofprint. "Then we better scout it out good before we go in."

"Let's go," said Simms, turning his horse and kicking it out ahead of them.

They rode hard until they topped a low rise and spotted the front gates of the Burdine spread and the shell of the house two hundred yards beyond. Looking through his telescope, Sullivan Hart let a low whistle at the sight of debris. "It looks like a war was fought in there," he said, scanning the yard front and rear. "If there's anybody around, they're well hidden." He lowered the lens from his eye and passed the telescope to Roth with a puzzled expression. "Take a look. There's big crater holes in the ground everywhere."

Roth scanned the house and the yard, then passed the lens on to Simms. "Beats me what they've been doing," Roth said.

Simms took the telescope, eagerly looking through it, then passed it back to Sullivan Hart. "Have they been practicing with dynamite?"

"Why would they be?" Hart asked.

As one, they nudged their horses forward and, leading their spare horses behind them, they rode down cautiously, spreading out once they got past the gates. Keeping a few yards between them as they neared the house, they saw the Mexican woman step out from behind the small shed, with a rifle pointed at them. "Do not come any closer or I will shoot," she warned them in a shaky voice.

Sullivan Hart called out to her from thirty yards away, "Ma'am, we're federal marshals, in pursuit of the men who burned a stage and killed the driver over in Indian Territory. Lower the rifle; we mean you no harm."

As Sullivan Hart spoke to the woman, Simms edged his horse away, giving his full attention to the large craters in the ground, drifting from one to another, examining closely the deep hoofprints and drag marks from one hole to the next. At the fourth hole in the ground, he stopped and pushed up his hat brim, smiling to himself as the sound of Sullivan Hart's and the Mexican woman's voices resounded from the front of the house.

When Hart and Roth finally convinced the Mexican woman to lower her rifle, they walked with her through the downed roof timbers and broken furniture as she babbled in mixed English and Spanish about what had happened the day before. At the spot where the kitchen had stood, they looked down at a blanket on the ground and saw the half-naked body of Clarence Ames lying flat on his back with the handle of a butcher knife standing from his chest as if it had grown there. Ames's dead eyes stared blankly at the sky. Hart and Roth looked at the woman, getting the picture. "He was going to make me lie down with him."

"You needn't explain, ma'am," said Hart. "The others left him here to ambush us, *sí*?"

"*Sí.*" She nodded. "There were three of them, but the other two left. I think they will be waiting for you along the trail. I hear Señor Priest tell them he will pay them much money if they kill you."

"*Gracias*, ma'am," Hart said. He turned to Roth. "Priest left them here to ambush us, but the other two saw it was a losing situation. They'll be waiting somewhere ahead."

"Yep," said Roth. He looked all around, then asked, "Where's Simms?"

"I don't know . . . out back somewhere," said Hart. "Last I saw, he was following the holes in the ground."

Simms saw Hart and Roth step out of the open rear of the house, looking all around for him. He waved and called out to them from sixty yards back, along a stretch of scrub brush and cottonwood trees.

"There he is," said Roth. "What's he standing on?"

"I don't know," Hart replied, stepping up into his saddle, "but he looks excited."

Simms had kicked away the remaining brush and tree limbs from the safe and stood atop it with his hands on his hips. Hart and Roth rode up and sidled their horses through the scattered brush Simms had thrown away from the safe. The two deputies looked the safe over, then looked back along the ground, their eyes going from one hole to the next, putting things together.

"I don't believe it," Hart said finally, looking back at Simms. "They've done all this trying to blow open a safe?"

"That's all I can make of it," said Simms. "Evidently, they didn't do much good." He tapped a foot on the scarred and smoke-blackened safe beneath him. "Looks like they bounced it all over the place, and still haven't put a dent in it."

Roth shook his head. "So they gave up and just hid it back here, hoping to come back to it, I'd guess."

"Oh yes, J. T. Priest will come back for it," Simms said, the crafty look coming back into his eyes, the look that had been missing since he'd heard that Priest was holding Kate McCorkle hostage. "He must think there's something pretty important in it, as much trouble as they went to trying to get it open." He nodded at the ground where the broken handles of two picks and a sledgehammer lay in the dirt. "Priest never could handle a safe. But you can bet it's got his interest. It must be driving him crazy leaving it here."

Hart moved his horse in close and ran a hand down the front of the safe. "Is this the one I think it is? The one that's been missing since the big train robbery in Kansas?"

"It's the one all right," said Simms, bouncing down from atop the safe on his good foot and dusting his hands together. "It's this baby that's going to turn the tables on J. T. Priest and set Kate free."

Hart and Roth just looked at one another.

Simms smiled and patted the big steel door of the safe. "Leave it to J. T. Priest to get everything going his way, then let his greed get the better of him."

"What are you thinking, Simms?" Hart asked. "That Priest is going to come back here for that safe, and we'll just stick around here waiting for him?" Hart shook his head. "We're not going to do that. We're on his trail and I'm not stopping. It could be months before he comes back here."

"Don't worry, Hart, we're not getting off his trail," Simms said. "But it's not going to be months before he comes back for whatever's inside here. I'll see to that, I promise." He patted the safe. "Priest said for me to come to him alone if I want to see Kate alive? Good enough. That's exactly what I'm going to do."

"Don't be a fool, Simms," said Roth. "Priest will kill you the minute he lays eyes on you."

"Have you got any better idea?" Simms looked back and forth between the two of them. When neither one answered, he said, "I didn't think so."

"But still, Simms," said Hart, "you can't play this thing Priest's way. He won't even listen to what you've got to say. You said so yourself back in Fort

Smith. He'll kill you before you get a chance to make him listen."

"I know what I said back in Fort Smith," Simms replied, "but things have changed since then. All I'm concerned with now is getting Kate back in one piece. I'll make him listen. He won't kill me now, not if he ever wants to get this safe open. He'll go out of his way to keep me alive . . . me and Kate both. By now, he's figured out that there's no way he's ever going to blow this safe, or bust it open. Now he's got to have somebody who knows how to spin it, listen to the tumblers and pick it open."

"Are you saying you can open this safe?" Roth asked, giving Simms a dubious look. "Don't you think you better try it first just to make sure?"

"No," said Simms, nodding at the safe. "We'd have to turn it over to get to the dial—that'd take us all day. I don't have time. What I need to do is to ride back to Mobeetie, and see if the bank there has what I need."

"What do you need?" asked Hart.

"I need a couple of empty bank bags, one that's plain and one that's marked 'U.S. Government.' I need some paper money bands, too, and a stack of new dollar bills . . . about a thousand dollars' worth."

"I don't like this, Simms," said Hart. "You're not going to convince Priest you can open this safe with a few dollars and some empty bags."

"I've got to," Simms said with determination. "Not only do I have to convince him I can open this safe, I've got to make him believe I'm the only person in the world who *can*."

PART 2

Chapter 11

"I don't like nobody telling me what I can or can't do with a woman," Big Joe Macon growled under this breath. He turned to Roundhouse Eddie and Pete Lamburtis, who sat atop their horses beside him, the three of them watching Jake Coak and Kate McCorkle from across the camp along the west bank of the Rio Grande. "Besides, now that we're in *Mejico*, I don't think it's even against the law."

"Joe," said Pete Lamburtis, "what you're wanting to do to that woman is not only against the law of *Mejico* . . . it's probably against the law of nature."

Big Joe Macon scratched his neck as he replied, "Come to think of it, you might be right. But there ain't a man here not wanting to do the same thing. They already would have if it wasn't for that cockeyed peckerwood keeping so close to her. You'd think they were betrothed to look at them."

"Cockeyed, huh?" Pete Lamburtis raised his brow slightly, watching Jake Coak hand Kate McCorkle a cup of coffee beside the low campfire. "Is that what's wrong with his eyes? I always just figured his one eye was blind."

"Naw," said Big Joe, "he's cockeyed as a goose." He

shook his head and spit in contempt. "Look at him. He's cockeyed, stoop shouldered, damn near bald, don't look like he'd have sense enough to hammer a cork in a bunghole. And here we sit, ain't a one of us made a move on him."

Pete Lamburtis nodded. "You're right, we haven't. But the way I figure, he's just making our job easier on us. As long as she ain't trying to get away, I don't care if he pours her coffee, or even powders her nose for her. We told Priest we'd bring her to him. That's what we're doing. If Coak wants to wet nurse her all the way to Sonora, let him have at it."

"But it don't feel right," said Big Joe, "us not keeping her tied up and on the end of a rope."

"Then hop right on down, go over and tell him, Joe," said Roundhouse Eddie. "Then after you and him beat the living hell out of one another, you can sit up all night watching her."

"He ain't seen the day he could beat the living hell out of me," said Big Joe Macon. "It's that rifle that keeps me in my saddle. I ain't ashamed to admit, I'm no fancy gunman. But bare fists, toe-to-toe, I'd stand on his boots and bat his head back and forth like it was on a spring."

"Is that a fact?" Pete Lamburtis gave Roundhouse Eddie Jenkins a wink, then said to Big Joe Macon, "Then why didn't you do that the other night when he gave you that look?"

"What look?" Big Joe asked, staring across the camp, his eyes turning harsher, more cold toward Jake Coak.

"Aw, come on, Joe, you saw it," Lamburtis said, teasing the big man. "Hell, the whole camp saw it. Everybody just figured maybe you didn't want no part of Mister Jake Coak." Pete Lamburtis shrugged. "So we all let it pass."

"He gave me a look? A dirty look?" Big Joe Macon grew incensed at the thought of it. "He didn't give me no *look*—he don't want to either, if he knows what's good for him. Without that rifle, I told you what I'd do to him."

Lamburtis stifled a laugh, glancing at Roundhouse Eddie, winking again without Big Joe seeing it. "We know you used to be a bare-knuckle demon, Big Joe," he said. "But let's face it, that was a few years back. Everybody starts to slip a little with age."

"Age hell! I ain't but thirty-three!" Big Joe snarled.

"Easy, Joe," said Lamburtis. "Nobody's making fun of you . . . not really anyway. We all understand how it is."

Big Joe turned in his saddle, facing Pete Lamburtis. "Who's been making fun of me?"

"Nobody, Joe." Lamburtis shrugged. "That's what I just said, didn't I?"

"Yeah, but I heard how you said it." The big man's shoulders leveled. He drew his wide stomach in. "I can see you're just trying to edge me into something. But you don't have to. For two cents, I'd step down right now, walk over there and beat something green out of Coak's ears!"

Roundhouse Eddie chuckled, reached into his pocket, pulled out two copper pennies and pitched them into Big Joe's lap.

At the campfire, Kate McCorkle sipped her coffee, speaking low near Jake Coak's ear. "He's stepping down now. He handed Roundhouse Eddie his reins."

"Don't worry about it," said Coak, sitting cross-legged beside her, his shoulders slumped, his hands folded around his coffee cup. He reached down, drew his sawed-off rifle from its holster, looked at it as if inspecting it, then laid it down a few inches from his side. "Now what were you saying about you and Simms?"

"Not now, Jake," Kate whispered, looking surprised at his calmness.

Coak looked a few yards away to his right where a double-bough pinyon tree swayed in a hot noon breeze. He seemed to be judging the distance to the tree. Counting steps to it? Kate McCorkle asked herself, studying Coak's face as Big Joe Macon came stomping toward them. "Whatever you do, don't make a move for the rifle," Coak whispered to her.

"What if it gets out of hand . . . if they try to kill you?" Kate whispered hurriedly, placing a hand on Coak's forearm, seeing Big Joe Macon coming closer.

"It's been tried before." Coak patted her hand and removed it from his arm. He looked at her with his strange off-center gaze. "I want no harm to come to you, Kate. That's all that matters to me."

Their eyes lingered for only a second, but in that second, Kate McCorkle saw that Jake Coak had gotten much closer to her over the past week than she'd intended. She felt like telling him right then and there not to lead himself to believe there was anything between them except their present situation. They'd gotten close, but it was only out of necessity. Wasn't it? she had to ask herself. Perhaps the only reason she thought Jake Coak might have become infatuated with her was because *she* had been feeling something toward him. But there was no time for such thoughts right now.

"Get up, Coak," Big Joe Macon growled, hovering over him. "I saw that look you gave me!"

"That what?" Coak raised his eyes to Big Joe as he sat his coffee cup aside in the dirt. The other men around the campfire had seen it coming as Big Joe stomped across the ground. Now they scooted and stepped aside, giving a wide berth to what was about to happen.

"You heard me, Coak! Get up! You cockeyed, slab-sided idiot! I'm going to take you apart and put you back together the right way!"

"Back off, Big Joe Macon," said Coak. "I don't want to hurt you over a bunch of nonsense." He slid a glance at Pete Lamburtis and Roundhouse Eddie, letting them know he understood who had started this. The counting started in Coak's mind even as he spoke—but he wasn't using the rhythm for a shooting this time. This time, he was pacing himself as a way to stay out of Big Joe's reach. Systematically, Coak had to get Big Joe going in the direction he wanted to take him.

"Get up, or I'll drag you up!" Big Joe reached down with both hands for Jake Coak, but Coak rolled to one side, coming to his feet and moving a step back toward the double-bough pinyon. Big Joe staggered a step as he turned to face him. Before Big Joe could catch his balance, a left jab caught him in his side, not hard, but not intended to be, as Coak sprang a step farther away from him.

"Oh, one of those hit-and-hide fighters, eh?" Big Joe wasn't fazed by the punch. "If that's your best lick, you better hope I get—"

His words stopped short as two more sharp jabs hammered against his chin, the first one hammering his head back, the second landing harder, catching the big head as it bounced forward. Coak bounced a step farther back, standing silently, seriously, his shoulders slumped even more than usual. He looked apelike, his fists hanging down at his sides, his arms looking too long for his body.

"Jesus!" Pete Lamburtis winced. "Come on, nail him, Joe!"

One thousand . . . two thousand . . . Jake Coak rocked back another step, then another, seeming ready to turn and run. Big Joe ran a hand across his chin, feeling the smear of warm blood. "All right, you monkey-looking son of a—"

Another jab caught Big Joe's nose. He staggered backward a step, then caught himself and lunged forward, seeing Jake Coak back farther away. "Stand still and fight! Damn you! I'll break every bone in—"

This time, it was a hard cross that came as if from out of nowhere, the force of it landing full on Big Joe's jaw, knocking him sideways. He started down, but caught his hand on the ground and shook his head. Blood poured from his chin, his nose, and now from the cut on his cheekbone. "You ain't . . . got no punch," Joe said, his words slurred as he raised himself to his feet. "Now I'm gonna—"

"Lord have mercy," Roundhouse Eddie cried out, almost turning from the sight of Big Joe Macon's head whipping side to side, blood flying with each solid punch Jake Coak landed.

"Why don't he shut up *and fight*?" asked Pete Lamburtis, a stunned look on his face.

Big Joe righted himself, standing in a wobbly low crouch, too low, his big feet spread too far apart, his eyes wandering aimlessly for a second as Coak backed farther away and took what looked like a firm stand. "All . . . right! That's it . . . for you, Coak! Now . . . I'm gonna finish you off!"

"My God! He will *not* keep his damned mouth shut!" Pete Lamburtis shouted, shaking his head in disbelief.

Coak stood firm this time, giving Big Joe Macon a target. Big Joe saw it and took advantage of it. He lunged forward, a hard right coming all the way around from behind him, everything he had riding on it. "Die, you son—"

But Jake Coak wasn't there—nothing was there but the looming double boughs of the pinyon, about shoulder high on Big Joe Macon. His full weight thrust him forward. His thick arm shot between the vee in the boughs and he slammed into the trunk with a loud grunt. Jake Coak grabbed his arm from the other side of the vee and yanked him forward again and again, Big Joe still trying to talk and curse, his face taking in rough bark each time it slammed against the thick trunk.

The men drew closer in a half-circle, speechless, their mouths agape. But Bob Herns stayed back from the others, a faint trace of a smile on his face, his thumb hooked in his pistol belt. The sound of Big Joe's head pounded the tree trunk like the rhythms of a war drum. Coak stood with one boot raised and propped against the tree trunk, still holding Big Joe's thick arm as he turned to the gathered men. "See this?" Coak shouted. "This is all because he couldn't stand keeping his hands off the woman!"

The men looked at one another, some nodding, others only staring.

"Any time there's a woman in camp . . . there's trouble! I've never met J. T. Priest, but I'm having second thoughts about him!" He looked at Lewis Prior. "Would you do this? Bring a woman in here, cause this kind of trouble?"

Prior didn't answer, but he didn't have to. Jake Coak had made a point to every man there. He knew he'd just raised some doubts about J. T. Priest. In doing so, he also knew he wouldn't have to worry as much about Kate McCorkle from now on. Big Joe Macon was the biggest man in the camp. It had to mean something to the others.

"I joined because you invited me to, Prior," Coak said, still hanging on to Big Joe's limp arm, Big Joe knocked cold and hanging on the other side of the tree. "Am I going to have any more trouble over her?" He nodded at Kate McCorkle. "Because if I am, I'll straighten it out one at a time with everybody here." He looked around at the faces of all the men. "Who's next?"

The men shied back a step, avoiding Coak's harsh crooked stare.

"You've made your point, Coak," Lamburtis called out, his hand resting on his pistol butt. "Now turn him loose."

"What about you, Lamburtis?" Coak called out, making no attempt at letting go of Big Joe's arm. "You keep sitting over there looking like you've got something on your mind. You want to take up where Joe left off? Huh, do you?" Coak shook the limp arm, staring at Pete Lamburtis.

"See what he's doing?" Pete Lamburtis whispered to Roundhouse Eddie beside him.

Roundhouse whispered in reply, "Yeah, he's offering to beat the hell out of you, too."

"No," said Lamburtis, looking a little embarrassed, "I mean the way he's playing for the crowd. He's making sure nobody else makes a play for the woman."

"Yeah, maybe that, too," said Roundhouse. "But I think he really wants you to step in there and go at it with him. Go ahead if you want to. I'll hold your pistol for you."

"Shut up," Lamburtis hissed. "He'd love to see us turn against one another."

"I'm not turning against you. . . . I'm just offering to hold—"

"Not today, Jake," Pete Lamburtis called out, ignoring Roundhouse Eddie. "Maybe some time when you're not all tuckered out."

Jake Coak dropped Big Joe's arm and let the man slide down the other side of the tree. "I'm not tired at all, Lamburtis," said Coak, taking a step forward, his arms spread in an accommodating gesture.

"*Tuckered out*? Hell, he's still got his hat on," said Roundhouse Eddie. "He never broke a sweat! I don't think Big Joe even hit him, did he?"

"Not that I saw," said Lamburtis in a low tone to Roundhouse Eddie. "Big Joe never shut up long enough to hit him." Then he raised his voice to Jake Coak, saying, "You don't have to worry about the woman, Coak. All I want to do is get her to Priest. It's between him and Simms what happens to her."

"Good enough for me." Jake Coak nodded, knowing he'd made some big gains for himself and Kate McCorkle among the men. He dusted his hands together, walked back to the fire, sat down and picked up his coffee cup. He sipped it and turned to Kate McCorkle, who sat looking at him, stunned. "That's that," he said, sipping his coffee. "Now go on with what you were telling me before he butted in . . . about how long you and Simms have been together."

Once the camp had settled and Lamburtis and Roundhouse Eddie had dragged Big Joe Macon away from the tree, Bob Herns came to the small campfire and stooped down to pour himself some coffee. Knowing others could be watching, he didn't speak directly to Jake Coak, but rather said above the rim of his cup as he stood up to walk away, "Good work, teacher."

When Herns had walked away, Coak turned his eyes back to Kate McCorkle. "See? You're going to be all right from here on."

"Until we get to J. T. Priest, anyway," Kate replied. She sipped her coffee, looked Jake Coak up and down and decided this was the time to make it clear where they stood with each other. "Jake," she said gently, "I appreciate all you've done for me." She hesitated, then added, "But I think I need to tell you something—"

"Sssh," said Coak, stopping her from continuing, "you don't have to explain. I understand."

She gave him a curious look. Coak smiled slightly, looking down at his cup, rubbing a thumb along the rim of it as he spoke. "I know you're Quick Charlie Simms's woman. Nothing we're doing here is going to change that—I wouldn't allow it anyway. It would be like taking advantage of you, under these circumstances."

She placed a hand on his. "I just thought I should mention it."

He nodded and fell silent for a moment. Kate could see he had more to say and was searching for the way to say it. She gave him the time he needed. "I— I will admit I could easily have some powerful feelings for you, Kate." He paused, then said, "But I have no expectations. I know who I am, and I know that a man like me isn't meant to have a woman like you. So there." He shrugged as if letting go of something. "I just like being near you . . . for a while. That's all there is to it. Call it wishful thinking. I do it sometimes. What's the harm in it?"

She studied his face as he gazed away from her. "A man like you? A woman like me?" Kate shook her head softly. "Jake, a woman would be *most* fortunate to have a man like you."

"Aw, come on, Kate, you don't have to say that. I don't fool myself." He let out a breath as if in resolve. "There's men who women want, and there's men they don't want—guess which one I am?" He toyed with the cup in his hands, reflecting. "I've never had a real woman, someone who cared enough about me to want to see me come to the house every night at supper time. I saw a long time ago that somebody like that wasn't in the cards for me. But I've always wondered how that would feel."

"Have you ever stayed in one place long enough to give it a chance?" Kate asked, feeling a need to console him somehow.

"Nope, not for a long time anyway. I'm just not the kind of man that a woman notices and wants to get to know. I'm just plain Jake, a face passing by on a busy street. Once out of sight, I'm out of mind. But I accept that." He turned his smile to her, then looked away. "I'll tell you one thing though, if ever I do find somebody who cares for me the way you care for Simms, I'll spend the rest of my life at her side. I won't mistreat her, nor take her for granted. I'll work at whatever trade it takes to make her happy. She'd never have to wonder where I am at night, or who I'm with, or how I feel about her." His eyes had turned wistful. "When I touch her, I'll touch her the way a man touches a precious jewel."

"Jake?" Kate said softly.

"Hmm?" he turned, facing her.

"I really *am* Charlie's woman. And believe it or not, I *am* faithful to him." She smiled knowingly. "So you can save it for another time."

Coak looked at her, puzzled for a moment, then as he saw what she was implying, he nodded, and let out a short chuckle. "So, you're not buying any of this?"

"Buying it? I wasn't even shopping for it." She squeezed his hand affectionately, then turned it loose. "But you're good. You had me going there for a second."

"Well, thank you, ma'am," Coak said in a mocking tone. "That's good to hear. Sometimes it works, sometimes it doesn't." He tipped his hat brim, stood up and dusted off his trousers. Seeing Lewis Prior walking toward him from across the camp, Coak slung the coffee grounds from the bottom of his cup and set it on a rock near the fire.

"Damn, Coak, you beat that man senseless," said Prior, grinning and thumbing over his shoulder to where Lamburtis and Roundhouse Eddie had propped Big Joe Macon against a stand of rock.

"You saw it, Prior. He brought the fight to me. I wasn't looking for it."

"I know," said Prior, "I've got no complaints. I'm glad to have you riding with me." He paused long enough to rub his chin, then said, "I think some of my boys are wondering where you stand, though. They were a little skittish of you anyway, you having been a lawman and a bounty hunter. After seeing you whup Big Joe, they don't know what to think. Neither do I, to be honest."

"Really?" Coak looked around the camp, seeing Bo Romans, Tommy Kendall, and Bob Herns watching them. "What do you want me to do?"

"It wouldn't hurt if you said something, you know, let them know you're just one of us?"

Coak nodded. "Hey, Romans. Hey, Kendall," he called out. "Think we ought to be friends?"

Romans and Kendall looked at each other, then back at Coak with blank expressions.

"What about you, Herns?" Coak called out. "You want to make up and be pals?"

Herns slowly shook his head no and kept staring at him.

"You still wanting to kill me?" Coak asked.

Herns nodded yes, his expression unchanged.

Coak spread his hands in a show of submission. "All right then. What if I write a nice letter to your daddy, tell him it was all a mistake about that bell?"

"Crazy sonsabitch," Bo Romans said, chuckling, speaking in a lowered voice to Tommy Kendall and Bob Herns. "Come on, boys, Coak's all right. He's one of us. Just keep your hands off the woman." They walked forward and stopped three feet from Coak and Lewis Prior. Bo Romans cocked his head to one side and asked, grinning, "I got to know one thing, Coak. Why the hell did you hang him in the fork of that tree? You already had him whipped."

"I didn't realize it at the time," said Coak. "Besides, a big sucker like that, once you get to beating on them it's hard to stop."

The three men laughed, Lewis Prior joining in. "Ain't that the truth?" Bo Romans agreed.

Kate McCorkle sat quietly, watching and listening from her spot on the ground. Jake Coak was a hard man to read, she thought, seeing him now, the way he hadn't really said one thing to warm up to the others, but how whatever misgiving they had now seemed to be gone. Now, for some reason, she wondered if she had been right a while ago, calling him down for trying to feed her a line. Had he been playing her along? She wasn't sure, now that she thought about it. Maybe he had been truly speaking his mind, and she was so used to the con and the hustle that she hadn't recognized honesty when it stared her in the face.

A puzzling man, that Jake Coak, she thought, watching him without his knowing it. *Another place . . . another time, maybe?* She looked away from the men, across the camp at Pete Lamburtis and Roundhouse Eddie, at Big Joe Macon lying battered on the ground. This was no time to think of such things. Coak was busy keeping things level, doing his job, looking out for her and himself as well. That's all there was to it . . . and what else really mattered? They would soon be in Sonora. That's what she'd better be thinking about.

Chapter 12

Denton Howel stood on the stone walk outside of *La Rosa Negra Posada,* a sprawling new adobe structure on the outskirts of Sonora. Howel gazed out at the band of riders coming in from the east in a low cloud of dust as he spoke to the man beside him. "You worry too much, Juan. I can see where you might very well develop stomach problems running this kind of business." Behind them, inside *La Rosa Negra Posada,* the sound of crashing glass resounded. Juan Jerea panicked at the sound and, cursing under his breath in Spanish, turned and ran back inside.

Denton Howel laughed to himself and kept his eyes trained on the coming riders. When Howel and the eight gunmen riding with him had blown into the *Rosa Negra* three days earlier from the Mexican desert flatland, the owner, Juan Jerea, had met them at the open stone doorway. Nervously wringing his hands, Juan Jerea had welcomed the men and presented his new establishment the way an artist might present a newly completed portrait. Juan had explained that *La Rosa Negra Posada* was his lifelong dream, a creation of his own hands. The inn was the largest, the newest, and perhaps the grandest drinking, eating and lodging establishment west of Juarez. Yet, as Denton Howel, Max Sheppard and the others looked around the elaborate surroundings, Howel dropped a cigar stub to the shining tile floor, crushed it out with his dirty boot heel and said, "The Black Rose Inn, huh? I don't see nothing black about it."

"Where's any rose?" Max Sheppard had asked, looking around, slapping dust from his chest with his hat brim.

"Just one more beaner flea-trap, far as I can see," said Joe Cherry, stepping out from the other riders, slinging his rifle down on the polished-stone bar top with a solid thud. "Where's all the whores? Where's all the mescal?" He swiped a stack of wineglasses from the bar with the sweep of his forearm. "Where's a man to get a bag of something he can snuff up his nose?"

Howel gave Juan a menacing look, snatching him by his shirt, saying, "I better warn you now. I don't eat goat, ole man . . . and I don't eat nothing that grows from the ground or hangs from a tree. Anything goes into my belly has to have been *alive* at some time or other. *Comprende*?"

By the end of the first day, women had shown up from a brothel in town. Their pimp had brought with him a large, carved wooden box filled with the powerful derivative of the cocoa plant. Later that night, when the pimp had not returned to town, the woman who ran the brothel had ridden out to *La Rosa Negra* and inquired about him. "Where is *el alcahueta*? What has happened to him?" But the men leaning along the wet, sand-streaked bar had only shrugged. They didn't know.

By the end of the next day, a whore had left the *Rosa Negra* with a broken leg and a fork prong lodged in her hip. A family's pet milking cow had been reported missing from a nearby stable. Two other young whores had battered one another bloody and senseless in a fistfight. Thirty yards behind the inn, buzzards began to circle above a pile of sandstone and loose boards. For no apparent reason, a checkered tablecloth had burst into flames. Fire streaked up the side of the dining room wall. The men put out the fire by pelting the wall with bottles of wine and the contents of a brass spittoon. Juan Jerea had pleaded and cried, and moved his wife out of their living quarters, taking temporary refuge in a toolshed out back.

Now, on the third night, alone out front in the waning light of evening, Denton Howel whispered as if Juan Jerea was still standing beside him, "Juan, you ain't seen nothing yet." Howel turned slightly and called up to one of the windows above him where broken shards of glass still clung to the frame and where the shattered remnants of a wooden chair lay in a heap on the long, clay-tiled roof. "Joe, you up there?"

A second passed, then Joe Cherry stuck his disheveled head through the broken window, the pimp's carved wooden box tucked under his arm. "Yeah, I'm here. What?" As he spoke, Cherry shoved a woman's arm away from his bare shoulder. Red wine glistened in his beard stubble. He wiped a hand across his sweaty face, smearing the residue of brown powder beneath his nose.

"Pull your drawers on and get on out here," Denton Howel called up to him. "Bring the boys with you. Looks like Priest and Macklinberg's coming. Let's make 'em welcome."

Joe Cherry grumbled as his head disappeared back inside the window. Denton Howel leveled his gunbelt and lit a fresh black cigar. In a moment, the sound of heavy boots crunched through shattered pottery and scraps of furniture, moving across the floor of *La Rosa Negra*. The men sauntered out, some of them taking their gunbelts down from their shoulders and strapping them on, others stuffing their shirttails down into their trousers. Juan Jerea rushed out behind them and over to Denton Howel, saying in an excited voice, "*Por favor*, let there be no shooting, *por favor*!"

"Damn it, Juan"—Denton Howel chuckled, clamping his teeth down on the black cigar—"you're the most worrying man I've ever seen. These are friends of ours . . . the ones I told you we'd be meeting. Now get yourself back inside and you and your wife can clean this pigsty up a little. I don't mind telling you the place has grown rank as hell." Looking back at *La Rosa Negra*, Howel shook his head in disgust at the sight of Max Sheppard's big roan gelding stepping out through the wide arched doorway. "Shit, I give this place six months at best," he said to himself.

Joe Cherry stepped out beside Denton Howel and held a cupped hand in front of him. "Here, suck this up," Cherry said, grinning, his red-rimmed eyes lit and shiny.

Denton Howel looked down at the small mound of powder in Cherry's palm. "Get that away from me. I got better sense."

"Yeah?" Cherry laughed. "I recall seeing you once raise a goat up a flagpole outside of Mexico City, blowing this stuff up your nose."

"That's *why* I've got better sense," Howel replied. "Save it for Tuck Priest. He might appreciate a little upturn, after all that time in jail."

"I still don't see why we're getting back in with

Priest," Cherry said, closing his hand on the small mound of powder. "We've been doing all right without him. You've got something in mind, don't you?"

Denton Howel didn't answer. Instead, he took a step forward and watched the riders draw closer in the evening light. He looked back, past Joe Cherry, at the seven others who stood abreast on the stone walk of *La Rosa Negra Posada.* Max Sheppard had collected the reins to his big roan gelding and pulled the horse over to his side. Next to Max Sheppard stood Phillip Oates and Monty Osbourne. To their left, stood Eli Drake, Little Bit Collier and Buddy Raines. Off to the side, stood the half-breed, Buck Dehoney. The group looked haggard and sodden from three days and nights of drinking and whoring.

"Boys, look sharp now," Howel called back to the grim-looking faces. "Let Priest know he's getting the best. Any of you that ain't rode with *Los Pistoleros* before . . . you're getting ready to meet the man who helped start it all."

The men milled. Two newcomers, Little Bit Collier and Buddy Raines, straightened their clothing and looked themselves up and down. "Are you as drunk as I am?" Little Bit whispered to Raines.

"Oh, hell yes, drunker," Raines replied under his breath.

Nearing the *La Rosa Negra,* Rance Macklinberg turned to J. T. Priest riding close beside him. For the past two days, Priest had been quiet and sullen. Seeing the solemn look on Priest's face, Macklinberg asked, "You doing all right, Boss?"

"I'm all right," Priest said without facing him. R. Martin Swan was once again riding double behind J. T. Priest. The mule Swan had been riding never recovered as it should have from the blast of dynamite. Once across the Rio Grande, Priest had stuck a pistol in the young attorney's hand and forced him to put the poor animal out of its misery. Swan flopped back and forth behind Priest like a bundle of rags.

"It's that safe, ain't it?" Macklinberg said to Priest. "It's still on your mind."

Damn that safe, Priest thought. He didn't like being reminded of it, having been able to think of little else the whole ride across the Mexican sands. Priest turned a dark gaze to Macklinberg and lying in a raspy voice, he said "I put the safe out of my mind the minute we left there. I know where it's at when we want it." He kicked his horse harder, almost angrily, speeding it up toward Denton Howel and the men out front of the inn. At twenty yards, Priest slowed his horse and stepped it closer, drawing it into a quarterwise canter, saying over his shoulder to Swan, "Ever been to Sonora before, Swanny-boy?"

"No," Swan replied, "but I've always thought I'd—"

"Well, you're there now," said Priest. The sidelong lunge of the horse cut Swan off, and he hurriedly placed his hand down atop his bowler hat to keep from losing it as J. T. Priest spun the horse and stopped it in front of Denton Howel.

"Welcome," said Denton Howel, looking past Priest at the others as they stepped down from their horses. "Is this all the men you brought?"

"I left three men back in Texas to take care of some federal deputies," Priest said, reaching around and swinging R. Martin Swan down from behind him. "But I've got others coming. Roundhouse Eddie and Pete Lamburtis are bringing Simms's woman, Kate McCorkle, with them. She ought to make for some good sport." Priest grinned. He swung down and tossed his reins to Joe Cherry, who in turn passed them along to Little Bit Collier.

"Who's this little strip of skin?" asked Joe Cherry, thumbing toward R. Martin Swan.

"This is my brilliant young attorney, R. Martin Swan," said Priest. "If it hadn't been for him and his colleagues, my neck would be seven inches longer right now." Looking around at the *La Rosa Negra Posada*, Priest added, "This place looks brand new." Then his eyes swept across the broken windows and the furniture strewn along the roof overhang. "But I see you boys have made yourselves at home."

"Hell, you know us," Joe Cherry said, holding his closed hand up to Priest, "we're at home anywhere we go. Try some of this; it'll get your hooves pounding." He shook his closed hand back and forth.

"Maybe after a while," J. T. Priest said, stepping away from Joe Cherry. "I want to say howdy to everybody first."

As Priest stepped past Cherry to the others, Rance Macklinberg followed, looking down at Joe Cherry's closed hand with a dark expression. "I see nothing's changed with you."

"Nothing needs to," said Cherry, shaking his hand back and forth in front of Macklinberg. "Want to suck it up?"

"Get away from me, Cherry. We're here to talk some business. Keep that stuff to yourself."

"We'll talk business once we get to Diablo Canyon," said Joe Cherry. "Meanwhile, I'll do as I damn well please." Glaring defiantly at Rance Macklinberg, Cherry raised his palm to his nose and inhaled the brown powder. Then he shook a leather bag hanging around his neck by a leather string. "There's plenty more where that came from."

Macklinberg gave a grim look of disapproval and walked away behind Priest and Howel, into *La Rosa Negra Posada*. R. Martin Swan stood staring, frightened, unable to conceal it.

Joe Cherry laughed, looking him up and down with glassy bloodshot eyes, and threw an arm around the young attorney's shoulder. "You better stick with me, lawyer-boy, this bunch will eat you up for supper."

Swan asked in a shaky voice, "That stuff, what does it do for you?"

Joe Cherry jiggled the leather bag on his chest, holding Swan close against his side. Swan smelled sour breath full of mescal and the recent sickness that usually came with it. "This stuff? My God, man! This stuff is home to the homeless, religion to the sinner, and hell to a soul in peril." He pulled the reluctant R. Martin Swan to the side, away from the others. "Come with me, *mi amigo nuevo*, I'll show you all about it."

After dark, when Juan Jerea's wife, Soledad, and her elderly cook's helper, Maria, hadn't prepared the food as quickly as Denton Howel and some of the others felt they should have, some of the men threw lassos around the large stone-and-earth chimney out back and pulled it to the ground. Then they fed all the bundles of mesquite onto the open fire at once, along with armfuls of hay from the stables and furniture from the dining area. When the fire raged high into the night, so close to the rear wall of *La Rosa Negra Posada* that the coating on the structure's hand-carved facade and trim blistered and peeled from the heat, Joe Cherry stepped back with a bottle of mescal hanging from his dirty fingertips and yelled, "By God, that's more like it!" Sparks spiraled and raced away on the wind as half of the freshly slaughtered milk cow lay sizzling on an iron slab grill.

R. Martin Swan let out a hysterical laugh and rubbed his sore and reddened nose, his eyes shining and crazed in the shimmering glow of the fire. Joe Cherry shoved the bottle of mescal into Swan's hands, saying, "Here, throw this back. It'll keep your teeth from grinding." Off in a dark corner of the rear yard, Juan Perea, his wife, and their grown son, Lorenzo, stood watching in anger and humiliation as their lovely *posada* was pillaged before their eyes.

"Papa, we must do something," said Lorenzo. "I beg of you, let me get the rifle and chase these animals away from here! You did not build this place to be trampled beneath the hooves of pigs!"

"No, my son, I did not," said Juan, gripping his son's arm. "But neither did I build it to be a place of sorrow, and that is what it will always be to me, if you die here. I sent the old woman into town to bring back the *alquacil*. He will stop them."

"The town constable?" Lorenzo said, astonished. "But he is old and frail and will do nothing! He will only anger them!"

"He will bring help with him," said Juan.

"What help, Papa? There are no *federales* in Sonora. They are off chasing the Apache!"

"We must have faith, Lorenzo," said Juan. "It is all we can do. These men will not stay long. They will soon go off to do the terrible things they do. Stay silent until this passes. We will repair what they destroy."

But at midnight, when the town constable rode up out front of *La Rosa Negra* in a black, open-topped buggy, three men with rifles in their hands stepped forward as he rose up from his seat and demanded of them, "Who are you men? What is going on here?" He pulled back his wrinkled white linen suit coat, revealing a copper badge.

Max Sheppard replied boldly in a whiskey-lit voice as he cocked his rifle, "We're *Los Pistoleros,* Mister *po-lice-man.* We're just having ourselves a little party, you might say."

The old constable looked stunned. *"Los Pistoleros?"* He sat back down.

"Sí, Los Pistoleros," said Sheppard.

From the balcony on the far upper end of the building, J. T. Priest watched the buggy turn a circle on the walk stones and speed away into the night toward the lights of Sonora. Turning back to the soft candlelight, he picked up a wet towel from a porcelain water basin, wrung it out and pressed it to his hot face. His nostrils were raw and throbbing from inhaling the powder Joe Cherry had given him before he'd retired upstairs with two young women in tow.

"Come back to bed," said the woman who was still awake. She lay naked in the small circle of soft light and patted a hand on the damp side of the bed where Priest had been lying. When J. T. Priest walked over, then only turned his back to her and slumped down on the side of the bed, she scooted over closer to him and drew a thin line down his spine with her fingertip. "What is wrong, *mi gran amante hombre*? Does my sister and I not satisfy you?"

Great lover man . . . "Ha," said Priest, "you whores are the same everywhere." He pressed his face to the towel and scooted forward an inch, getting away from her fingers on his sweaty back. He spoke into the moist towel. "Do you ever wonder what a half million dollars looks like, up close, in a pile? With both your hands buried in it?"

She didn't answer for a moment, and when she did, all she said was, "No . . . I have never dreamed of so much money."

Earlier when he'd taken the brown powder, she'd watched how it had affected him, the way she always watched men and what their eyes and actions said to her. He had been a brute, making demands on her and her sister that only a man with much violence and madness would make. It had taken all their cunning and the skills of their profession to keep him from hurting them. Then, when the powder had begun to wear off, he had been like a sick, brooding child. He had grown distant and wrapped in his thoughts. Now that his mind was settling, he would need to talk, to tell her things that she would listen to and agree with, even if she did not want to hear, even if she did not understand.

"What do you know about anything?" he said in a muffled voice, his face still buried in the towel. "What could a whore ever know about what a man goes through? I was going to hang last week, bet you didn't know that. I was going to hang because I killed a man and cut off his ears . . . that's all, nothing more. It was no different than a string of ears I cut off a dozen other men over the past twenty years. But they didn't get to hang me." He chuckled. "Not me. I was too much for them . . . damn them all." He raised his face and took a deep breath, then lowered it back into the towel, this time not covering his lips with it, allowing himself to speak more clearly.

"You know what my downfall was? I loved a damn

woman. I loved her so much I stole her from another man—hell, I stole everything else in life, what did it matter? I sent him to jail for a crime *I* committed. You think I give a damn about anything? Well, I don't, I never did. She'll show up here before long, that woman. And I'll kill her when I'm through with her. I'll kill her and that man she loves . . . the man she betrayed me for. They're both as good as dead right now."

He raised his face and looked over through the open balcony doors at the wide sparkling sky above the desert floor. After a moment's pause, he said to himself, "Shit, it's coming apart though, I can feel it. There's money back there in a safe, buried upside down three feet deep. I can feel that, too. . . . And damn it, between the two, the money and the woman, I can feel it all coming apart on me."

He stood up, slung the towel down to his feet, picked up a black cigar, walked naked back out onto the cool stone balcony floor, and struck a match in his cupped hands. He worked on the cigar until the tip glowed red in the night. Then he studied the cigar's tip and blew his breath on it. "Get your sister up and both of yas get out of here. Get out now, or I'll kill you both!"

As the two women scurried naked from the room, one of them managed to peel a blanket from the bed and throw it around herself. Priest looked down at the stone walk below to where R. Martin Swan ran screaming and laughing, his arms spread wide toward heaven, buck naked save for his black necktie fluttering back over his shoulder.

"Damn you to hell, Quick Charlie Simms," Priest said to the endless night sky. "Come on and get me.

Come get me quick, Simms, or so help me God . . . I'll kill her graveyard dead."

He stood for the next hour in a drifting gray stream of cigar smoke, telling himself the safe was full of money, making himself believe it was there and at the same time warning himself *not* to even think about it.

Sometime before the first sliver of light mantled the horizon, he watched R. Martin Swan walk back out of the blackness below, in silence, his thin arms wrapped across his naked chest. Priest shook his head and walked back inside the room. He stretched out across the bed, but lay with his eyes wide open, staring down at the floor. Knowing sleep was not going to come to him, he sat up, reached for the small leather bag Joe Cherry had given him earlier, squeezing it to gauge its contents, then reached for his clothes hanging over a chair.

Downstairs, Rance Macklinberg sat at the only table left standing in the wide dining room. He looked up as J. T. Priest walked toward him, past the men who lay sleeping atop the bar and past R. Martin Swan, who lay stretched out on the floor with his trousers back on, but down around his knees. An old horse pistol lay on Swan's chest.

Swan looked up at Priest and asked in a hollow voice, "Is it time to go yet?"

"I'll tell you when, Swanny-boy," Priest said, kicking aside an empty bottle.

"Couldn't sleep, Boss?" Rance Macklinberg asked as Priest righted a chair and flopped down on it at the table.

"No, not much," said Priest, letting out a tired breath and combing his fingers back through his tangled hair. "That damned Cherry and his powder."

Macklinberg sipped wine from a bottle and slid the bottle over to Priest. "Still thinking about that safe?"

Priest stared at him, then said, a bit put out, "No, but you must be. It's all you've talked about since we left there."

"It's a powerful lot of money, if it's really in there," said Macklinberg. "More than we could make in a long while, provided we didn't have to share it with anybody else."

"Yeah?" Priest took a sip, then set the bottle down, considering it. "It's even more if only one man had it all to himself." His gaze turned suspicious.

"That ain't what I was thinking, Boss. You know me better than that." Macklinberg shrugged. "I was just thinking maybe after Roundhouse and Lamburtis get here . . . and you get settled with the woman and Simms, if Simms even shows that is."

"Simms will show," said Priest, "and I'll kill him."

"And the woman, too?"

"I've been giving her some thought," said Priest. He looked away and rubbed his inflamed nose.

"Well, I'm just saying, Boss. Once you get settled on things, we could figure out what to do about that safe. It won't blow, we've seen that. But maybe find somebody who knows how to spin it open."

"It's hard to find somebody like that," said Priest. He stood up, dismissing the idea, getting restless, not liking what had just passed across his mind. "Where the hell's the owner of this shit-hole?" Priest call out across the ravaged dining room. "Can we get some coffee over here?"

Chapter 13

No one out front of *La Rosa Negra Posada* noticed the black dog when he slipped forward out of the wake of looming dust and sat twenty yards away for a moment, watching Jake Coak swing down from his saddle. Jake Coak caught a glimpse of Buster and resisted the urge to shoo him away. But when Coak helped Kate McCorkle down from the saddle, then looked back toward where the dog had been sitting, Buster was gone. Coak breathed in relief, then said to Kate, standing close to her, "Are you going to be all right with this?"

"Just watch me," she said firmly, smoothing her hands down her dusty riding skirt.

"We'll take her now," said Roundhouse Eddie, stepping in, wanting to let Priest know that he and Lamburtis had some control. He started to grab Kate's arm, but the look on Coak's face stopped him. "Come on then," Roundhouse said to Kate, taking a step back, giving her room to walk in front of him and Lamburtis.

Watching from beside their horses, Bo Romans said to Bob Herns and Tommy Kendall, "You got to admit, it took some gall, him telling them straight up that the woman was riding with him until we got here. Whatever else a person says about Jake Coak, he sure as hell ain't bashful."

Bob Herns looked at each man, feeling better now that they had formed some sort of acceptance of Coak. Not wanting to give in too easily he said, "I hate to say it, but I might have been mistaken all these years about him."

"Mistaken?" Bo Romans raised a brow. "You mean after all this time, maybe you was in the wrong?"

Herns feigned a look of embarrassment. "Maybe."

Tommy Kendall stifled a laugh and shook his head.

Bo Romans looked closer at Bob Herns. "Let's settle this once and for all." He raised a finger for emphasis. "Did you or did you not steal that damned bell?"

Herns squirmed in place, rubbing a boot toe on the ground. "Let's put it this way . . . the bell ended up in my hands some way. I was young at the time; it ain't all that clear to me."

"Well shit," said Romans in disgust, "you've been packing a mad-on over nothing."

"All right, maybe I have," Herns admitted. "But I'm over it now. If he's good with you fellows, he's good enough for me." He stepped toward *La Rosa Negra*, seeing Priest and the others file out and join Joe Cherry on the stone walk. "Come on, let's meet the gang."

After the fight with Big Joe Macon the other night, and after Romans and Kendall had given in and become more friendly with Jake Coak, Herns had managed to get Coak to the side and let him know where he stood. While the others had gathered around a water hole, Herns had revealed to Coak that he was indeed working undercover for the Pinkerton Detective

Agency. He'd been working his way in with Lewis Prior in hopes of it leading him to *Los Pistoleros.*

"I figured as much," Coak had said, barely above a whisper. In the few moments they had alone, Coak let him know the whole story, about J. T. Priest, about Hart, Roth and Simms being on the trail. "So, we're not going to be by ourselves for long," Coak added when he finished. "Just be ready to take them down when the time comes."

"I'm ready," said Herns, passing a glance over toward the others, making sure they weren't watching. "Only one thing I need to tell you . . . I usually work alone."

Coak had smiled. "So does everybody else I've run into lately."

"I don't share rewards with anybody," Herns told him.

"You always was one of my favorite students," Coak had replied wryly. "We'll settle up when the time comes. . . ."

Herns thought about it now, looking around at the faces out front of *La Rosa Negra Posada.* There was more at stake than just the reward money, but the reward money couldn't be dismissed. Before him stood the same faces he'd seen in the new rogues' gallery files at the Chicago office. He'd spent night after night studying these same faces assembled before him. He'd committed them to memory; and now as he saw them in the flesh, his mind began clicking, putting together the particulars of each man's crimes, and the price on their heads. As he added dollars in his mind, he caught a glimpse of Coak looking at him and wondered for a second if Coak had been doing the same. Then his attention was drawn to Kate McCorkle as Pete Lamburtis gave her a slight shove forward and J. T. Priest caught her by the shoulders.

"Well, just looky here," said Priest, holding her back at arm's length. "My old, long-lost flame . . . my best ole warm, soft—"

"You son of a bitch!" Kate's nails slashed across his face. The men almost gasped. Priest slung her around backward with one arm and held her pinned to him, his free hand going to the red scratch marks on his face. Kate struggled against him. In the doorway of the inn, one whore giggled to another, both of them concealing their lips with their fingertips as they whispered in Spanish.

"Jesus!" Priest said. "Why's her hands untied?" He glowered at Lamburtis and Roundhouse Eddie, catching only a quick glance at Big Joe Macon's battered face, standing partly hidden behind them.

"Ask him," said Pete Lamburtis, jerking a thumb toward Jake Coak.

"No, by God," said Priest, "I'm asking you!" Reaching into his coat pocket, taking out a wadded bandanna, Priest blotted it against the trickle of blood on his cheek.

Roundhouse Eddie Jenkins stepped forward saying, "We just figured you would want her comfortable is all, Boss, knowing she used to mean something to you."

Priest released his hold on Kate just enough to allow her to settle down, which she did, cursing him under her breath. J. T. Priest chuckled and lowered the bandanna. Not wanting to appear weak in front of the men, he said, "All right, no harm done." He nodded at Big Joe Macon. "What got ahold of his face?"

"Ask him," Lamburtis repeated, again jerking his thumb toward Jake Coak.

"Stick that thumb at me again," Coak said in a low growl, "and watch you lose it."

Priest stared back and forth, bemused, then asked Lamburtis pointedly, "Who the hell is he, and why must I ask *him* every damn thing?"

Before Pete Lamburtis could answer, Lewis Prior moved forward, wanting to deflect any heat off of Coak and at the same time make sure he kept himself level with J. T. Priest. "These are my men, Priest," he said. "This is Bob Herns, Bo Romans, Tommy Kendall and Jake Coak." He started to jerk a thumb toward Coak, but then thought better of it and nodded at him instead. "Jake here joined up with us on the trail. These others have been with me a while."

Priest looked the men over, then turned his gaze to Coak. "I've heard of you, Coak . . . a lawman ain't ya, or a bounty hunter?" As Priest spoke, Joe Cherry and Max Sheppard seemed to brace forward behind him, glaring at Coak.

"Yep, I used to be." Coak smiled. "Now I'm mostly looking for something to get into."

"Want to turn outlaw, huh?" Priest eyed him, noting the sawed-off rifle and the ease in which the man managed to keep his hand near it. "Figure you're tough enough?"

Coak nodded at Big Joe Macon, saying to Priest, "There's some reference if you want to see my work."

A ripple of laughter stirred across the men as Big Joe Macon looked down in humiliation, his eyes the color of fruit gone bad, and swollen almost shut.

"Damn!" Priest whistled low, looking Big Joe up

and down. "I've never seen you in such a shape, Big Joe."

"It ain't over with," Big Joe said through cracked and swollen lips. "Next time, I swear I'll take his head and pound it till his brains go—"

"See?" said Lamburtis, cutting Big Joe off. "That's all he did, was talk about what he was *going* to do!"

Priest closed his eyes for a second, grinning, then he opened them and said to Lewis Prior, "Coak is your man. Just keep him in line."

"What about him being a lawman?" Joe Cherry asked, still glaring at Coak.

"Go fill your nose, Cherry," said Priest. "Hell, I was almost a congressman myself once. Now look at me." Priest turned his eyes back to Coak. "I hope you didn't harm your gun hand any?"

"Never used it," said Coak, tapping his fingertips on his sawed-off rifle stock.

Laughter roared. Big Joe Macon tugged his hat brim down on his sore forehead and lowered his face.

Against J. T. Priest's chest, Kate McCorkle let herself relax a bit, seeing Coak had just handled it the way he should. She caught a glance from Bob Herns and saw that he was thinking the same thing.

"Boys," Priest called out as the laughter settled, "make yourselves at home for the day. This place is a dirty rag, but it's the best we got. Tomorrow we head out of here." He turned, with Kate still pressed to his chest. "Come on, you're coming with me!"

Coak forced himself to look away lest he lose control at the sight of J. T. Priest, the way he held Kate McCorkle, the way he forced her along. Coak allowed himself to turn and look instead at Herns. Their eyes met, then kept moving, both of them taking in the men, judging the gang's strength, getting a feel for the task ahead. . . .

Upstairs in the room, Priest shoved Kate to a corner and walked over and closed and locked the balcony doors. He turned to Max Sheppard and nodded toward the hallway. "Stay right out there, Max. I want some privacy."

"You got it, Boss," Max Sheppard said, ducking his eyes and stepping back out into the hall.

As soon as the door closed, J. T. Priest turned to Kate McCorkle. She looked into his eyes and said in a low, menacing rasp, "Try it, and I'll kill you, J. T. So help me *God* I'll kill you!" Her mind went to the straight razor up under her arm, but she held back from reaching for it. She wasn't going to risk her life or the lives of Coak and Herns . . . not if she could keep from it.

"Kill me? You still don't get it, do you, Kate?" Priest tapped himself on the chest. "This is my world now. You and your grifter boyfriend, Simms, made your run at me and you missed! If there's any killing here today, it'll be me doing it. Don't think you can't die, Kate." He attempted a step forward, but stopped as her fists closed at her sides.

"Don't think we can't *both* die here, J. T.!" she hissed. "I'm willing if you are. Let's get to it!"

"I can have you tied up," Priest said in a strong tone.

"That would be your style," said Kate. "I'm surprised you didn't think of it before, back when I was sharing your bed. It might have added something, instead of it always the same ole—"

"Don't, Kate," he said, taking a step back, turning his face from hers, looking almost hurt by her words.

He stood in silence for a moment and Kate used the pause to look around the room, checking things out, weighing what moves she might make if she had to.

Standing with his back to her, Priest said barely above a whisper, "Can I ask you one thing, Kate, just the two of us here?"

"Why not?" she said, bitterly mimicking him. "After all, this is *your* world now."

"Why?" he asked, not facing her, his shoulders slumped as if in humiliation.

"Why what?" she responded.

"You know what I'm asking, Kate," Priest said, half turning to her, then stopping himself. "Why did you do it to me, turn from me to Quick Charlie Simms. I had everything then . . . it was yours, too."

Kate let her shoulders drop and let out a breath of disbelief at his words. "My god, J. T. . . . you framed him for murder, for robbery. He was going to hang! You only got me out of jail to win me over. I was just a bauble to you, something for you to dangle in front of your men!"

"That's not true, the bauble part. I had strong feelings for you, Kate. I did. All right, so he was going to hang. But that would have been the end of it. . . . You would have gotten over it in time. Then look what we could have had, the two of us."

"Jesus, J. T." Kate shook her head. "Listen to what you're saying. And you wonder why I turned back to Simms? I can't believe you're this crazy."

"If I'm crazy, you drove me to it." He turned facing her now, his eyes drawn and bloodshot, his face ashen.

Kate turned her eyes away from him and crossed her arms on her chest. "Look at you, J. T. What have you been doing to yourself? You're drunk and sick and look like you haven't eaten in a month. I don't know what keeps you alive . . . I never did."

"I— I wanted to talk some, Kate."

"No you didn't, J. T. You didn't want to talk! You wanted me here, begging for my life . . . but I won't. You wanted me to beg for Charlie's life . . . but I don't have to. Guess what, J. T. He's not coming."

"He'll come," J. T. Priest said, regaining some of his harshness at the thought of Quick Charlie Simms. "He knows I'll kill you if he doesn't show up."

Kate let go with a dark smile. "That's just it, J. T., Charlie doesn't know I'm here. He wasn't there when your idiots came and grabbed me. He'd already left town. He never saw the note Lamburtis left behind. So there, you fool!"

Priest looked stunned, but only for an instant. "That means nothing. I planned for that. I sent two cowboys back to let him know. I'm sure they met him on the trail."

"Well, they might have," she said, lying, "if they were on their way to New Orleans! I tried to tell your monkeys that was where he was headed, but no, they wouldn't listen. So to hell with all of you. So go on and kill me, J. T., you stupid bastard! I'm all you're going to get!"

Once Quick Charlie Simms, Twojack Roth and Sullivan Hart had crossed the border, Simms stopped his horse and turned it crosswise in the trail. He looked back past Roth and Hart at the prisoner, Leonard Hergo, who they had captured two days earlier as he and Huey Moss tried to ambush them. Huey Moss had died with his gun in his hand but Leonard Hergo had been sitting, quietly smoking a cigarette when the deputies surrounded him. "I think you two need to stay back here," said Simms, turning back to Hart and Roth. "If this goes the way I've got it planned, I'll bring J. T. Priest to you, I promise."

"And if it doesn't go the way you've got it planned?" Hart asked.

"It will, Hart, you've got to trust me," said Simms. "You heard what Hergo said. Priest couldn't stand not getting into the safe. Now that he's had a few more days thinking about it, it's driving him loco. I can promise you that, too. Give me three minutes alone with him, he'll change his mind about everything if I'll open the safe for him."

Hart thought about it. "Why don't we ride a little closer to Sonora with you just in case you're wrong?"

"Because if we get too close to Sonora, we'll risk running into some of his men, or he might sight your tracks on our way back here. I can't take that chance. He's got to think I came alone."

"I don't like it," said Hart. He turned to Roth. "What about you, Twojack?"

Roth gazed ahead along the barren desert floor for a moment, thinking about it. "Simms does have a way of causing Priest to trip over his own boots."

"Yes, but—"

Sullivan Hart's words were cut short by Simms. "Either we agree on doing this my way, or I'll bust on ahead and do it my damn self. You both know that! Why not go along with me for once? We're on the same side here."

A silence passed, then Hart let out a breath. "I hope you know what you're doing, Simms. If you don't, Kate is dead. You, too." He pointed a gloved finger.

"I know what I'm doing," said Simms, "and don't

forget I'll have Jake Coak there backing me if worse comes to worse."

"Then get on out of here," Hart said, nodding at the distance. "We'll hold up along that high stretch of rock."

Simms started to bolt his horse forward, but he stopped as he turned it and said sincerely, "Thanks, both of you. I won't let you down. Just make sure Kate is riding with me and Priest before you spring any traps, all right?"

"We'll do our best, Simms, you can count on it," said Hart.

Roth stepped forward, leading their spare horses. "Here, pick one or two. You'll need to put some long ground behind you."

Simms took the reins to two of the spare horses and without another word, turned and sped away in a rise of dust.

"I've never seen him so shaken up," said Hart, watching Simms's dust drift and settle.

"Me neither," said Roth. "He sure loves that woman. I hope it's not going to get him killed."

Chapter 14

In the middle of the night, Jake Coak slipped away from the others as they ate, drank, gambled, danced and played with the whores in *La Rosa Negra*. Bob Herns noticed him leave, but Herns only glanced around making sure no one else had. Outside the inn, Coak eased into the darkness and crept along the adobe wall. Near the far corner of the building, Coak stopped and crouched down at the sound of someone moving toward him from out of the blackness. Coak let out a breath of relief and spread his arms when he heard the panting sound of Buster move in close to his face.

"Good boy," Coak whispered, rubbing the dog's head. "How're you holding up out there?" As Coak whispered, he ran his hands along Buster's gaunt flanks. "Not too poorly . . . could be better." He pulled the dog's face to his, hugged him, then turned him loose as Buster's dangling tongue made a swipe at his cheek. "Soon as this is over we're going to fatten you up."

Buster whined quietly, showing restraint, as if knowing better than to raise his voice. "I know . . . I miss you, too," said Coak. He pulled the dog to him again, then pushed him back gently. "Get back out there, Buster; we're still on the job."

Coak stayed crouched until the darkness engulfed the dog. Once Buster was out of sight, Coak raised up slightly, moved the rest of the way to the corner of the building, reached up and pulled himself atop a low roof. Once up, he walked quietly up the half-round roofing tiles to where the low roof met the wall of the building. He moved along the wall to the edge and looked down fifteen feet to the stone walk beneath him. He reached out with one hand and grasped the length of ornate metal trim running along the edge of the balcony. He shook the metal, testing it, then swung out on it with both hands and pulled himself up over the balcony rail and dropped down into a crouch. He listened for a moment to the silence to make sure he hadn't been heard. Then he moved over to the balcony doors and eased one of them open a few inches.

The room looked empty, the bed unslept in, with no sign of J. T. Priest. In the darkness he whispered, "Kate it's me, Jake."

"Over here," Kate whispered in reply.

As Coak slipped over in a corner beside her, he saw the handcuff around her right wrist attached to the iron frame of a tall oaken wardrobe. He also saw Kate close the razor in her hand and hide it inside her blouse. "Kate, are you all right?" Coak brushed her hair back from her face and looked at her in the darkness.

"Yes . . . don't worry about me," she whispered, placing her fingertips to his lips. She nodded toward the door. "J. T. left a guard out there." She looked back at Coak's eyes, whispering, "You shouldn't be here."

"I had to check on you," he said.

"Thanks." She moved her hand from his lips, but cupped it on his cheek.

"Maybe this isn't a good idea. Maybe we should get you out of here, grab the horses and go."

"No," she whispered. "We're going to play this out. As long as Priest is alive he'll be after Charlie—I can't have that."

"But—"

"Sssh," she said, silencing him, listening to the sound of a boot squeak outside the door. They both looked at the crack of light beneath the door. Even in the darkness, they saw the brass doorknob turn slowly.

Dim light spread slowly through the few inches of the narrowly opened door. Max Sheppard eased his head inside and looked over at the sleeping outline of Kate McCorkle in the corner. When Kate turned a sleepy face to him and pushed back a strand of hair, Sheppard only nodded, withdrew his head and closed the door behind him.

Jake Coak eased back across the floor from beneath the bed, and this time placed his lips an inch from her ear as he whispered, "I can't stand the thought of you up here."

Kate turned her face to his ear and cupped her hand. "Don't worry, J. T. won't bother me—we've already settled that."

Coak drew back an inch and looked into her eyes, not certain what she'd meant. He started to say something more, but her hand slipped gently over his mouth, stopping him. "I'm all right. Now go," she whispered.

Kate watched him move silently across the floor. When the balcony door made a faint squeak behind him, she held her breath for a second. But in a moment, when Max Sheppard didn't respond to the sound, she relaxed, hearing nothing but the muffled laughter and coarse language from the bar below.

Coak made his way back down to the lower roof, crept down to the edge and lowered himself to the ground. No sooner had his boots touched the dirt, than he felt the cold solid jab of a pistol barrel to the back of his head. "Hold it right there," said the slurred voice of Joe Cherry. Behind them, Coak heard the sound of paws running across the dirt and he braced himself, knowing what Buster was about to do. Yet, in an instant, the sound of the paws stopped. Behind Coak, Cherry let out a grunt and sank to the ground.

"Come on, Coak!" Bob Herns whispered, grabbing Coak's arm and turning him around. But Coak hesitated, looking around for the dog.

"He's back there," said Herns. "I'm lucky he didn't take my leg off!"

"Not Buster," said Coak. "He always knows . . . don't ask me how but he always knows." On the ground at their feet, Cherry moaned and rolled over onto his side.

Slipping away in the darkness, Herns whispered over his shoulder to Coak, "How's she doing?"

"She's holding up good," said Coak. "I asked if she wanted to clear out of here. She turned me down. She's a tough woman, that one. I admire her a great deal."

"Yeah, I noticed," said Herns as they stopped and stood in the darkness looking back at the lights of the inn from twenty yards away. When Coak turned and gave him a questioning look, Herns added, "It's none of my business, Jake. I'm here to do what I set out to do. I watch your back, you watch mine."

Coak nodded. "That's good, because I—"

"But I've got to tell you, Jake, there's nothing can get a man into something over his head worse than a woman."

Coak let out a breath. "See? I knew you was going to make some remark."

"Sorry," said Herns. "I won't mention it again." He nodded back toward the corner of the building where they had left Joe Cherry lying on the ground. "Did he get a look at your face?"

"No, I don't think so," said Coak. "He's so drunk and powdered up, I doubt he'd remember it anyway."

"Let's hope not," said Herns. "Once we get out of here and to *Los Pistoleros'* hideout, I say we put an end to this thing before something really goes wrong."

"I had to see her, Bob," said Coak, catching an implication that may or may not have been intended.

"I understand, Jake. But we can't afford to take too many chances. Things are going good for us right now, but these boys can turn deadly in a heartbeat. We both know that."

"Thanks for covering me," said Coak quietly, nodding toward the corner of the building. "Looks like I owe you one."

"Good, I like that," said Herns with a slight smile, "having you owe me one. I expect we'll both owe one another *several* before this is finished."

In the morning, the men drifted to the stone walk out front of *La Rosa Negra*, arriving one, two and three at a time at the sound of Max Sheppard calling out to them, "Move your asses! Get on over here!"

Jake Coak held back, having risen from his spot on

the ground near his dapple-gray's hooves and rolled his blanket, deliberately taking his time, seeing Joe Cherry stagger in place beside Max Sheppard, holding a wet towel to the back of his head. Coak instinctively loosened his sawed-off rifle in its holster, looked around at Bo Romans, Tommy Kendall and Lewis Prior, who had already started to walk toward Sheppard and the others. "Ain't you coming, Coak?" asked Prior.

"Yeah, I'm coming." Coak pitched the blanket atop his saddle on the ground and turned, walking a few feet behind Lewis Prior and Bo Romans. "Where's Herns?" Coak asked.

"He's around somewhere." Romans looked back over his shoulder at Coak. "Why? You don't have to watch your back anymore . . . he's not out to kill you."

"I know," said Coak, "just wondering."

They walked on, seeing J. T. Priest step out through the arched doorway and strike a match down the front wall. Rance Macklinberg stepped out behind him, pulling Kate McCorkle along by her cuffed hand. J. T. Priest lit his cigar as Max Sheppard called out, "All of yas listen up! Boss has something to tell you."

"Men," Priest called out, stepping forward, the black cigar in his fingers, "last night, somebody was prowling around outside my room. When Joe Cherry caught him sneaking back down from the roof, somebody got the drop on Joe and knocked him cold." Priest looked around from one face to the next, judging the men's expressions, seeing what he could read from them. "We caught one of the men, but there's another one involved."

Coak glanced around, looking for Bob Herns, not seeing him anywhere. He let his hand rest on the butt of his sawed-off rifle and waited, and tensed as J. T. Priest turned back to the doorway of the inn. "Go drag him out here, Mack," Priest said to Rance Macklinberg.

Coak stared, then winced at the sight of the swollen bloody face as Macklinberg turned Kate McCorkle loose, reached back inside the doorway and jerked the rope tied around the blood-streaked neck of Lorenzo Jerea. Oh no! Coak said to himself, not him! Macklinberg held the man's face up by a twist of hair, long enough for everybody to see. Then he slung Lorenzo out onto the stone walk.

"He won't admit to it," Priest said, stepping forward, popping a boot up on Lorenzo's back, "but we know it was him, don't we, Cherry?"

"Yeah, that's the sneaking bastard all right." Joe Cherry spat down on Lorenzo, keeping the wet towel pressed to his head. "Now I want to get my hands on the man who did this to me." He glared at the faces of the men through red-rimmed eyes. "I figure it was his old man, Juan, since nobody seems to be able to locate Juan or his wife this morning!" He drew back a boot and kicked Lorenzo in the ribs. "Was it your daddy? Huh? Was it?"

"Nada, por favor! Por favor!" Lorenzo rasped through bloody lips.

No! My God, no! Coak's mind raced. He looked around once more for Bob Herns, but still didn't see him. He stepped forward a step and to one side, getting into position. He shot a glance at Kate McCorkle and saw the warning there, telling him with her eyes to keep quiet, that it was too late. . . . Nothing he could do now would help. And Coak knew she was right. Last night he'd made a mistake going up to the room.

Now any move he made would only make matters worse for himself, and in turn for Kate, and for Herns.

J. T. Priest reached down, grabbed Lorenzo by his hair and pulled him up onto his knees. Lorenzo wobbled back and forth, his head bowed.

"I hate this kind of stuff before breakfast, don't you?" J. T. Priest called out to the men. He spread his hands, a wide grin on his face. "I mean, after all, we're not animals!" He turned to Joe Cherry and nodded down at Lorenzo Jerea. "Finish him off, Joe," he said in a matter-of-fact tone.

"My pleasure." Joe Cherry laughed, lowering the towel from his head. He moved a step around in front of Lorenzo's bowed head. Lorenzo shook his head back and forth slowly as if trapped in some dark nightmare from which he'd never awake. Cherry drew his pistol from the holster hanging from his shoulder. He took his time cocking it, torturing Lorenzo, making sure the doomed man heard the sound of it. Lorenzo tried to raise his bloody shaking hands to make the sign of the cross on his chest, but Joe Cherry kicked his hands away.

"Huh-uh, none of that last-minute religious stuff. You're going straight to hell, if I've got any say so!" Cherry pointed the pistol down, an inch from the bowed head and cupped his free hand down behind the hammer to shield himself from the back blast of brain and bone matter. "So long, *Lo-ren*—"

"Wait!" Jake Coak shouted, stepping forward, the sawed-off rifle coming up and levering around into the chamber. "He didn't do it!" All eyes turned to him. Coak stared at Priest and Cherry, not wanting to catch even a glimpse of Kate McCorkle's face.

"Oh, really now?" Priest grinned, blowing a long

stream of smoke, as if extremely satisfied with himself. "And what makes you say that, Jake Coak?" Joe Cherry stood glaring at Coak, the pistol still an inch from Lorenzo's head.

Jake Coak pointed the rifle barrel toward Priest, catching the sight of hands going to pistol butts among the men as he readied his hand on the rifle lever. *One thousand, two thousand . . .*

"You know why, Priest," Coak said, "because it was me up on the roof." *Four thousand, five thousand . . .* "Now let him go."

But Cherry and Priest only smiled. Behind Priest, Macklinberg pulled Kate McCorkle to one side and stood with his arm around her shoulders as if using her as a shield. "Life's not that simple where I live, Coak," Priest said. He drew on the cigar, hooking his free hand on one of the pistols in his waist belt. "What exactly were you doing, up there . . . peeping into my room, no doubt?"

"That's right, Priest, I was peeping into your room. Now let the Mexican go . . . he didn't do anything."

"Who was with you?" Priest demanded.

"Nobody was with me," said Coak.

"Somebody hit Cherry from behind. . . . Who was it?"

"Cherry was so drunk he couldn't hold his head up," said Coak. "He tried to grab me and almost fell. I cracked his head with my rifle barrel. If I wanted to, I could have killed him." He shot Joe Cherry a cold stare. "It's still not too late." He wanted to say something to cause Cherry to turn the pistol from Lorenzo, even if it meant having it pointed at himself.

But Joe Cherry kept the pistol pointed at Lorenzo's

head, a smile on his face as if he knew what Coak had just tried to do.

"Nice try, Coak," said Priest. "Now, *why* exactly were you peeping into my room?"

Coak allowed himself to stop counting. "I wanted to see that the woman was all right, Priest, that's all." He feigned an embarrassed expression. "Can't you see she's gotten to me?"

"Do say." Priest chuckled. He turned to Kate and shook his head in reproach. "Kate, you naughty girl. Once again someone has been smitten by your charm."

Kate snarled, "Go to hell, J. T., you rotten murdering bastard!"

"It's certainly easy to see why!" Priest continued to Coak, gesturing toward Kate McCorkle as she stood staring wild-eyed at him. "She has such a lovely grace about her." Priest stepped closer to Jake Coak, his smile disappearing like sunlight behind a black cloud. "Give me the rifle, Coak," he hissed.

Coak stood firm. "You know better than that, Priest."

"Then the man you've gone this far to save is going to die anyway," said Priest. He raised a hand and held it toward Joe Cherry. "When my hand drops, Joe, let the hammer fall with it."

"You got it, Boss," said Cherry, steadying his gun-hand toward Lorenzo's head.

Coak shot a glance around the stone walk, across the men. Now Bob Herns had appeared back behind the others. Herns's hand was on his holstered pistol like everyone else's, yet Coak knew it was for a different reason. The message in Herns's eyes was clear. One move from Coak and the killing would start. Coak cut his glance to Kate McCorkle, seeing Rance Macklinberg's pistol rise slowly and cock, a strange look coming to Macklinberg's face.

"All right," said Coak, "I'll hand it over . . . soon as I see the Mexican get around the side of the building."

"Huh-uh, that would be giving up my advantage, Coak," said Priest.

"Then you and I are going to die together, Priest." Coak let Priest see the resolve in his eyes, his finger drawing tight on the rifle's trigger.

"Wait," said Priest, seeing nothing but cold determination ready to snap at any second. He kept his hand raised and said over his shoulder to Joe Cherry, "Help him up, Joe . . . run him away from here."

"But, Boss," said Cherry, "you told me I could be the one—"

"Damn it to hell, Joe!" Priest barked. "Do like I tell you! I learned what I wanted to know! Get the Mexican out of here!"

Coak waited, watching until Lorenzo Jerea staggered out of sight around the far corner of the building. Then he eased his hand off the rifle stock, lowered it and held it out to J. T. Priest.

Priest snatched it and looked it over. "Hell of a fighting weapon, Coak. How many people have ever handled this besides you?"

"Just you, Priest," said Coak.

Priest held the rifle down at his side, then held his palm flat out to Coak. "Now lift that pistol under your arm with one finger and give it over."

When Coak had given up his pistol, Lewis Prior stepped in beside Priest and said to Coak, "I'm damn disappointed in you, Coak."

Priest shoved Prior back with his forearm and said

to Coak, "So am I. Nobody but a lawman would have stepped forward and acted that way."

"Old habits are hard to break," said Coak.

"What did you care if we shot that boy?" Priest asked, cocking his head, studying Coak's eyes, wanting to see some fear there, but finding none.

"If you've got to ask a thing like that, Priest, there's no answer you could understand." Coak stood facing him, his shoulders level, his eyes unyielding.

"Oh, I get it," said Priest, "it's some sort of morality question, I suppose. Well, I never did believe in morality; always thought it was just some sort of rumor." He grinned and put the cigar in his mouth. "I hate shooting a man with his own rifle, but I'm sure you understand."

"That rifle will never kill me," said Coak. "It wouldn't know how."

"Well, let's just give it a try and see." Priest shrugged nonchalantly. "It's probably something we'd both like to know." He leveled the rifle a foot from Coak's stomach and braced for the recoil.

"Don't shoot, J. T.," Kate McCorkle called out from the stone walk, unable to step forward with Rance Macklinberg still holding her against his chest. "It wasn't his fault . . . I made him do it."

Priest half turned to her. "Did you now?"

Coak could tell by the gleam in Priest's eyes that he was enjoying all of this, standing center stage, all eyes on him, everybody hanging on thin strings, waiting for his next move. Coak resisted the urge to spit in his face. "She never made me do a thing, Priest," Coak hissed.

"Shut up, Jake," Kate shouted, struggling against Macklinberg until a nod from Priest set her free. She ran quickly forward, stopping a few feet from J. T. Priest. "It's the truth, J. T. I made him do it. I've been leading him on."

"Oh, I see," said Priest, "he just happened to have fallen head-over-heels for you on the trail coming here? Sorry, Kate, there's more to it than that." He started to turn the rifle back toward Coak. "She tried"—he chuckled—"you have to give her that."

"No, J. T., it's true," Kate, talking fast, making it up as she went, "but it wasn't something that started on the way here. Jake and I were lovers back in Fort Smith. He left there because of me. When I broke off with him, he quit his job. We just happened to run into him when Lamburtis and Roundhouse Eddie brought me with them."

Priest looked to Coak for an answer. "She's lying, Priest. I saw her in town with Simms . . . that was all. We never spoke three words to one another until we met on the trail. Do whatever you need to do. Leave her out of it."

Priest looked taken aback by the look on Coak's face.

"Jake, you fool," Kate hissed. She turned to Priest. "Can't you see it, J. T.? He'll do anything to protect me. He's crazy! That's why I ended it with him. He got too serious, followed me everywhere I went. I couldn't breathe. Last night, he came to the room, and I begged him to get something and cut the handcuff loose, but he—he wouldn't do it." She looked down as if in submission.

Priest considered it, rubbing his hand back and forth on his brow. Then he looked at Coak and said, "She must be telling the truth, you poor sorry bastard you. Nobody would stand here and put their life up for a woman unless he's a love-struck fool." Priest leveled the rifle again. "It's just as well I get you out of your misery." Out of the corner of his eye, Coak saw Bob Herns's hand start up from his holster.

"Riders coming, Boss," Dick Witt called out before Priest could pull the trigger.

"Damn, now what?" said Priest, turning, seeing the column of *federales* as they swept in quickly and circled the front of *La Rosa Negra.* At the sight of the riders, Buster the dog turned his attention from J. T. Priest and slunk back a step from where he stood ready to lunge forward from beneath the overhanging tentacles of a *cacto caido* plant. Beside the tall *federales* captain sat Juan Jerea on a big chestnut barb, his wife, Soledad, sitting behind him, pointing over Juan's shoulder at Priest and his men as she rattled in angry Spanish.

The men spread out as best they could, given the close quarters the *federales* horsemen held them to. There were a dozen mounted soldiers, each of them with his rifle drawn and ready, pointing down at Priest's men.

"Jesus," whispered Little Bit Collier to Buddy Raines, the two standing side by side, their hands on their pistols, "this ain't at all good, is it?"

"Nope, not that I can tell," said Raines.

Chapter 15

In spite of the tension, and the violent confrontation about to erupt, the tall *federale* craned his neck and looked all around *La Rosa Negra Posada* at broken furniture, broken windows and broken bottles and glasses strewn about. He looked down across the faces of the men, then settled his gaze on J. T. Priest, Jake Coak and Kate McCorkle. Taking note of the handcuff hanging from Kate's wrist, his question went to her. "What is the trouble here?"

Butting in, Priest spoke before Kate could respond. "Trouble? There's no trouble here, Captain," Priest said. He spread his hands as if offering the captain a closer look.

"I see." The captain nodded. Seeing that he wasn't going to get the truth out of these people, he went on to reveal the purpose of his visit. "Señor Jerea and his wife have registered a complaint in Sonora. They say you men have destroyed their inn and made several threats against their personage. Now I must ask you to lay down your weapons and come with me."

No one made an attempt to lay down his weapon, and from the look on the men's faces, it didn't seem likely that they were going to. The captain hesitated, then said, probing the situation in hopes of avoiding bloodshed, "What has been going on out here? The constable in Sonora said one of you men told him you are the dreaded *Los Pistoleros.*"

J. T. Priest looked surprised and smiled. "*Los Pistoleros*? My goodness, Captain, do we look like gunmen to you?" Realizing that was exactly what they looked like, Priest added hurriedly, "I'm afraid your constable must have misunderstood. His English is probably not good. . . . But no, we're not *Los Pistoleros.* I'm down here looking around at business opportunities."

The captain looked away from Priest as if he weren't there and said to one of his mounted soldiers behind him, "Corporal, prepare to fire at my command."

"Hold on, Captain!" Priest said, drawing the man's attention back to him. He gestured his free hand at Jake Coak, then at the sawed-off rifle in his other hand. "Captain, I'm afraid you've just arrived at an awkward time. But let me assure you these men all follow my orders. If you came riding in here looking for—"

"Thank God, you've arrived, Captain!" Kate McCorkle blurted out, stepping forward, looking almost straight up at the mounted captain. "My husband and I came here to enjoy the desert air and celebrate our marriage. But then this man"—she pointed a finger in the direction of both Priest and Coak—"this man who used to be my fiancé, tracked us here and tried to force me to go with him." She shook the handcuff hanging from her left wrist, for effect. "He even stole my husband's rifle!"

Seeing what Kate was about to do, Coak almost breathed a sigh of relief; and he would have were it not for the many hands clasped around pistol butts, Priest's men ready to spill blood, the mounted *federales* ready to do the same with their cocked rifles.

But then Coak took on a strange bemused look, seeing Kate McCorkle step over to J. T. Priest and slip her arm into his, speaking quickly. "We'll gladly make payment for any damage we've done here and, of course, we apologize for any trouble we've caused the Jerea family. But if anybody here should go to jail, it's *this* man." Her finger pointed at Jake Coak. Coak reeled in surprise, staring at her, stunned for a second. Then he turned his face to the captain.

"She's lying," he said. "This is not her husband! She's only saying that to protect me!" As soon as he'd said it, Coak realized how little sense it made, in spite of the fact that it was true.

The captain looked puzzled. Before he could speak, Kate cut in, her finger still pointed at Jake Coak, "See? Hear how he talks? He's crazy! He can't get it in his head that my husband and I are happily married, that we came down here to—"

"Enough of this!" The captain sliced a hand through the air, cutting all conversation off. He looked once more across the faces of the men with their hands ready on their pistol butts. Considering the gravity of the situation, he turned to Juan and Soledad Jerea on the horse to his right. "Are you willing to let these men make settlement for the damage they have done?"

Juan Jerea nodded. "Sí, provided they leave afterwards and never return."

The tension among Priest's gunmen lightened up some. The captain saw it and said down to Kate McCorkle and J. T. Priest, "Are you willing to come to

Sonora and bring charges against this man?" He nodded at Jake Coak as he spoke.

"No," said Priest.

"Yes, of course," said Kate.

The captain's jaw tightened. "Which is it, yes or no?"

"The answer is yes, Captain." Kate McCorkle squeezed J. T. Priest's forearm, letting him know she could change this whole situation if he didn't go along with her. But she also knew if she tried leaving here with the captain and his men, the bloodshed would start. "As soon as I freshen up, I'll gladly ride in and file whatever charges it takes to get this man out of our lives. Right, dear?" She turned her eyes to J. T. Priest, squeezing his arm harder. "It's the best you're going to get," she whispered in Priest's ear.

Priest only nodded up at the captain with a sullen expression.

"Corporal Ramirez, get up here!"

"*Sí,* Captain Luna!" said the corporal, gigging his horse, pushing it up beside the captain as he kept his thumb over his cocked rifle hammer.

"Arrest this man." The captain pointed at Jake Coak, then said to Corporal Ramirez, "Send him on ahead to Sonora with two guards. We will stay here and see to it these people are compensated for their losses."

"*Sí,* Capitan." The corporal made a hand signal to two of his men.

The two soldiers stepped down from their saddles and over to Jake Coak. As they grabbed Coak's arms, Coak gave a quick glance toward the *cacto caido* plant, knowing the dog was there and knowing the dog would make a move if he wasn't stopped. "Easy, Buster, no!" he said in a firm tone.

"See? He's out of his mind!" Kate McCorkle said, drawing the captain's attention back to herself, away from the spot Jake Coak had spoken toward.

"Perhaps a few days in our jail will clear his mind," said Captain Luna to Kate McCorkle. "But you must come and prefer charges, or else he will be released. Then your trouble with him will start all over."

"Don't worry, Captain, I'll be there shortly," said Kate.

"Can I at least ride my own horse?" Jake Coak asked through clenched teeth.

"No," the captain replied sharply. "It is not that far. You can walk." The two soldiers pushed him forward.

Kate McCorkle took a breath, easing down now. She was still J. T. Priest's prisoner, but at least Jake Coak wasn't going to die here. Sorry, Jake, she said to herself, seeing him cast her a sidelong glance in passing.

In moments, the two soldiers were out of sight, rounding a turn in the trail toward Sonora. Jake Coak walked in front of them, his shoulders slumped and his head bowed. A few hundred yards along the trail, Coak looked over to a stretch of brush and said in a tight muffled voice, "No, Buster, no!"

The two soldiers looked at each other. One shrugged and tapped a finger to his temple. The other soldier nodded in agreement, then said, "Those men back there, I think they are *Los Pistoleros*. I think they only lied to the captain."

"*Sí*, I think so, too. But the captain is no fool; he knows what they are. He only goes along with it to keep from spilling blood. He will chase them back toward the border and be rid of them."

"But they will come back, those *gringos*," the other soldier responded.

"*Sí*, they will come back. They always do." He looked forward at Jake Coak, watching his worn-down boot heels raise a low swirl of dust with each step.

Outside *La Rosa Negra Posada* the tension had lessened even more, now that a sum of money had been agreed to between Juan Jerea and J. T. Priest. Ten yards away, Bo Romans saw the embarrassed look on Priest's sweaty face. "This whole damn thing has made Prior and us look bad," said Romans. "I reckon you was right about Mister Jake Coak all along, Herns."

"Why?" asked Tommy Kendall. "Just because the man fell for a pretty woman?" He spread a lurid grin. "Hell, I'd like to fall for her myself for an hour or two."

"I hope to God you didn't fall for that story, Tommy," said Romans.

Kendall only shrugged.

"As soon as these soldiers clear out of here, I'm taking his horse," Herns said, "if nobody's got any objections." He looked back and forth between Kendall and Romans. "I always wanted a big dapple-gray."

"Take it," said Romans, "but it'll be hell to pay if he ever shows up and sees you with it."

"I'll worry about that," Herns replied. The three of them stood watching Rance Macklinberg count sweaty money into J. T. Priest's hand. Macklinberg had taken off his right boot, where he carried his cash, and now stood with his toes showing through his ragged sock. Captain Luna stood with Juan Jerea, watching as Priest turned to Juan and laid the money in his hand. The soldiers still sat atop their horses, their rifles still poised toward the gunmen.

"You are satisfied with this amount?" Captain Luna asked Juan Jerea.

"*Sí.*" Juan Jerea recounted the money and nodded his satisfaction as he folded it and put it inside his shirt. "It will take many days to put our inn back in order. But this will help." He patted his shirt.

"Very well." The captain turned back to Kate McCorkle and J. T. Priest. "Now, I demand that all of you leave this place and never return. Fortunately for all of you, no one has been physically injured." He turned slowly, looking at each face in turn as he spoke. "Had there been, you would all be brought to justice."

As Captain Luna spoke, some of his men turned their eyes to the bloody face of Lorenzo Jerea as he came staggering around the far corner of *La Rosa Negra* and caught himself against the wall to keep from falling. "Papa," Lorenzo gasped.

Soledad Jerea looked at her son and screamed, running to him.

Juan Jerea shrieked and turned to J. T. Priest with his fists balled.

Captain Luna took a step back, appalled at the sight of Lorenzo Jerea as he fell forward into his mother's arms.

"Oh shit . . ." said Joe Cherry, falling back a step toward the arched stone doorway of *La Rosa Negra*, his hand coming up with his cocked pistol in it.

At the sound of sudden steady gunfire erupting a mile behind them, the two soldiers jerked their horses around and looked back along the trail. One of them drew a pistol from his holster as he wheeled his horse back around toward Jake Coak. Coak threw his hands in the air. The soldier shouted something at Coak in Spanish, then spun his horse again and fell in behind the other soldier, both of them racing away, back to join their column.

Jake Coak dropped his hands and stood alone in the dust. Buster slipped from behind the stretch of brush and trotted over to him, the dog's eyes looking back toward the inn. "Good boy, Buster." Jake Coak sighed and rubbed the dog's head. "Come on, let's get back there, see if there's anything left to save." Above the rest of the gunfire, Coak heard his overload rifle cartridges pound out a long volley of explosions. He winced and stepped up his pace, the dog trotting along beside him.

On the stone walk, Dick Witt had been the first to fall, a young soldier getting a shot off before Max Sheppard lifted him from his saddle with a .45 slug to his forehead. The young soldier's horse reared and fell back into two other horses, causing soldiers to spill from their saddles in a tangle of reins, stirrups and horses' hooves.

"Run, *Mamacita*!" Juan Jerea shouted, darting toward his wife and injured son, his arms flailing wildly in the air. J. T. Priest had dropped Coak's rifle and grabbed Kate McCorkle, using her as a shield. Even as bullets whistled past him, Priest couldn't resist the urge to put a bullet in Juan Jerea's back. "Spend that money in hell!" Priest screamed, firing three quick rounds at Juan, two shots going too wide, the third lifting a tuft of hair on top of Juan's head. But Juan only let out a shriek, never slowing as he threw a hand to his scalp and followed his wife and son around the corner of the building.

On the ground, Captain Luna had taken a bullet from J. T. Priest as the fight began, but he'd rolled across the sawed-off rifle where Priest had dropped it. He'd come up with it, firing steadily, taking down the Hubbs brothers, and wounding Joe Cherry. Now the captain was up on one knee, blood spewing freely from his chest. He aimed at Priest, but held his shot, afraid of hitting Kate McCorkle.

"Shoot! Damn it! Shoot!" Kate screamed at Captain Luna as she struggled against J. T. Priest.

But Captain Luna still hesitated; and J. T. Priest laughed as he put another bullet into the captain, before falling back into the arched doorway. Captain Luna reeled backward, hit the ground, then forced himself over onto his side, still firing, not giving up. Another shot hit him high in the shoulder, this one coming from Max Sheppard, who'd dove behind a long water trough beside the doorway. Chunks of wood and water flew high from the trough as Sheppard ducked down.

As the fight had commenced, Bob Herns had ducked around the side of *La Rosa Negra*, circled the building and raced over to where his horse stood beside Jake Coak's dapple-gray. He hurriedly gathered the reins to Jake Coak's horse, then leapt atop his own horse and gave it heel, sending it bolting away from the inn and speeding along the trail. Herns came within a few feet of meeting the two soldiers who came back to join the fight. They didn't notice him as they slid their horses to a halt, jumped down with their pistols drawn and ran forward firing.

Corporal Ramirez made his way through three

wounded soldiers who crawled hand over hand across the bloody ground. Bullets licked at his back as he dove behind a downed horse, raised his rifle over its back and fired. Rance Macklinberg jerked back a step, the rifle shot hitting him in his thigh. But he remained standing, two pistols hammering out rounds, taking down three soldiers, holding three more pinned behind dead horses until his pistols both clicked on empty chambers. "Damn it to hell!" He dove sidelong as the three soldiers rose up as one from the ground and fired, none of their shots hitting anything but the bullet-ridden facade of *La Rosa Negra Posada.*

Less than four minutes had passed, yet Bob Herns could already hear the shooting subside as he raced along the trail toward Jake Coak and the dog in the distance. By the time he reached Jake Coak—Coak and Buster both running forward to meet him—the firing had ceased altogether. "How bad is it?" Coak asked, swinging up onto his saddle even as Herns turned both horses back toward the inn.

"Real bad! Close quarters like that—they should have dismounted right away!"

"Think he had any idea what he was dealing with, that captain?"

"If he didn't, he does now," said Herns.

"What about Kate?" Jake asked, drawing the dapple-gray up beneath him, his boots poised and ready to send the horse forward.

"Kate?" Herns said, an incredulous look on his face. "Hell, who knows?" They kicked the horses back toward the inn, Buster loping along in their wake.

Out in front of the inn, Rance Macklinberg walked forward, pointed his pistol down at the wounded soldier whose breath only came in short gasps. "I believe you're the one who did this to me, ain't ya?" Macklinberg raised his cupped hand from the flowing blood in his thigh, looking down at the dying soldier's face.

"Misericordia, por favor . . ." the soldier pleaded, his voice trailing down to a whisper.

"Yeah, I thought you was him." Macklinberg cocked the hammer back on his pistol.

J. T. Priest stepped out through the arched doorway as the single shot resounded in the ringing silence. With Kate still clamped to his chest, he looked around through the low drift of gun smoke and called out, "Who's up?"

"I'm up," said Bo Romans, rising to his feet and dusting off his trouser leg.

"Me, too," said Tommy Kendall. Lewis Prior only nodded at Priest as he finished loading his pistol and shoved it down into his holster.

Kendall looked all around. "Herns? Are you still up?" When he heard no reply, he looked around once more, then shook his head. "Can't win 'em all, Herns," he said, almost to himself.

Joe Cherry came limping in from behind a bullet-riddled rain barrel. A streak of blood showed through the bandanna he'd tied around the graze on his right leg. "Whoohee," he said, chuckling, "that weren't so bad now, was it?"

Denton Howel stepped in and shoved Joe Cherry to one side. "Shut up, Joe, we've got men dead here."

J. T. Priest looked across the carnage—dead horses, dead and dying soldiers, and at the faces of the gunmen rising up like creatures from some netherworld. Dean Spence and Harry Turpin moved in from the right, along the stone path. Other faces came forward: Big Joe Macon, Pete Lamburtis and Roundhouse Eddie

Jenkins stepped over from the left, Roundhouse Eddie holding his wounded arm. "Damn, they blew Earl's face clean off," said Roundhouse Eddie, looking down at where the Hubbs brothers lay dead on the ground.

"Mack," Priest called out to Rance Macklinberg, "send somebody over for the horses."

"You got it, Boss," Macklinberg replied. "We better make tracks out of here. Once word gets back to the *federales*, this place is going to look like the Alamo."

Dark, low laughter stirred across the remaining men. J. T. Priest walked over and started to pick up the sawed-off rifle from beneath Captain Luna's body. But seeing all the blood puddled around the captain, he turned and cursed under his breath and walked away, dragging Kate behind him. "See all the trouble you caused here, Kate? All this just because you had to have a little fling with that cockeyed Jake Coak. I hope you're damn well satisfied." He jerked her along gruffly. "That poor captain might have been a family man."

Kate McCorkle didn't answer right away. In J. T. Priest's warped mind, he'd found a way to make this her fault. She thought about the straight razor up under her arm, but forced herself not to make a grab for it. "You haven't *seen* trouble yet, you rotten bastard," she hissed.

Chapter 16

"Where is this Diablo Canyon?" Bob Herns asked. He and Jake Coak stopped their horses at the edge of the trail out front of *La Rosa Negra* and looked to the south where a tall wake of the riders' dust stood slantwise and drifting on the air.

"I don't know," said Coak, "and it doesn't matter anyway. Diablo Canyon is not where they're headed. If it was, Priest wouldn't have mentioned it."

Herns felt a twinge of embarrassment for not having realized that before. "You're right, Jake. Where do you figure their hideout is then? Nobody's ever found it that I know of. If they did, they never lived to tell about it."

"Maybe nobody's ever been this close on their trail before. We'll be able to track them from here."

They stepped their horses over in the yard near the stone walk where the dead from both sides lay together now, peaceful in the Mexican sun. "Nothing we can do here," said Herns. "We just as well get on their tracks."

"Give them a few more minutes," said Coak. "Let them think nobody's behind them. If Priest is smart, he'll have some men drop back and cover their trail."

Coak swung down from his saddle and walked around, looking for his rifle on the outside chance it would still be here. When he spotted the bloody rifle barrel sticking out from under the captain, he stepped over and reached down for it. Yet, as he tried to raise it from under the captain, he heard a moan and a soft murmur. "Bob, bring some water over here, quick. . . . Give me a hand, the captain's still alive!"

Bob Herns snatched a canteen from his saddle horn, looking over in disbelief as Coak turned the captain over onto his back and propped him up against his knee. "Here," said Herns, stooping down, and pouring a trickle of water into his cupped hand and wiping it across Captain Luna's brow. Even as Herns did so, Coak saw the captain's bloody hand inch toward a pistol lying in the dirt beside him. Coak reached down and pitched the gun away.

"Take it easy, we're not a part of that bunch, Captain," said Coak. "If we were, we wouldn't be here." Coak spoke as Herns tipped a thin sip of water to the captain's lips. "The woman was lying to save me, Captain Luna. You were right, those men are *Los Pistoleros.* They were about to kill me when you and your men showed up." As he talked, Coak picked up his sawed-off rifle and, without wiping it off, stuck it down into his long holster.

"It is a good and powerful weapon," the captain said in a strained voice, looking at Coak's holstered rifle.

"I'm glad it was in your hands, Captain, and not theirs," said Coak.

The captain swallowed water and turned his eyes to Jake Coak, whispering in a weak voice, "You two are *Americano* lawmen?"

"Yes, Captain," said Coak. "I'm a U.S. Federal Deputy with Judge Parker's court in Fort Smith. Herns here is a detective working for Allen Pinkerton. I know we have no authority here, but we'll get these men, Captain . . . you have my word."

"*Sí*, your word." The captain's eyes glazed a bit.

"Let's get him inside," said Herns, reaching around and looping the captain's arm over his shoulder.

At the far end of the building, Coak caught a glimpse of a straw sombrero and the tip of a shotgun barrel as he helped Herns pick the captain up. "Don't shoot," Coak called out. "Juan, if that's you, get over here—the captain needs your help!"

"Why should I trust you?" Juan's voice called out. "Look at what you have done to my place—to my son!"

"We weren't a part of them, Juan. You've got to believe me, for the captain's sake," Coak called out, he and Herns moving as he spoke, carrying the captain through the arched doorway of *La Rosa Negra*.

As Coak and Herns laid Captain Luna on the bar top, Juan Jerea and his wife slipped in warily through the doorway and over to one side of the disheveled dining room. The shotgun in Juan's hands stayed poised toward them. "Ma'am," Bob Herns called over to Soledad Jerea. "Can you get us bandages and hot water? We've got to stop this bleeding."

Seeing that the two men really were trying to assist the captain, the woman whispered something to her husband. As he nodded in reply, she hurried away toward the rear of the dining room. In a moment, she returned with strips of white tablecloth hanging over her forearm. She moved in between Coak and Herns. "Here, let me do this." She loosened the dirty blood-soaked bandanna Herns had used as a tourniquet, and replaced it with a clean strip of cloth. Coak and Herns stepped back and gave her room to work.

Stepping over to Juan Jerea with his hands spread in a show of peace, Coak said, "Señor Jerea, we are American lawmen. I know you think you have no reason to trust us. We're not even supposed to be on this side of the border. But we're out to bust up that gang and see to it those men face justice. There are some other men who will be coming through here most any time. They'll be looking for me and the woman. Tell them I have an ally now, a Pinkerton detective." He gestured toward Herns. "Tell them we are on the trail and point them in our direction. Will you do that, *por favor*?"

Juan Jerea only nodded, still wary, keeping his hands tight around the shotgun. Coak looked all around at the destruction and shook his head. "I'm sorry this misfortune befell you . . . I truly am."

Coak and Herns left *La Rosa Negra Posada* and swung a few yards wide of Priest and his men's tracks leading northwest, keeping out of the settling dust still hanging in the hot air. Buster trotted alongside them.

An hour had passed when the two men drew their horses up at a place where hoofprints gathered close and into single file and headed upward through a narrow crevice to a higher plateau. "He'll have left some men up in there," said Herns.

"Yep, it's perfect for an ambush," said Coak. He looked around at the dog. "What do you think, Buster?"

The dog stepped forward in front of them and lifted his muzzle toward the upward trail. He looked back at Coak as if in anticipation. "Good boy . . . take us up," Coak said.

The dog slipped forward and to one side of the narrow crevice trail, climbing off to the left along a smaller crevice where he seemed to vanish out of sight. Coak drew his bloodstained rifle from his holster and began cleaning it with his gloved hand, checking the load. "Now we give Buster a few minutes to scout the trail before we go up."

Bob Herns only nodded, his attention given to any sound or movement above them. "He works quiet, doesn't he?" Herns commented.

"All Catahoulas do," said Coak. "The good ones, anyway."

Coak judged the time as he finished cleaning and reloading his rifle. Beside him, Herns did the same with two big Colt pistols. When Jake Coak slid his rifle back into his holster, he said to Herns, "Time to go. As long as we don't see Buster, we'll know everything's all right. If he shows himself along the trail, we stop right there and find out why."

"He's your dog . . . lead the way," said Herns.

They traveled slowly and quietly up along meandering natural switchbacks through rock and sandy soil. Rock facings on either side of them reached up as high as fifty feet in some stretches, then dropped all at once to ground level. In the dirt beneath them they saw only horses' hoofprints. No sign of the dog's paw prints were visible, as Buster made his way through smaller crevices and animal paths that no man on horseback would dare attempt. But when they did see the dog's paw prints lead down from what appeared to be a sheer rock ledge ten feet above them, Coak stopped his dapple-gray abruptly and backed it a step. He drew his rifle and stepped down silently from his saddle. Herns did the same without asking why.

Following Coak, Herns led his horse forward. A few feet ahead where the trail turned sharply left, Buster slipped out from behind a low spill of rock and stood with his muzzle lifted to the still air. Coak eased forward, ran his hand back along the dog's head and whispered, "Good boy."

"What's he got up there?" Herns whispered, slipping in beside Coak, rubbing his hand down his horse's muzzle to keep it still and quiet.

"Just what we expected," whispered Jake Coak. He backed away and stepped over behind the cover of an out-thrust of rock. Buster moved back with them and lowered himself down in a small space between the horses. "Here's the deal," said Coak, only raising his voice enough for Herns to hear, "there's probably only two men at the most up there in the rocks along the top edge. But that's all Priest needed to leave behind. Once the firing starts, J. T. Priest and the rest of them will hear it up ahead. They'll break up and disappear on us."

"An old Indian trick," said Herns.

"Yep," said Coak, "and one that always works."

"But not this time, thanks to Buster," Herns said, looking at the dog, then back to Coak.

Coak reached down and slipped the knife from his boot well. He ran a thumb along the blade, then looked at Herns with a grim expression. "Have you ever done this before?"

"No," Herns said flatly. He swallowed a dryness in his throat.

"You can stay here and keep the horses quiet," Coak suggested.

"What you're asking is if I have the stomach for it," Herns said.

Coak gave him a questioning gaze.

Reasoning it out in his mind, Herns said, "If the men are on both sides of the trail, while you get one, the other will have a chance to fire. So, yes, I have the stomach for it. It's our only way."

"Got a knife?" Coak asked.

Herns searched through his trouser pockets and came out with a small jackknife. He opened it and clutched it tight in his fist as if judging it. "This will have to do," he said.

"Huh-uh," said Coak. "Too risky." He reached into his vest pocket, took out a rolled-up length of rawhide and shook it loose. He wrapped each end around his hands and tested its strength. "Which do you want?" he asked. "This or the knife?"

Herns folded his pocket knife, put it away, and took the length of rawhide from Coak. He looked into Coak's eyes, saying, "All the months I spent in that schoolhouse . . . who could imagine the two of us ever doing something like this?"

"I know," said Coak, his expression indiscernible. Then he turned and ran a hand across the dog's head. "Stay here, Buster, watch about the horses."

They climbed the rock and earth silently on either side of the trail, hand over hand until they both reached a thin ledge a few feet from the top. Coak caught one last glimpse of Bob Herns as Herns reached up, found a handhold and lifted himself up and over. Once he saw Herns was over the edge, Coak did the same, then moved out across a small stretch of flatter ground before circling wide, moving forward fifty feet. As he moved back toward the edge in a low crouch, he scanned back and forth until his eyes caught a glint of sunlight streak along a rifle barrel.

Coak dropped down for a second, then rose up cautiously, this time gazing out across the deep crevice, seeing the gunman, Bo Romans, on the other side. Coak saw no sign of Bob Herns over there, but he didn't need to. He and Herns had been moving at about the same pace, anticipating one another, each knowing they needed to strike at the same time.

Coak dropped back down and inched forward on his belly, the big knife in his right hand. When he raised his head again, he could see, on his side, the rifleman's broad back and shoulders less than ten feet from him. *Sorry, Big Joe . . .* Coak rose up onto his haunches like a mountain cat ready to pounce. Yet, no sooner had he prepared to spring forward, Big Joe Macon jumped straight up and shouted across the crevice to Bo Romans, "Look out! Behind you!"

Big Joe Macon's rifle snapped up against his shoulder, taking aim at Bob Herns. But before Big Joe got the shot off, Coak came in fast, sweeping upward, then down onto Macon's back, an arm encircling the big man and knocking his rifle out of his hands.

Big Joe slung Jake Coak back and forth on his back like a rag doll, until Coak managed to get his legs wrapped around Macon's waist. They tumbled backward onto the ground as the knife found its target and Jake Coak sank the blade in to the hilt.

Across the crevice, Bob Herns sank down onto his knees with Bo Romans's weight against his chest, the rawhide drawn deep and tight around Romans's throat. Herns was glad Romans never saw his face. Romans's fingers scratched and dug at the rawhide, but found no way to stop it from doing its job. In a few struggling seconds, the clawing fingers fell limp, but Herns held firm until the rest of Bo Romans sagged downward against him. As Bob Herns unwound the rawhide strip from Romans's throat, he looked across the open span of air and earth between them and watched Jake Coak stand up from the body on the rocky edge and wipe the knife blade across Big Joe Macon's shirt.

Jake Coak moved forward to the edge of the crevice and looked back and forth along it. Seeing no signs of other men lying in wait, he stood up, waved Bob Herns down toward the horses, then turned and moved away quickly out of sight.

"Jesus," said Bob Herns in a whisper to himself, looking down at Bo Romans's body lying in the dirt. "I never want to do something like that again."

Moments later, they met at the horses and, seeing the look on Herns's face, Coak asked, "Are you all right, Bob?"

"No, not really," Herns said, a slight tremor in his voice, the strip of rawhide still wrapped around one hand, having been there even as he climbed back down the wall of the crevice.

Coak reached out and loosened the strip from Herns's hand and rolled it up and put it away. "First time you ever had to use something like this?"

"Yes, I—" Herns swallowed and found his words. "That is, I never felt a man die against me that way."

Coak just stared at him, his eyes asking for more.

Herns offered it. "To be honest, I've never killed a man. I had to shoot a bank robber in Chicago last year—but only in the leg."

"What were you going to do back there when J. T.

Priest had my rifle in my belly?" Coak asked. "I saw you ready to draw."

"I would have done whatever I had to," said Herns. He nodded upward toward the higher ledge where they'd killed the men with their hands, up close, and left their bodies lying in the sun. "But that, up there. I never—"

"Put it out of your mind, Bob," Coak said, cutting him off. "It might have been a little easier if you hadn't known the man, hadn't ridden with him—but that's not how it played. Just remind yourself that he'd have done the same to you without thinking twice."

"I know," said Herns, "and that helps, some." He turned, walked to his horse, and took down his canteen, opening it with shaking hands. Coak watched him take a long drink of tepid water, then pour some into his hand and run it on his neck.

"You can turn back, Bob," Coak offered flatly.

"Nope, I'll stick around. . . . Besides, it's done now, and can't be changed. I'm still on my job."

"Then let's ride," said Coak, "and think about it no more. I've got a feeling nobody's ever gotten this close to *Los Pistoleros* before. By the time they realize these two men aren't coming, we need to be in position to do some serious damage."

Both the horse he was riding and the spare horse on the rope behind him were badly blown by the time Quick Charlie Simms turned off the trail and onto the stone walk of *La Rosa Negra Posada*. Evening shadows stretched long across the dark stains of dried blood on the ground. Lorenzo Jerea did not see Simms ride in from the east, nor did he hear any sound until the horse beneath Simms snorted and scraped a hoof on the stone. As Lorenzo turned, his hand gripping the stock of the double-barreled shotgun, from around the corner of the building the old constable stepped out with a big Russian revolver cocked and aimed.

"Raise your hands!" the old constable called out.

But Quick Charlie Simms didn't even look toward him. Instead, Simms winced at the sight of Lorenzo's face and said, "Goodness, Lorenzo! What happened to you?"

Lorenzo let out a tense breath and waved the old constable forward from the end of the building. "It is all right, Raoul . . . I know this man. He is a friend of my family."

"And you know me, too, Raoul," Simms called out to the old constable. "Come over here where you can see something. You ought to know better than to put somebody between you and the sunlight."

"Quick Charlie?" Raoul said in surprise, his pistol lowering as he stepped forward. "It *is* you? What are you doing here?"

"What's the matter, Raoul?" Simms smiled, swinging down from his saddle, dusting his sleeves. "Can't I come to visit my old friends when I take a notion? I've been hearing about the new inn here. Juan always said he'd build a place of his own someday. Hope I'm not intruding?"

"Of course not! You are always welcome here." Raoul holstered his pistol, he and Lorenzo stepping forward as one. "But, Charlie, *mi amigo*. This terrible thing has happened here today. Many people have died here!"

"I heard the shooting from a long ways off," said Simms, his eyes going from Raoul to Lorenzo. "Are your folks all right?"

"*Sí*, they are both unharmed," said Lorenzo. "They are with the captain of the *federales* in Sonora. He is badly shot. Several of his soldiers are dead." Lorenzo pointed down at the long marks in the dirt where he and Raoul had dragged the bodies to a wagon and hauled them to town. "This might be a dangerous time for a *gringo*—" Lorenzo stopped himself. "I mean for an *Americano* like you, to be traveling here."

"I appreciate your concern, Lorenzo," Simms said, "but I feel welcome most places I go." Simms looked around at the inn. "It so happens I'm looking for the men who did all this. Think you can lend me a horse and point me in their direction?"

"You know these men?" Raoul asked.

"Oh yes, I know them all right, some of them anyway," said Simms.

"Why are you looking for them?" Lorenzo asked.

"Well, some things have changed since the last time I saw you or your folks, Lorenzo. I'm a U.S. Federal Deputy Marshal now."

"Ha, always you make a joke," said Raoul, "even at a time like this."

"No, it's no joke," Simms said, giving the old constable a patient look. "I've been working for Judge Parker, not that it means anything down here. But these men have taken a woman hostage, and I've come to get her back."

"The woman," said Lorenzo, "I saw her! She is with them against her will? You know this woman?"

"Yep, I know her. She's the real reason I'm here," said Simms. "Now what about that horse?"

"Of course, you can have a horse. You can take my father's riding horse."

"Are you sure?" asked Simms. "It might be awhile before I bring it back."

"*Sí*, I am sure. My father would insist you take the horse if he were here."

"*Gracias*," said Simms.

"And you will need a gun," said Raoul, seeing no pistol or holster on Simms's hip, "for these men are all killers." Raoul reached for the horse pistol in his holster, but Simms stopped him.

"I won't need it, Raoul, but thanks." He looked back around the shattered windows, the bullet holes in the walls. Then he asked Lorenzo, "Did you happen to notice a man riding with them who had a strange look in his eyes?"

"*Sí*, they all have such a look!" said Lorenzo.

"Never mind," said Simms. "This man's name is Jake Coak. He carries a sawed-off rifle, always has a black dog traveling with him."

"I see the rifle but no dog," said Lorenzo. "This man is the one who stood up to the others. They were going to kill me, but he stood up and took the blame for the things they accused me of doing."

"Yep, that would be Jake Coak all right," said Simms. "Was he with them when they left?"

"No, the *federales* took him to Sonora, but then the fight started and he must have gotten away. Him and another man came back. They asked my father to keep an eye out for *Americano* lawmen. But we had no idea they were talking about you!"

"Well, now you know." Simms smiled. "There might be a couple of other lawmen coming this way. I need you to keep them here if you can."

"How will I do that?" Lorenzo shrugged.

"Tell them I'm bringing the man they want to

them," said Simms. "I asked them to wait for me back at the border, but I figure they'll have gotten too restless by now and are headed this way."

"*Sí*, I will tell them to wait here for you," said Lorenzo. "But do you not want their help?"

"No," said Simms, "I want to shut this thing down with no more gunplay than necessary."

Lorenzo gave him a knowing look, saying, "This woman, she is more than just someone you know, *sí*?"

"Exactly," said Simms, and for the first time since he'd arrived, Raoul and Lorenzo were able to look past the carefree smile and the easygoing manner, and see the concerned, almost frightened look in Quick Charlie Simms's eyes. "I'm doing my best to keep real calm here, Lorenzo . . . for her sake."

Chapter 17

When Simms and Raoul had finished saddling Juan Jerea's big chestnut barb, Simms filled his canteen and accepted a bag of food Lorenzo had prepared for him. Before Simms swung up onto the saddle, Loenzo looked across the darkening land and asked, "Are you sure you do not want to wait until morning? You are welcome to stay here."

"No, thanks, Lorenzo, I'll push on tonight," said Simms. "I'd like to reach the place they're going to as soon as possible."

"You know where this place is?" Lorenzo asked.

"No, but I've got a good idea." Simms smiled and swung up into the saddle, leveling his hat on his brow. "The closer I get to them, the better that idea will be."

"But you will not catch up to this Jake Coak tonight," said Raoul. "And even if you catch up to him, together you will not catch up to those men you are after."

"I might know a shortcut," allowed Simms.

"A shortcut?" Lorenzo and Raoul looked at one another, then up at Simms. "How can you know a shortcut when you do not know where they go?"

"Call it odds and intuition," said Simms, pulling the

chestnut barb back a step, checking how it responded to the reins. "Once I know the direction they're headed in, it's not that hard to figure where they're going." He turned the chestnut barb with a tap of the reins to its neck, and in a moment had ridden out past the first turn in the trail.

"Always he talks so strange, our friend Simms, eh?" said Lorenzo to Raoul. "Do you think he will be safe?"

"*Sí*, he will be safe. He is always safe." Raoul considered things for a second, then added, scratching his chin, "But I have never seen him so worried. I wish he had taken my pistol with him. It is not good that he goes unarmed."

Lorenzo smiled. "He did not say he was unarmed . . . only that he did not need your pistol."

"But I did not see a pistol on his hip or a rifle in his saddle scabbard," said Raoul.

"*Sí*, I know," said Lorenzo, and offering nothing more on the subject, he turned and walked back into *La Rosa Negra*.

In the waxing light of a three-quarter moon Simms only followed the hoofprints out across a short stretch of flatland until he got his bearings and judged where the men were headed. A black outline of foothills loomed in the northwest, the prints in the sand leading in that direction. Yet, this was not the direction he would take. Instead, Simms reined the chestnut barb straight north, a trail that would be straighter, steeper, and more difficult. But once above the crest of a three-mile climb, the land would even out. His trail northwest from there would be flat and less rocky for as much as fifty miles or more.

He stopped the chestnut barb for only a moment

and patted its neck. The chestnut pranced high hooved and restless beneath him, as if telling Simms he knew what was expected and was ready to give whatever it took. Simms spun the horse, reining it high with the reins, getting a feel for the animal and its capabilities. As the barb's front hooves touched the ground, Simms collected it, tapping it forward with his boots to its sides. He did not stretch the horse out the mile and a half distance to the foothills, but rather held it back, giving it just enough of a workout to reach the upward trail, feeling loose and ready.

"Take us up," Simms said, letting the horse move at its own pace as its hooves bit upward into the loose sand and dirt. For an hour, the horse pulled the ground back beneath them, its breath pumping deep and steadily in the otherwise silent night. When they had ascended the high crest where the flat land lay westward between the foothills and the beginning of the mountain lines, Simms heeled the barb forward at a walk until he felt it grow rested and nimble hoofed once again. Then he tightened his hat down on his forehead, collected the horse quickly and batted his boots to its sides, relaxing the reins this time as the horse bellied low to the ground, the ride turning into a smooth fast glide along a ribbon of sand and silk.

"When I said Sonora, Quick Charlie Simms knew what I meant," said J. T. Priest to Kate McCorkle when she'd asked him how he expected Simms to find them out here in the Mexican hill country. "Besides, I thought you said he wasn't coming, Kate." Priest smiled and lifted the bottle of whiskey to his lips. He sat at a small wooden table inside the weathered wood-and-adobe shack built against the side of an upthrust of rock. Kate

McCorkle lay on the floor, her wrists cuffed around a thick support column.

When Kate didn't answer, J. T. Priest chuckled under his breath and wiped his hand across his mouth. "Why so quiet all of a sudden, dear Kate? Could it be you've just realized that I've caught on to how you and your grifter boyfriend work?" Light glowed from a miner's lantern in the center of the table, giving Priest's face a ghastly drawn appearance. Outside, the men slept around the glow of a campfire, the light sheltered by the walls of the rock canyon surrounding them.

"He'll come for you, Kate," Priest added, "and this time when he and I meet, there won't be any talking . . . just killing. He won't get the chance to work his fast-talking charm on anybody."

"Look at you, J. T., you poor sick-minded fool. You act as if killing Charlie Simms is the only thing that matters in your life. Do you think that once he and I are dead, your problems will be over? What about Sullivan Hart? Do you think he'll forget all about you killing his father? Do you think Judge Parker will stand still for you and your attorneys making his court a laughingstock?" She shook her head. "Do you think Jake Coak just threw up his hands and gave up?"

"I figure the *federales* probably killed your friend Coak when they heard the shooting and came riding back to it."

"Where in the world do you get these ideas, J. T.?" Kate asked, astonished.

J. T. Priest tapped his temple. "Because that's what I would have done if I were them. See? Charlie Simms is not the only one who can anticipate what goes on in the other person's mind and take advantage of it. I've dealt myself the upper hand here. I've outsmarted all of you—Judge Parker, Hart, Simms—all of you. It's too bad you won't live long enough to realize it. All those nights in jail, Kate, I had plenty of time to figure out what I did wrong the last time. I was too eager, moved too fast and made too many mistakes. But not anymore. From now on I play it calm and easy. I lay back like a spider and let all of you walk into my web."

Kate only stared at him in the flickering glow of the lantern, hoping he really believed everything he'd just told her. As Priest drank more whiskey, she turned her eyes from him and gazed out through the small open window and up at the stars.

A thousand yards away in the thin light before dawn, Jake Coak and Bob Herns lay atop an overhanging rock and looked down at the small circle of firelight in the canyon below. They had drunk tepid water from their canteens, and ate the stiff jerked beef that Herns had been carrying in his saddlebags for a long time. Behind them stood their horses, still damp and winded from the long ride that had only ended after prowling the hillsides for the better part of the night before Herns had spotted the campfire. Beyond the horses, Buster stood watch on the trail. Moments earlier, when the dog had let out a low growl, both Coak and Herns had tensed and listened closely for any sound coming out of the blackness of the rocks behind them. When no other sound came from either the land or the dog, Coak raised his hat brim and said in a quiet voice, "He must've caught a wisp of cat on the air." They turned back to the light below, Coak laying out a line of cartridges and checking each one. "I figure our best chance at getting Kate out of there alive is for you to lay back and cover me down there. I'll slip in at dawn, get her out and make a run for it."

"He'll have a guard watching her, Jake," said Herns. After a hesitant pause, Herns added, "Are you sure you're not letting your feeling for her get the best of your judgment?"

"No, I'm not, Bob." Coak looked at him in the darkness. "I made a mistake back at the inn . . . I admit it. But now my mind is clear. This is strictly business from here on. If you've got any better plan, I need to hear it."

Herns let out a breath thinking about it, then said, "No, I have no better plan in mind. I just thought you ought to—"

"I do," said a lowered voice behind them, interrupting Herns and causing him and Coak to both spin toward the sound with their guns cocking. "Easy, gentlemen, it's me, Simms. You don't want to fire a shot right now and give yourselves away."

"Simms!" Jake Coak hissed. "How in the world . . . ?" Coak's voice trailed as he saw Simms step forward in the pale starlight, Buster at his side, Simms's hand resting near the dog's head, patting it. Coak stared at Buster in disbelief.

"Don't blame him," said Simms. "I have this real gift with animals." He stooped down with Coak and Herns and gazed at the light of the campfire and the glowing light in the small window.

"Buster, you and I are going to have a long talk after this is over," Jake Coak said to the dog. Buster whined slightly.

Simms smiled in the darkness, watching the light below as he spoke to Jake Coak. "And you and I might have a talk about these *feelings* you seem to have developed for Kate McCorkle."

Coak looked at Simms's shadowed face. Simms stood at ease, looking down into the canyon as if this whole situation had been waiting for his arrival—Quick Charlie moving in and taking control. "How long have you been standing back there listening, Simms?" Coak asked.

"Not long," said Simms. "I wouldn't have found you at all if it hadn't been for the dog." He reached a hand around and scratched Buster's ears. "Who's your partner here?" He nodded toward Bob Herns.

Coak moved Simms's hand away from Buster's head. "This is Bob Herns, he's with the Pinkertons. We go a ways back, me and Bob."

Sims and Bob acknowledged each other. Simms said, "Pinkertons, huh? I once met Allen Pinkerton . . . shot billiards with him."

"Billiards?" said Bob Herns, dubiously. "Mister Pinkerton doesn't shoot billiards. He's no gambler."

"You can say that again." Simms chuckled.

"What's this better plan you have, Simms, or were you just saying that for effect?" Coak asked, already irritated at Simms's cavalier attitude.

Simms looked back down at the glow of firelight, saying, "Since you're both far better with a gun than I am—especially you with that rifle—it's better I slip in down there and get Kate. You two cover me. Once Kate and I are in the clear, you can get in there and collect whatever bounty these men are wearing. That's what you were after, right, Coak?"

Coak hesitated before saying, "Yeah, that's right. We want the rewards. So, now that you're here, you figure you'll just ease in and out, not raise a fuss? Not make a sound? You'll be Kate McCorkle's saving angel?"

Simms caught the bite of jealousy in Coak's words. "She's her own woman, Coak. Where she goes after I get her out of there, or who she goes with, it's up to her. As far as me not raising a fuss down there, don't count on it. If I thought I was that good, I wouldn't have come here—I would already have Kate out and gone by now, and left you two sitting here with your guns in your hands." As he spoke, he placed his hand back on the dog's head, rubbing it.

Again, Coak removed Simms's hand from the dog and said, "You'll take the woman, and Bob and I get left to bear the brunt of the fight. It figures."

Simms turned his eyes from the campfire below and, facing Coak, said, "Kate's been with me a long time, Coak. . . . For her sake, don't fool yourself. But if you want to do it different, tell me how, right now before the sun comes up."

"He's right, Jake," Herns cut in, keeping his voice lowered. "We've got to make a move here pretty quick."

"Go on then, Simms," said Coak. "As soon as we see the two of you get out of sight, we'll come down and finish things." He ran a hand along his short rifle barrel.

"There'll be more than the two of us, Coak," said Simms. "But whoever you see us ride out with, let us go."

"What are you talking about, Simms? This is no time for your slick grifting ways. If you get down and cause her any harm, you've got the rest of your short life to outrun me." The sawed-off rifle levered in his hands as if for emphasis.

Simms looked into Coak's eyes and saw that there was no way to explain what he was about to do. Jake Coak wouldn't go along with it if he knew. Simms stood up and stepped back from the edge. "Take the bounty rewards, Coak. It's all you've got coming." He turned to leave.

But Coak called out in a whisper, "Simms, are you armed?"

"Only with truth and righteousness." Simms smiled, moving away, Coak holding the dog back as if afraid Buster might follow him.

As Simms slipped out of sight, Jake Coak and Bob Herns stood up, ready to move down closer for a better fighting position. "He's too cocksure of himself to suit me," Coak said, reaching for his horse's reins.

"That's not what I saw at all," said Herns, holstering the pistol he'd just checked and spun in his hand. "He's not sure of anything right now. He's scared to death and playing this by ear."

"Yeah, maybe," said Coak. "It's hard for me to tell anything about him. I think he realizes he played this thing wrong from the start, but doesn't want to admit it to himself. We should have come in full force, Hart, Roth, Simms, and any other deputies we could round up."

"Do you really believe that, Jake?" Herns asked.

"I don't know what I believe right about now. Come on, let's take the bounties. Like he said, it's all we're going to get."

As a silver-gray thread of sunlight painted the horizon, J. T. Priest stood up, pitched the empty bottle into the pile of other bottles and old debris from times past, and called out to Rance Macklinberg on the other side of the door, standing guard, "Mack, come in here."

The door creaked open. "What is it, Boss?" asked Macklinberg.

"Stay here. Keep an eye on her while I go relieve myself." He gave Macklinberg a knowing glance. Kate caught the look pass between the two of them and wondered what it meant.

As if on cue, Macklinberg replied, "Why, Boss? Hell, she ain't going nowhere."

"Watch her anyway," said Priest. He swung his hat up atop his head and walked out the door. Passing through the men who lay asleep around the campfire, Priest looked down at the face of R. Martin Swan and shook his head in disgust. As if actually feeling the scorn on Priest's face, Swan drew in a snoring breath and threw a forearm over his closed and sleeping eyes. "Another one bites the dust," Priest growled to himself, noting the scraggly beard forming on Swan's cheeks and the stain of whiskey on the young attorney's dirty lapel. A rusty pistol lay in a worn-out leather holster across Swan's stomach. The sleeping man's free hand caressed the pistol chamber absently, his dream seeming to examine what dark possibilities lay within. Priest leaned down slightly and whispered, "Just once I'd like to meet a man who's more than just an outlaw in the making." When he'd walked away, R. Martin Swan's eyes opened for an instant, then his lids fluttered in search of something he'd missed and closed again in the darkness.

Behind a deadfall of juniper, J. T. Priest relieved himself, then stood for a long moment before turning and taking his time going back to the shack. On his way back, he made no attempt to keep his footsteps light through the coarse, dry bracken at his feet. He stopped suddenly, but not seeming too surprised when he felt something hard pointed to the back of his head. He felt Simms's forearm sweep around his face, keeping him from calling out to the guards at the edge of the camp or the men asleep around the fire.

"Not a sound, J. T.," Quick Charlie Simms hissed in his ear. "Keep walking."

At the door, J. T. Priest stopped, even though Simms tried pressing him forward. Without struggling, Priest raised his hand to Simms's forearm and lowered it from his lips. He whispered to Simms over his shoulder, "I doubt that's even a gun . . . probably just your finger."

"Want to bet your life on it, Priest?" Simms whispered. "All you had to do was ride away. You were free, you poor fool! Now open the door, and take what's coming to you."

"I can take what's coming to me, Quick Charlie. Can you?" Priest lifted the wooden handle and opened the door slowly, speaking as he did so, stepping inside. "Because if you can take it, Simms, here it is."

In the middle of the dirt floor stood Kate McCorkle. Behind her was Rance Macklinberg, his pistol cocked and pointed up under her left breast. "Step around from behind him, Simms," Macklinberg demanded in a low tone. "You just lost this game."

Part 3

Chapter 18

Rance Macklinberg's hands felt up and down Quick Charlie Simms's sides, searching him. He pulled out a folded cloth bank bag from inside Simms's coat and stepped back looking at it. "He's clean, Boss," Macklinberg said, his big Colt still pointed at Simms's belly.

"Told you he'd come." Priest grinned at Kate McCorkle and held up the small derringer he'd snatched from Simms's hand. "He even armed himself. A *derringer* of all things? Just to show he cares, I suppose."

Rance Macklinberg stood, glancing at the folded cloth bag in his hand, holding it by its top and letting it roll open. "Take a look at this, Boss."

J. T. Priest snatched the bag from Macklinberg, his hand shaking in exhilaration. "Now go on and shoot him."

"Right now?"

Priest opened the top of the bag. "Yes, right now, before he starts running his mouth." Reaching down inside the bag, Priest drew up a flat, banded stack of dollar bills.

"Jesus, Boss!" Macklinberg looked stunned. "That must be a thousand dollars there."

"Expense money," Simms offered.

"Shut up, Simms." Macklinberg reached out with his pistol barrel and tapped Simms on the forehead.

"Shoot him, Mack, like I told you to," Priest commanded, turning the flat stack of money in his hand, looking it over good in the faint glow of the lantern light.

"I'm sorry, Kate," said Simms, his hands chest high, looking over at her, his eyes lost and helpless. "I lost my head . . . couldn't think straight knowing they had you hostage—"

"I mean it, shut up, Simms!" Macklinberg's pistol barrel tapped a little harder this time. Simms winced and drew his head to one side.

"Shoot him, Mack! Damn it!" Priest ruffled the stack of money, noting the crispness of the bills, the paper band around it never having been slipped, never wrinkled. "I've seen this man work too many times. You ever let him start talking, he'll get you, somehow, some way—now shoot him!"

"Whatever you say, Boss." Macklinberg shoved Simms to one side, raising the pistol to his forehead, levelling it a few inches back to keep Simms's brains from splattering on him. Kate McCorkle struggled, her cuffed hands going up under her arm. She braced herself, preparing to spring forward as the sound of Macklinberg's pistol cocking filled the room.

But even as her hand tore at her dress and reached for the razor, she stopped abruptly as Priest said, "Wait, Mack! Just one damned minute . . ."

Priest stepped over in front of Simms, the stack of bills in his hand. "Expense money? From a miser like Judge Parker? Still in a federal mint band? How stupid do you think I am, Simms? Where'd you get this money? Don't try to lie!"

Simms's eyes widened in fright, but he said nothing. Priest cocked the small derringer, swung an arm around and pointed it at Kate McCorkle. "Make me ask you again . . . see if I don't put a bullet in her mouth."

"J. T., it's the truth," Simms said, talking fast, "it's expense money from Judge Parker. He wanted you real bad, gave me an open hand to hunt you down. Said if that wasn't enough, there was plenty more where that came—"

"You're lying, Simms!" Priest pulled the trigger, the derringer pointed at Kate's face. But the hammer only clicked. "Empty! You son of a bitch! You came here with an empty *derringer*? So help me God, Simms!" Priest jerked one of the pistols from his waist belt and cocked it quickly toward Kate McCorkle. "Bet me this one won't blow her head off! Now, one last time—where'd you get the money?"

The empty derringer had shown Simms how serious Priest was. "All right, J. T.! Hold it! I'll tell you. This time it's the truth."

"It better be," Priest warned.

"Uh, Boss," said Macklinberg, quietly reminding Priest, "you're letting him talk."

"I know it, Mack, shut up!" said Priest. "This is different. He's done for and he knows it." He swung his eyes back to Quick Charlie Simms. "Now spill it, Simms . . . where'd it come from?"

"What's the use?" Simms asked himself aloud. Then he said to Priest, "You already know where it came from. Don't act like you don't, J. T."

Priest's faint smile of satisfaction turned in an instant into a wide grin of delight. "Hear that, Mack? This grifter peckerwood opened that damned safe!"

"What? No, he didn't," said Macklinberg.

"Oh, yes, he did, Mack. I know he can. I know he found it where we left it. And I'll bet you every dollar in my pocket he spun that baby and opened it wide!"

"Boss, you said awhile ago not to listen to him, not to let him start talking—"

"Mack, do I have to draw you a picture of what happened back there? That's why he came alone! That's why Hart and Roth aren't with him! He didn't want them to know. Simms cracked the safe."

Simms whispered across the room to Kate, "I'm sorry, Kate. It would have been ours . . . yours and mine—"

"Now that's damn touching," Priest said, cutting him off, "but where'd you stash the money?"

Simms gave him an incredulous look. "Why, it's back in the safe, of course." He shrugged. "What better place to keep it? Nobody can open it . . . except *me* that is."

"Now you're lying again, Simms!" Priest swung the pistol back at Kate. But this time Simms knew it was all a bluff on Priest's part. One shot, and every man around the fire would be up and in on the money.

"J. T., you can shoot Kate, you can shoot us both. But there's nothing else I can tell you—the money is back in the safe, all seven hundred and thirty-eight thousand dollars of it. Maybe it was a mistake putting it back in there with all the lawmen, the outlaws and the Apache wandering back and forth, but that's where I left it."

"Sev— seven hundred thousand dollars?" J. T. Priest's pistol sagged, but then he caught himself and leveled it back on Charlie Simms. "What's the numbers, Simms? Mack! Get a pencil and paper, write this down!"

"Where the hell will I get a pencil?" Macklinberg asked, looking all around the adobe shack.

"The numbers? Oh, you mean the combination?" Simms said. He stalled. "Are you going to shoot us, J. T.?"

Now Priest stalled. "That all depends, Simms. Seven hundred thousand dollars is going to make up for a whole lot of hurt feelings between us."

"Then what's our share going to be?" Simms asked, bold as brass.

Priest stared, stunned by Simms's words. "Your *share*? I just said I might not kill the two of you! What more could you want?"

"Boss," Macklinberg said, "this whole deal is moving a little too fast. How do we know he's telling us the—"

"Because, Mack, damn it! Do you think this snake would be trying to cut himself in for a share if it wasn't true? Now what's the combination, Simms?"

"Four right, seven left, six right . . . uh, ten left," Simms said, tossing the numbers out as if knowing them by heart.

Priest stared at him, his eyes looking more shrewd. "Better repeat that for me, Simms. I didn't quite catch all of it."

Simms hesitated, then said, "Uh, five right . . . seven left, six left, uh . . ."

"Never mind," Priest said, "you're going with us!" Jerking Simms forward and slinging him over beside Kate McCorkle, Priest said to Macklinberg, "Think you can gather some horses without waking the whole camp?"

"You mean . . . just the two of us, sharing all the money? A two-way split?"

"You're catching on, Mack." Priest nodded at him without taking his eyes off of Kate and Simms. "Get three horses, keep these lovebirds riding double. And Mack?" Priest's voice went down a notch. "Be sure and cut the rest of the horses loose. We'll scatter them on the way out."

"Damn, Boss, that'll leave everybody stuck here. What if the *federales* come?"

"Mack, if we leave their horses, they'll follow us. They'll round the horses up before the day's over. Do you want to share that money with the whole damned world?"

"What about the two men standing guard, Boss? What if they see us and try to stop us?"

"Mack, anything a man does that's worth anything involves a certain amount of sacrifice. I hate that, but it's the damn truth."

"But still, Boss, double-crossing our own men?"

"Listen to me," said Priest. "There are very few times when you can hear destiny calling out your name. We'll get that money first, then we'll have the rest of our rich lives to feel bad about double-crossing somebody."

Kate and Simms stood silently, watching Rance Macklinberg disappear through the open door into the first gray light of morning. Once Macklinberg was out of sight, Simms whispered, "Nice touch about the horses . . . I wouldn't have thought of it. You must have learned a few things in jail, J. T."

Priest gave him a venomous stare. "Shut up, Simms,

this is none of your business. Shoot straight with me on this and there's a slim chance I might let you and your girlfriend go free. Cross me and there's not a doubt in the world I'll leave you both dead in the sand."

"We won't cross you," Kate said, "you have my promise. But let me ask you one thing, J. T., just for old times sake? Why are you going to split all that money with a fool like Rance Macklinberg?"

Bob Herns caught the first glimpse of the three horses moving through a sparse line of juniper and mesquite clinging to the walls and the floor of the canyon. He and Jake Coak had climbed down and taken position a hundred yards away from the adobe shack, ready to move in and start the fight. "There they go," Herns whispered. "Looks like Priest and another man are riding with them."

"What about Kate?" Coak asked. "Does she seem to be all right?"

"Yep, her and Simms are riding double." Herns looked through the lens a second longer and saw two more men on horseback come easing along the same path as Priest, Macklinberg and their prisoners. "Oops, there goes two more men, following them . . . looks like Denton Howel and Joe Cherry."

"What's Simms up to? Think he even knows the other two are following him?" Coak tried watching with his naked eyes through the grainy morning light.

"Here, take these," said Herns, handing him the lens. But Coak turned him down.

"This is no time to wonder what Quick Charlie Simms is up to now," said Coak. "We'll give them a few minutes to clear out of here, then we make our play."

Herns looked back through the lens for a moment, then said to Coak, "Now here's something strange . . . the rest of the horses are scattering, making their way down a trail."

"What? Let me see!" Jake Coak took the lens and looked through it. "Priest and Macklinberg are cutting out on the rest of the men! What do you suppose that's all about?"

"Beats me," said Herns. "I just hope nobody leaves who's got a bounty on their heads."

On the narrow trail through the coarse juniper and mesquite, Denton Howel held his horse at a slow walk, grabbing Joe Cherry's reins as Cherry tried stepping his horse around him. "Damn it, Joe!" Howel hissed, "Stay back, don't let them see us." He looked Joe Cherry up and down, seeing the wild glassy look in his eyes, and the leather bag still hanging around his neck. "Are you up to doing this?"

"Hell, yes, I'm always up to making some money. If Priest thinks he's going to cut us out of the deal, he's got another think coming."

"Oh, he thinks it sure enough," said Denton Howel. "Never once did he mention the safe they found at Burdine's spread. Luckily the Hubbs brothers let it slip the other night while we were drinking. Priest is playing everybody for a fool. Look at those horses scattering up into the rocks. Think Priest gives a damn who he caused to get killed here?"

"Well"—Cherry grinned, his eyes swimming a bit—"it ain't going to be us." They moved their horses slowly upward until they reached the long stretch of flatland.

* * *

By that time, Priest and Macklinberg were a thousand yards ahead. Macklinberg kept Simms's horse in front of him, forcing Simms along at a fast trot. Kate McCorkle clung to Simms's back, with her cuffed hand holding on to his waist.

"I was beginning to wonder if you were ever going to show, Charlie," Kate whispered near Simms's ear. "What safe is J. T. talking about?"

"It's a long story, Kate," Simms replied. "Right now, all we've got to think about is getting as far from here as we can. Coak and a fellow named Herns is back there getting ready to take down *Los Pistoleros.*"

"Jake got away from the *federales* then," said Kate. "I'm glad to hear it."

"So it's *Jake* now?" Simms asked, looking over his shoulder into her eyes. "Is there anything you want to tell me about you and *Jake*?"

"He's a good man, Charlie, that's all you need to know. He looked out for me, and he treated me like a lady."

"No talking up there," Rance Macklinberg called out to them.

Simms gazed forward into the gray of morning, heeling the big chestnut barb along the steep trail.

Chapter 19

R. Martin Swan was the first man to rise up from his blanket near the low campfire. He rubbed his eyes with both hands and ran his fingers back through his dusty tangled hair. It was purely by chance that his eyes caught sight of Bob Herns moving into position thirty yards to the right, in the cover of rocks and scrub juniper above the adobe shack. Catching Swan's glance and knowing he'd been seen, Herns raised his rifle to his shoulder and aimed it. But before he could get off a shot, Swan dropped back down to the ground, jerked his blanket over his back and scurried across the ground like a rat. Looking down at Swan, Pete Lamburtis chuckled and said to Roundhouse Eddie Jenkins, who had just stood up beside him, "Look at the crazy lawyer! Think he's fooled with Cherry's powder so much it's caused his mind to slip a notch?"

"Hell, who knows?" Roundhouse Eddie yawned and stretched, spreading his arms wide. "Alls I know is, if today ain't no better than yesterday, I just as soon lay back down and call it quits—"

The shot from Bob Herns's rifle hit Roundhouse Eddie Jenkins in the chest with the impact of a forging hammer, clipping his words and lifting him backward into the fire. Smoke and sparks billowed upward.

"What the—?" Lamburtis ducked into a crouch, his pistol coming out of the holster hanging from his shoulder and fanning back and forth. "Eddie's shot!" he bellowed. His pistol scanned the rock and brush, his eyes searching for a drift of barrel smoke.

Men scattered from around the campfire, guns springing from holsters and rifle scabbards, saddles being snatched up from the ground for cover. Before Lamburtis could get a shot off toward Bob Herns, Jake Coak's rifle began to pound from the opposite direction, the first shot hitting Lamburtis high in the shoulder, spinning him in place. The shots walked from left to right across the campsite. Philip Oates stopped hurrying away long enough to turn and fire toward Coak's position, but then one of Coak's shots nailed him to the ground.

"Son of a bitch!" Monty Osbourne screamed, stooping down in his flight and checking on Oates, then scrambling away when he saw Oates was dead.

When the first deadly volley of crossfire lulled for a second, Roundhouse Eddie and Philip Oates lay dead, and Lamburtis was sprawled out wounded behind a saddle on the ground. As the next hard volley began, the other men had found cover, three of them managing to spill through the door of the adobe shack and return fire from the window. One of the men in the shack was Buck Dehoney, and he wasted no time going to the back wall, stepping up onto a wooden chair and hammering his rifle barrel against the earth and plank ceiling, opening a hole large enough to climb through.

"The hell's he doing?" Little Bit Collier asked Buddy Raines.

"You'll have to ask him!" Raines levered a fresh round into his rifle chamber, turned and fired.

Hearing them talk, Buck Dehoney looked around, sand and bits of clay clinging to his hat brim. "I'm getting up where they are, see if I can't get behind these bastards!"

Outside, Roundhouse Eddie's body lay sizzling in the fire, the stench of burning flesh rising and spreading in greasy black smoke.

"Damn!" shouted Eli Drake. "Somebody get that stinking mess put out!" Shots kicked up dirt in front of his cover behind an abandoned wagon frame.

"You do it!" Max Sheppard screamed, firing from behind a large boulder sticking up three feet out of the ground. His voice seemed to summon two quick shots from Jake Coak, fragments of rock spraying up in the air as Sheppard ducked down to the ground. Recognizing the sound of the sawed-off rifle, Sheppard shouted toward the rocky hillside, "Coak, is that you? Are you mad at us for what Priest was going to do to you?" Sheppard reloaded his rifle as he asked in the brief lull of gunfire.

"It's me," Coak shouted in reply. "I'm not mad at nobody. I'm a U.S. Federal Deputy Marshal carrying out my duty."

"Your duty?" Monty Osbourne shouted from his position flat on the ground behind a mound of firewood and brittle mesquite kindling. "You're in *Mejico*, you damned fool!"

"Wouldn't matter to me if we were in Paris, France," Coak replied. "We're taking down anything that looks, sounds or smells like *Los Pistoleros*." His words were followed by two shots from his sawed-off rifle.

"Who's that with you, Coak?" Pete Lamburtis shouted. He'd pressed a bandanna inside his shirt to stay the blood of his shoulder wound.

But Coak didn't answer, and neither did Bob Herns. They both knew that part of the talking had been a way of sighting their positions. But as soon as Coak had spoken, he'd moved back six feet and a few feet to his left. Now he waited in silence as the firing resumed from the gunmen. He saw brush bending and a trickle of loose rock slide down the hillside a few feet from where he'd been. He waited with his rifle aimed until he saw Buck Dehoney's head appear in view, then he fired. But as he did, a bullet came whistling past his cheek, causing him not to see whether or not he'd hit his target.

At the edge of the clearing, Lewis Prior and Tommy Kendall came sliding through the dirt up beside Pete Lamburtis. "The sonsabitches have left us stranded!" Prior said, trying to catch his breath.

"What are you talking about, Prior?" asked Lamburtis, reloading his pistol across his chest.

"Priest is gone . . . so's all our horses!" Prior levered his rifle. Tommy Kendall lay beside him in the dirt, a pistol in each hand.

"Priest cut out on us?" Lamburtis looked startled. "He took our horses?"

"Yeah, either took them or scattered them—either way, all the horses are gone."

"So is Rance Macklinberg, Denton Howel and Cherry," said Tommy Kendall. "We've been left jack-potted!"

"Where's the woman?" asked Lamburtis as Coak

and Herns began to let loose another heavy barrage of fire.

The men ducked down until the volley ceased, then Prior continued, "Where do you think the woman is? They took her with them!"

"Damn," said Lamburtis, "we're in for a long fight here. What got into Priest, doing something like this? All he talked about was getting *Los Pistoleros* going full strength again."

"I don't know what got into him," said Prior, "but something sure changed his direction . . . that double-crossing low-down coyote!"

"Coak?" the voice of Little Bit Collier called out from the door of the shack. "Me and Raines are giving up . . . throwing out our guns. We surrender!"

"If they do, I'll kill them myself," Lamburtis hissed, raising his rifle toward the adobe shack.

"Sorry, boys, there'll be no surrendering today," Coak replied, moving again in a low crouch, to a new position as he spoke. "This is the end of a long, bad situation. Everybody lives or dies like what they are."

"It ain't fair!" Raines shouted, his voice almost sobbing. "We only just joined this bunch!"

"You should have given it more thought," said Coak. A shot from his rifle tore up a chunk of earth and splinters from the door jamb. Raines ducked away with his hands to his eyes, rubbing dirt from them.

"We'll have to get collected and rush them," said Lamburtis to Prior, "while there's still enough of us."

Prior rubbed his chin, wincing a bit at the thought of having brought Jake Coak into their midst. "Damn that Coak! I reckon it's once a lawman always a lawman."

"Humph," Tommy Kendall grunted. "Before this, all you said was 'Any man can change.'"

"That was then," said Prior. "This is now."

"We're gonna have to rush them," Lamburtis said again. "If we don't, they'll hold us out here till they either pick us off one at a time, or else a bunch of *federales* hears all this gunfire and come running."

Lewis Prior looked at Tommy Kendall, then at Lamburtis. "We're game when you are," he said.

Five miles away, on the flatland above the canyon, J. T. Priest stopped his horse at the crest of a low rise and looked back through the morning light. They'd heard the beginning of the gun battle four miles earlier, but hadn't even slowed down. Now J. T. Priest looked back in the morning light and said, "What do you figure, Mack? *Federales*, maybe?"

Rance Macklinberg caught the big chestnut barb by its reins and turned Simms and Kate McCorkle beside him. "I don't know, Boss, but I feel bad as hell, leaving everybody on foot."

"You'll get over that once you run your fingers through seven hundred thousand dollars, Mack," Priest spoke as he scanned the flatland and caught sight of a thin streak of sunlight reflecting off metal. "We've got somebody on our tails!" He looked at Simms. "Did you come alone?"

"What do you think, J. T.?" Simms asked.

Priest nodded as if ascertaining something for himself, then he said to Rance Macklinberg, "Yep, he always works alone. None of the deputies will work with him, I expect." He looked back toward the spot where he'd seen the streak of sunlight. "We're going to have to find a spot where we can get covered."

"But what if it's some of our men, Boss?" Macklinberg asked.

"So what? You want to face any of our bunch, after scattering their horses on them, leaving them in a gunfight?" Priest gave him a look of disdain. "Are you sure you're smart enough to *handle* a large amount of money?"

"Alls I'm saying is—"

Priest cut him off. "Alls *I'm* saying is, I won't be dogged from here to the border, whoever that is. Ride forward and find us a spot, Mack. Take the lovebirds with you. I'll wait here till I can make out who it is." Priest jerked his horse toward a shallow dry wash in the sand and cholla, grumbling, "Why can't things just go simple for once?" He stepped his horse down into the dry wash and swung down from the saddle as Rance Macklinberg slapped the big chestnut barb on its rump and raced forward behind it.

They rode hard for almost two miles before Simms finally checked the chestnut barb down and turned it, facing Rance Macklinberg in a low swirl of dust. "Keep riding, damn you!" His hand tightened on the rifle across his lap.

"All right!" Simms raised a hand in a show of submission. "But how much farther are we going to go before your boss back there thinks we've run out on him?"

"He knows better," said Macklinberg.

"Are you kidding me? J. T. Priest is walking on fire right now. He wouldn't trust his own mother—if he ever had one." Simms looked astonished, stepping the chestnut barb closer to Macklinberg until the rifle came up from the man's lap and leveled on him. Sitting behind Simms, Kate McCorkle's cuffed hands clutched his shoulder.

"That's close enough, Quick Charlie," Macklinberg warned, causing Simms to jerk the horse to a halt. "I know you've got more angles than a bag of broken glass. Now you figure you'll slip in between me and Priest and get us agin one another. Don't even try it."

"I won't," said Simms, "but unless you're as stupid as *he* thinks you are, you should realize, Kate and me are trying to get through this thing alive! I don't want Priest going nuts on us . . . come charging at us, thinking we've tried to double-cross him. You've seen how easily that could happen with him—he's just dangling on thin strings anyway!"

Rance Macklinberg stared at him. "Get moving!" He jerked his head toward a higher rise in the sand, a thousand yards ahead of them. "We'll hold up there . . . it's good cover."

"Whatever you say." Simms shook his head and booted the chestnut barb forward. They rode on in silence until, at the bottom of the rise, Macklinberg pulled his horse up beside the chestnut barb and grabbed its reins again.

"What did you mean back there?" Macklinberg asked. "As stupid as *he* thinks I am?"

"Hey, forget it, Mack," said Simms, seeing the wheels of suspicion turning in Macklinberg's mind. "It's none of my business which one of you kills the other."

On the other side of the rise, Simms and Kate McCorkle swung down from the horse and waited while Rance Macklinberg turned his back on them and looked over the edge back along the trail. Kate gave Simms a look and patted her cuffed hands on the razor up under her arm. But Simms quickly shook his head, stopping her. The move came just in time as Macklinberg realized what he'd done and spun toward them with a flat level stare. "Don't try nothing, I'm warning you," he hissed, his hands clutching the rifle.

Simms shrugged and spread his hands. "Hadn't given it a thought, Mack."

"And don't call me Mack. Only my friends call me Mack!"

"All right, *Rance*, anything you say," Simms replied, noting the man was becoming rattled, having too much to think about.

For the next few minutes, Macklinberg shot glances away from Simms and Kate only long enough to check the trail. Then his eyes would snap back to them. After a while Simms let out a breath of exasperation and said in a quiet tone, "We're not the ones you have to worry about, *Rance*. You can see us . . . you know what our intentions are—"

"Shut up! Damn you!" Macklinberg sweated streams. "Don't call me Rance either!"

"Then what do I ca—"

"You don't call me *nothing*! You sit there and shut your mouth, or I'll put a bullet in your eye!"

"Boy, wouldn't that make Priest proud of you," Simms said, calmly. "The one person who can put your hands on the money, you shoot in the eye?"

Macklinberg started to respond, but cutting a glance along the trail, he stopped himself and said, "Here he comes." Then his eyes took on a strange expression as he watched Priest appear up above the sand and cholla, along with two other horsemen. "What's this? He's not alone! Howel and Joe Cherry are riding with him!"

Simms gave Kate McCorkle a sit-tight look, and the two of them stood up and stepped over beside the chestnut barb. "Let me cut him, now! Charlie," Kate whispered. "We can make a break for it."

Simms only squeezed her forearm. "What, and miss all this? Stay with me, Kate. We're gaining ground every minute."

Seeing the look on Rance Macklinberg's face, Priest drew his horse to a halt, Denton Howel and Joe Cherry right behind him. "Luckily they made it, Mack," Priest said quickly. "I told you I better wait back there, make sure it was Howel and Cherry and bring them to us—good thing I insisted on it. It's a damned wonder they got out of there alive, thank God!" Priest was sweating even worse than Rance Macklinberg.

"Yep, thank God!" Rance Macklinberg took the hint, but he'd also noted the way Priest made it sound as if Macklinberg had been opposed to him waiting for the two men. "Boys, I was on my way back to warn you somebody had turned the horses loose, but the boss stopped me." He gave Priest a cold stare, letting him know two could play this game. "What the hell's going on back there anyway? *Federales*?" He looked back and forth between Denton Howel and Joe Cherry.

"What went on," said Cherry, "is I tracked wide and slipped in sideways up that dry wash. Caught Priest with his britches down, so to speak." He gave J. T. Priest a cold stare.

Priest swung down from his saddle and squatted down on the ground, catching his breath and mopping a nervous hand across his brow. "That's the damned truth, Mack," Priest said, agreeing with Joe Cherry in part. "There I stood waiting for them . . . worried to *death* about them. Damned if Joe didn't slip right up and—"

"All's well that ends well," said Denton Howel in a flat tone, cutting Priest off. His eyes went to Simms and McCorkle. "Howdy, Simms . . . I might have figured you played into this some way."

"Howdy, Howel." Simms smiled. "I'm not at all played into this. I'm what you call the innocent bystander."

"Oh, you just dropped down out of the sky?" Howel looked at Kate McCorkle and shook his head. "You know, she'd be a half-decent-looking woman if she'd do something with that hair, clean herself up some. But damned if I'd put it all on the line for her. Is she really *worth* all this?"

"Denton, ole buddy, you just can't imagine." Simms grinned, putting an arm around Kate's shoulders. "But realize this, neither Kate nor me asked for any of this. This wasn't my idea, calling a war on *Los Pistoleros*."

Denton Howel took his hat off and dried the inside of the band with a wadded-up bandanna. "Relax, Simms. I never had anything against you—never liked you after you winning my grandfather's pocket watch that time, but never really *dis*-liked you either." He nodded back along the dusty trail toward the direction of the canyon. "I don't blame you for what's going on back there." His gaze honed over onto J. T. Priest. "For two cents, we'd all ride back there and take our medicine with them."

J. T. Priest looked at the ground, a feigned sadness coming to his eyes. "Denton, you don't know how much I've had to fight myself to keep from doing that very thing. If I thought I could change anything, I'd be in there like a dart. But the cold hard truth is those boys are done for, from what it sounded like to me. The best we can hope to do now is to go on. . . . It's what they would have wanted."

"J. T.," said Denton Howel, "you sound like P. T. Barnum selling rain to a river rat."

A silence set in, nobody wanting to be the next one to say a word. Priest just kept staring at the ground, wanting desperately to snatch a pistol from his waist and get busy. After a moment, Denton Howel broke the silence, saying, "Well, are we ready to go?"

Now Priest raised his eyes, squinting in the sun's glare. "Go where?"

"To the Burdine spread, of course," said Howel, "to see if Quick Charlie is really that good at opening a safe."

Priest stood up, swallowing a knot in his dry throat. There was nothing he could say that would make things any better. He wasn't even going to try. Dusting off the seat of his trousers, Priest picked up his reins. But before he could raise his foot to his stirrup, Denton Howel stopped him, saying, "J. T. Why don't you and Mack there ride double for a while, give Simms's horse a little break."

Chapter 20

When the next heavy round of firing ended, Pete Lamburtis raised his head briefly, looking back and forth, getting his bearings. Next to him lay Lewis Prior and Tommy Kendall. "Once Coak shoots his rifle empty this next time, we make our run at him. Sounds like he's loading ten shots at a time."

"Why only ten?" Prior asked. "That model of rifle fires fifteen shots."

Lamburtis frowned. "I don't know, Prior. Maybe you can write to the manufacturer once we get out of here. The point is, Coak's doing most of the damage. The other shooter is mostly pinning us down while Coak reloads." As Lamburtis spoke, Harry Turpin rose up from the ground in front of them and made a run for the shack. A bullet from Bob Herns stabbed him in the side and dropped him. Turpin crawled a few feet and stopped dead.

"Well, he sure pinned Turpin," said Prior, "if that's what you're talking about!"

"Damn it," said Lamburtis, "if this keeps up, there'll soon be too few of us to rush them!"

"Then let's get it done," said Tommy Kendall.

* * *

Up in the rocks and brush above them, Jake Coak finished reloading his rifle and resumed firing, the idea being to wear the men down and force them to make a bold rush on his position. If he was right in his assessment of the matter, the gunmen were just about ready to try it. His main concern right now was the figure in the brush that he had shot at earlier. Coak wasn't sure if he'd hit the man or not, and he didn't like thinking that the man was still alive and might make a move on him at the same time as the others rushed him.

Coak glanced around for Buster but saw no sign of him. Then, seeing another man rise up from behind a saddle on the ground and make a run for the shack, Coak aimed at the dirt behind his running boots and followed him shot after shot until the man dove through the door of the adobe shack. "Good," Coak said to himself, "let them see you miss." He looked on in satisfaction, hoping the others would see him miss, take heart, and decide it was time to make their charge at him.

Pete Lamburtis counted the shots from Coak's sawed-off rifle, then turned to Prior. "He's down to three shots, get ready to signal the men! I'll keep the other rifle busy."

A face ventured forward at the window, then pulled back out of sight, but not before Bob Herns took a shot at it, kicking up a sliver of wood from the window frame. Pete Lamburtis aimed at Bob Herns's rifle smoke and opened fire as Lewis Prior waved a hand toward the opposite side of the hill. Then Prior and Tommy Kendall bolted forward, firing as they went.

Pete Lamburtis shouted at the shack as he fired on Herns's position, "Help them, damn it to hell!"

By the time Lewis Prior and Tommy Kendall had

crossed the clearing through the rise of smoke from Roundhouse Eddie's sizzling body, Max Sheppard, Dean Spence and Eli Drake had joined them. They charged the hillside, pistols and rifles exploding. From the door of the adobe shack came Buddy Raines and Little Bit Collier, both of them firing and screaming as they ran.

Coak's rifle stopped Buddy Raines in his tracks, then swung to Dean Spence and flipped him backward just as he started up the hillside. Even with Lamburtis firing on him, Bob Herns got off two quick shots, one going wild, but the other nailing Little Bit Collier in the back. Coak swung his rifle toward the advancing men and started to squeeze off a shot at Eli Drake. But before Coak got the shot off, he saw the figure rise up and spring forward from fifteen feet—the man he had missed earlier.

Buck Dohoney charged in across the rocky ground, firing his pistol at arm's length, giving Coak little time to take aim and fire. A bullet hit Coak low on his left side, causing him to jerk forward. As he straightened up and went for the shot, he saw the pistol barrel pointed in his face, less than eight feet away now.

From out of the brush came Buster, leaping into Buck Dohoney at such an angle that when the pistol fired, the shot caught the dog in midair as he sailed into Dohoney's face.

Coak had no time to see the outcome of the struggle between man and dog. The other men were moving up on him, shots kicking up dirt and chunks of rocks in his face as he flattened to the ground and fired round after round, hearing the steady explosion of Herns's rifle from across the clearing. This time when Coak's rifle was empty, he had no time to reload. Instead, he snatched the pistol from his waist and went to work with it, seeing men fall with each shot.

Through the cacophony of gunfire, Coak heard Buster let out a sharp yelp and swung toward him, seeing the knife in the dog's side as Buster staggered back and forth. The last shot from Coak's pistol slammed into Buck Dohoney's chest as Dohoney rose up and reached out with a bloody hand toward Buster's throat. Buster tried to move away, but his wounds were too severe. Buster sank beneath Buck Dohoney's dead weight at the same time as Jake Coak slumped forward on the ground. "Good boy . . ." Coak managed to whisper before the blackness closed in around him.

On Jake Coak's side of the hill the firing had stopped, but Bob Herns still had his hands full. He moved down fast, stumbling over rocks to get across the clearing toward where most of the men had charged Coak's position. Something had gone wrong; he knew it. In the black grisly smoke from the body on the campfire, Herns saw Pete Lamburtis stagger back and forth in front of him, Lamburtis's pistol up and firing.

The bullet grazed Herns's shoulder, but he pressed forward, his rifle empty and lying in the dirt behind him now. His pistol bucked in his hand and Lamburtis sank to his knees. But before Herns could go a step farther, Max Sheppard stood to his right in the terrible smoke, his pistol firing steadily, puffs of orange flame blossoming like flowers from some distant hateful netherworld.

As Bob Herns felt his legs go out from under him, his pistol responded in his hand. Max Sheppard fell backward in the dirt and rolled limply onto his side.

Herns crawled forward, feeling nothing from his waist down. He choked and coughed in the acrid smoke, seeing Lamburtis rock back and forth on his knees in front of him. "It's . . . not over . . . you son of a . . ." Lamburtis's words trailed down to a gasp, and he slumped down on his haunches and pitched forward on his face. Herns crawled past him, struggling to rid himself of the smell of burning flesh, not wanting to die in the rancid black smoke. "Jake?" he called out in a waning voice, moving forward slower now, an inch at a time, looking up at the bodies strewn along the rocky hillsides. "Jake . . . we got them . . . got them all. . . ."

There was no sound of any living thing in the small clearing, only the crackling and hissing of the fire, until at length, Coak's big dapple-gray stepped down from the hillside and whinnied long and loud toward the spot where both Jake Coak and the dog lay bloody and still on the rocky earth.

J. T. Priest and Rance Macklinberg doubled the rest of the day, Denton Howel and Joe Cherry cautiously staying a few yards back. In front of Howel, Simms rode with a length of rope leading back from his neck to Howel's closed fist. In front of Joe Cherry, Kate McCorkle rode in the same manner, Cherry making it a point to now and then to let the rope draw a bit tight, keeping Kate always aware of its presence. That night, having swung wide of Sonora and headed straight for the border, Howel and Cherry handcuffed Quick Charlie Simm's and Kate McCorkle's wrists together around the rough bare trunk of a cedar tree.

After warming some jerked beef and coffee, Denton Howel put out the fire. Within moments after eating,

Joe Cherry moved off to one side of the camp with a rifle across his lap. In the closing darkness, Simms watched Cherry raise the leather bag from around his neck, take out a pinch of the brown powder and snort it up his nose. By the time darkness had engulfed the small unlit campsite, the voices of the men had fallen quiet and the sound of snoring rose above their blankets.

"Charlie, what do you know about Denton Howel?" Kate asked, whispering to Simms, the two of them leaning close together around the tree trunk.

"At stud poker he was always steady as a rock," Simms whispered in reply. "Never seen him let too much rattle him." Simms seemed to run recollections through his mind, then said, "The only way to beat him was to outlast him. That's how I won his grandfather's watch. I let him win some small pots one after another. Finally had to wait for one big hand, then kick the betting up slowly. He played the odds against me having another king in the hole to go with the two already showing. By the time we got through betting, the pot was up to four thousand and he was short of cash. He couldn't turn loose, so I let him play the pocket watch."

Kate just stared at Simms's face in the moonlight. "I meant, what do you know about the kind of man he is?"

Simms returned her stare. "And that's what I've been trying to tell you. He's hard to beat, but I've beaten him before."

"Yes, at poker, that is," Kate whispered.

"This is no different." Simms shrugged. "But we've got to get a player out of the game. The sides are too even right now—that's dangerous. The way things are now, these boys could blow up and start killing one another. We don't want to be caught between them."

"Who do you say?" Kate asked, letting her eyes move across the sleeping men.

"Oh, Joe Cherry, no question about it," Simms replied.

"I'll have to do it," Kate said, fixing her gaze on the dark outline of Joe Cherry as he sat gazing up at the stars.

"No, Kate, stay out of it!" Simms hissed. "It's too risky."

"But how will you get rid of him?" Kate responded. "They're all watching you like a hawk."

"I don't know, Kate . . . but I'm working on it." Simms looked out across the darkness and fell quiet.

At dawn, they were up and back into their saddles, Priest and Macklinberg still riding double, Howel and Cherry once again holding the ropes in their gloved hands. When they stopped long enough at noon to water their horses at a thin runoff beneath a jagged sloping stand of rocky hillside, Kate saw Joe Cherry take a snort of his brown powder and sink back against his horse for a moment. She shot Simms a sharp glance, then said to Denton Howel, who was obviously now in charge, "I've got to go out behind the bushes."

"Not now you don't," Howel answered gruffly. "You can go the next time we stop. We'll be close to the border tonight."

"No, I can't wait that long," Kate snapped at him. "What's the border got to do with it? I've got to go right now."

"I'll take her," said Rance Macklinberg, "if it'll shut her up."

Quick Charlie Simms stood watching, knowing she was up to something, but unable to stop her.

"Go on then," said Denton Howel, "and hurry up about it." But as Rance Macklinberg grabbed Kate by her handcuffs and pulled her forward toward a stretch of green foliage up one side of the runoff water, Denton Howel seemed to grow suspicious all of a sudden. "On second thought, Mack, maybe you best let Cherry here take her to do her business."

"Me? Why me?" Joe Cherry looked incensed, his eyes lit and glassy. "I got better things to do than watch her pee-pee in the dirt!"

Denton Howel chuckled and shook his head. "Go on, Joe, don't give me any lip about it. That powder's got you acting like your wheels have slipped the track. Whatever you've got left in that bag you best use it up today. Tomorrow you're going on a long dry spell without it."

Simms stood waiting almost breathlessly as Kate and Joe Cherry climbed up the hillside out of sight. "You oughta see your face, Simms," Denton Howel said, laughing quietly. "Don't worry, Joe Cherry won't bother her unless she makes a run for it. His only interest is powder right now."

Simms only nodded and looked away. But he could not stand easy until Kate and Joe Cherry reappeared and started walking back down the hillside. Once they were back on the trail, even with the rope around his neck, Simms managed to let his horse drift close enough to Kate to whisper, "Kate, I see what you're up to . . . don't do it."

"It's the only way, Charlie, and you know it," she replied before a short jerk on the rope caused her to pull her horse away from Simms.

Quick Charlie Simms stared straight ahead, unable to argue with her. Kate was right, and all he could do was prepare himself for what was going to happen.

At the end of the day, when they'd ridden off the rolling flatland and made camp along a narrow creek amid high-reaching rock formations, Kate dipped the coffeepot into the creek with her cuffed hands and then sat the pot over the low flames. "Look at this," she said, staring down in apprehension at the soft sand along the water's edge. "There's unshod hoofprints everywhere."

"We saw them," Howel said matter-of-factly, "they're Apache. But they're a couple of days old and headed the opposite direction. Whatever is left of the men back there, the Apache will most likely finish off." He gave J. T. Priest a dark grim smile. "That's one more thing you can be real sad about."

J. T. Priest didn't answer. All he could do for now was bide his time, look for a way to shift the advantage back to himself. Denton Howel's remarks had grown more and more bold throughout the past two days, the actions of a man who knew he held the trump card. But that was all because of Joe Cherry being with him. Man to man, Priest figured he had a good chance at handling Denton Howel, but there was no way in the world Rance Macklinberg could handle wild-eyed Joe Cherry.

"Well, maybe Apache don't worry *you*, Howel," Kate said, her cuffed hands hanging in front of her, "but I've got to go to the bushes again . . . and I'm afraid."

"Bull! Unless I miss my guess, you've never been afraid of anything, Kate McCorkle." He turned to Joe

Cherry, seeing the streak of brown powder beneath both his nostrils. "Joe, take her out there."

"Huh-uh," said Kate, "he's too crazy. I'll just wait."

"Just wait till when?" said Howel. "We're heading out as soon as we eat and rest these horses. I want to be over the border and away from here by morning. We ain't going to stop just whenever you feel like it."

"I can at least wait until dark," said Kate.

Joe Cherry staggered forward, chuckling, his eyes shiny and dilated. "Why? Anybody knows the Apache can see in the dark just like a cat."

"There, you see?" said Kate to Denton Howel. "He's crazy and doped up and I'm not going out there with him." She hesitated then added indignantly, "Besides . . . he won't keep his hands to himself."

Howel looked at Cherry with a trace of a smile. "Is that true, Joe? Did you offend this poor defenseless lady?"

"She's a damn liar," said Joe Cherry, his hand going to his pistol butt, then stopping, realizing what he was about to do.

"Settle down, Joe," said Denton Howel. "Get yourself some grub, if you can eat. Soon as it turns dark, take her out there behind some mesquite brush. Any Apache shows up, tell 'em I said take her with them." He chuckled and relaxed back against a scrub cottonwood.

Simms managed to get around close to J. T. Priest and whispered near his ear, "What's it worth to you if we get you back on top of this thing? Will that get us cut in for a part of the money?"

Priest stared at him, then whispered, "What's going on, Simms?"

Simms only winked. "Just be ready to take control

when the time comes. You can do that, can't you, for seven hundred thousand dollars?"

"Just watch me," Priest hissed.

Darkness had fallen by the time the warmed jerky and coffee had been consumed, and the fire had been rubbed out on the ground. Joe Cherry had not eaten, but rather sat off to himself finishing the last of the brown cocaine powder. He sniffed and stood up and spun a wild circle. "Whooie! And they say man was never meant to fly!"

"Knock it off, Joe," Howel demanded, "and keep quiet, just in case there are more Apache prowling around."

"I'm ready to go now," Kate said in a quiet tone, standing facing Denton Howel with her cuffed hands folded.

"Figures," Howel said, "now that Joe couldn't take both hands and grab his own ass."

"It's not *his* ass I'm worried about him grabbing," Kate said in a sharp voice. "I told you I'm not going out there with him, not the shape he's in."

Denton Howel bristled. "You don't call the shots here, Kate McCorkle! Either you go with Joe or you cross your legs till we hit the border!" He turned in a huff from Kate McCorkle to Joe Cherry. "Get over here, Joe. Take her out there like I told you to!"

Simms, Priest and Rance Macklinberg watched as Kate and Joe Cherry walked away through the brush to the other side of the shallow creek bed. When the two faded into the dark, Simms said to Denton Howel, just to get his attention and keep him occupied, "So, Howel, do you really intend to share your part of that money with Joe Cherry, the way he's acting? What's he done to deserve any of it?"

Howel grinned, looking at Priest and Macklinberg as he replied to Simms, "All Joe has to do is be here. He might be doped and half crazy, but he's a real devil with a pistol . . . ask Priest here."

"I've seen better," Priest said grudgingly.

"Yeah, I bet," said Howel, "but not lately."

They stood in silence for a few minutes, Denton Howel shooting a wary glance now and then toward the darkness across the thin creek bed. Finally, it was Quick Charlie Simms who broke the silence, saying, "Shouldn't they be back by now?"

"Yeah, they should," said Howel, leaning slightly, staring, listening for any sound on the night air.

In the brush on the other side of the creek, when Kate McCorkle finished wiping her razor on Joe Cherry's shirt sleeve, she closed the razor and put it back up under her arm. She wiped her cuffed hands on a stand of stiff, coarse leaves and walked back toward the creek bed.

"Is that you, Joe?" Denton Howel called out, at the sound of Kate's footsteps across the shallow water and loose stones.

"No, it's me," Kate replied flatly. "Joe's dead."

"He's what? Dead!" Denton Howel's hand snapped around the pistol butt at his waist. He glared at Kate McCorkle, then looked past her into the darkness.

"Yes, I killed him," Kate said. "I tried to tell you he wouldn't keep his hands to himself."

"Joe?" Denton Howel called out across the thin creek. "If he doesn't answer, there'll be a killing here," Howel warned Kate McCorkle.

"If he *does* answer, there'll be a miracle here," Kate responded.

Denton Howel only scowled at her. "Joe, boy? Can you hear me?"

"Forget it, Howel, he's dead," said Quick Charlie Simms.

"I don't believe it. . . . I'm going to check on him!" Howel took a step forward, then stopped cold at the sound of two gun hammers cocking. He turned wide-eyed toward Priest and Macklinberg, seeing the pistols in their hands.

"Go see, if you need to, Howel," Priest said, "only leave the pistol here . . . don't want you stumbling around out there, maybe shooting yourself in the foot."

"Listen to me, Priest!" Denton Howel's hand only tightened on his pistol butt. "Me and Cherry didn't do you this way. We came in and caught you red-handed, running out on everybody! We didn't take your pistol, did we?" As the two faced each other, Kate McCorkle stepped back out of the way.

"No," said Priest, "but some folks are more tolerant than others. Now lift it on your finger and drop it. It's better this way, Denton. How would you have managed it, staying up all night, wondering when one of us was going to come slipping up on you? Go on and drop it. We'll take you up the trail and send you on your way."

"Like hell I'll drop it! You'll only get it if you pry it from my hand!"

"I understand," said Priest. Both his and Macklinberg's pistols exploded at the same time. Denton Howel flew backward and landed flat on his back in a spray of water and sand.

Kate took a step forward and leaned down slightly,

looking down at Denton Howel. "He's dead," she determined.

Priest grinned. "Was there any doubt? Now, step back away from his pistol, Kate. This doesn't change anything between us."

Simms said in quiet tone, "After her getting rid of Cherry? After me warning you, helping you get the drop on Howel? This doesn't mean anything?"

"Not a damn thing, Simms." Priest sneered. "This is about big money. In a dog-eat-dog world, I'm proud to say, I'm the hungriest dog of all."

"Let's all try to remember that from now on," said Simms, stepping back, looking at Rance Macklinberg, seeing the strange look come upon Macklinberg's face at the sound of his words.

"See what he's trying to do, Mack?" Priest said. "He wants to plant a seed of doubt in your mind, make you start thinking I'm out to double-cross you."

"Yeah," said Macklinberg, "the way you've done all the others."

Priest eyed him closely. "Can't you see the difference, Mack? You and I are in this thing together. There's no room for mistrust between us. Don't let this grifter make you think otherwise."

"I won't," said Macklinberg. But when they'd mounted and rode on, Simms noticed Rance Macklinberg managed to ride in a way that kept J. T. Priest in front of him at all times.

Chapter 21

For two days, Bob Herns was not sure if he was dead or alive, although logic dictated that if he truly were dead he wouldn't even be asking himself the question. Or would he? In his drifting state of consciousness, he wasn't sure of anything. Matters of life and death had little meaning. What was more important to him was the passing of time, something he'd had difficulty keeping track of since he'd fallen facedown in the dirt and heard the sound of the crackling fire grow distant and finally disappear. Now he wasn't certain how long ago that had been.

On what he thought must have been the first evening, Herns looked around the campsite as shadows stretched long out of the western sky. As if through a wavering gray veil he'd seen the faces of grim men with long black hair, who wore bandannas tied around their foreheads and spoke to one another in a language unfamiliar to him. The soft fall of horses' hooves moved back and forth in front of him. He heard laughter, low and muted, then once again the strange voices. Only when one of the men stood barefoot in front of him and took him by his hair and lifted his head did

Bob Herns realize that these men were Apache warriors.

The warriors were busy doing something; he didn't know what. All Herns knew was that he'd seen the glint of evening sunlight along the blade of a knife. Then he'd heard the sound of a shirt ripping, and felt something wet and hot settle heavily on his chest. Try though he did to raise a hand to defend himself, or to raise his voice to them, neither his body nor his voice had responded.

He had drifted back to sleep, to the soft fall of the horses' hooves; and the next time he'd awakened, there had been another strange face looming before him. This face wore a thin black mustache, and although the words still sounded strange to him, with much concentration he began to make them out, his mind translating them from Spanish. *"Americano, sí?"* the voice had asked.

"Sí, Americano," Herns had whispered, noting the gold braided epaulets on the man's shoulder. But then he had drifted again, for how long he did not know. It might have been for an hour; it might have been for a day. But the next time he opened his eyes, the same face was still there, as if it had never left.

"Habla Espanol?" the voice asked.

"Solo un pequeno," Herns replied, shaking his head slowly, his voice sounding weak to himself.

"Only a little?" said the voice. "Then I will speak to you in English. Who has done this to you? Who has attended to your wounds and kept you alive?" A hand patted Herns's chest.

Herns focused on the face for a second, seeing it more clearly. Then he looked down at the dried and flaking mud on his chest and tried to recall how it had gotten there. Nothing came to him, and once again he shook his head slowly.

"I will tell you who did this," said the voice. "Victorio's warriors, that is who."

"But . . . why?" Herns felt puzzled, his mind not yet working as well as it should.

"That is what we would like to know," the voice said.

"I can't tell you," said Herns. Looking past the man's face, Herns saw other men standing over him. They wore dusty black boots and *federale* uniforms. "There was another man with me . . . is he dead?"

"Dead? That one? Ha!" The *federale* captain stood up, backed a step and dusted his knees. "That one is even more lucky than you. And believe me . . . you are both very lucky! Victorio does not do this sort of thing for anyone! He is one savage Apache, that Victorio."

"Where— where is my friend?" Herns asked, trying to look around, past the dusty boots, toward the spot where he knew Coak had been during the gun battle.

"Oh, your *amigo*? *Sí*, he, too, is alive. So is the young *abogado,* the attorney."

"Good . . . thank God," Herns said in a whisper. "My *amigo,* can I see him?"

"He is still unconscious. He cannot hear you. He has lost very much blood. Do you wish to speak to the attorney? We will bring him to you."

Herns shook his head. "No . . . that can wait."

"Good, because he is very much frightened and makes little sense." The captain gestured a gloved hand toward the broad dark stain on the dirt surrounding Herns. "You rest now, we are taking you to Sonora. But when you have regained your strength, there is much for you to explain. Your *amigo* carries a

United States Federal Marshal's badge in his pocket. Is it so, he is a lawman?"

"*Sí*," said Herns. "He rides for Judge Charles Isaac Parker, out of Fort Smith. We fought *Los Pistoleros* here . . . and killed them all."

"*Los Pistoleros?*" The captain shot a glance at the bodies scattered across the clearing and hillside. "Just the two of you? You killed that whole gang of *desperados*?"

"*Sí*," said Herns. "We killed them all."

"There is reward money for some of those men," said the captain.

"Yes . . . me and my friend will be claiming it," Herns said.

"I do not think so." The captain looked perplexed. "I do not care that he rides for the hanging judge. He has no business coming here. We are the law in *Mejico*. If there is money coming, my government will claim it." He thumbed his chest. "But enough for now, we will talk later. You must rest and regain your strength."

Herns was too weak to argue about the reward money. Somehow the money didn't matter all that much anymore. "I understand, Captain . . . *gracias*," he said; and with that he lowered his eyes and drifted back to sleep.

Quick Charlie had noticed that ever since they'd stopped and had coffee before crossing the border and heading across Texas, Rance Macklinberg had turned jumpier than a squirrel. He'd even taken to carrying his pistol across his lap. From the look Simms had been noticing in J. T. Priest's eyes, Macklinberg's fears were well-founded. Both men were ready to throw down on one another at the slightest provocation. Simms liked that. He knew it bettered his and Kate's chances at staying alive. Although, as things now stood, Simms was less and less worried about his and Kate's safety. So long as Sullivan Hart and Twojack Roth showed up before J. T. Priest saw that the big safe had not been opened, but rather was still stuck down in the earth as he'd left it, Simms and Kate would be all right. All that bothered Simms now was the fact that he'd seen no sign of Hart and Roth. They should have been somewhere on the trail where he'd left them . . . but they weren't. He began looking around with growing concern.

Moving the tired horse along at a walk, Simms's thoughts were interrupted by J. T. Priest saying to Rance Macklinberg, "Mack, we'll be at the Burdine spread in another hour or so. It might be wise for you to stay back and keep an eye on our trail, make sure nobody else comes upon us unexpected."

At J. T. Priest's words, Rance Macklinberg stopped his horse in its tracks and stared hard at Priest, his hand resting on the pistol in his lap. "So, this is how you plan on doing it? You just leave me behind, pick up the money and cut out, eh?"

Before Priest could answer, Simms saw a chance to cut in and widen the distrust between them, and he took it. "No, Macklinberg, there's more to it than that," Simms said, talking in a hurry, needing to make every word count. "He'll make sure he kills Kate and me before he leaves the Burdine spread—just to make sure there's no one who can put you on his trail afterwards."

"Shut up, Simms!" Priest demanded. Throughout the day, Simms had been exceptionally quiet. Now, hearing the sudden outburst from him, J. T. Priest sat staring at him, stunned.

"Let him talk, Priest!" said Rance Macklinberg. "What's the matter? Can't you stand to know people are onto you? Sounds like he knows you pretty well." As Macklinberg spoke, his voice grew stronger and more enraged—all that suspicion and fear boiling beneath the surface, ready to blow, his words helping it along.

"Mack, get a grip on yourself!" Priest shouted. "What the hell's wrong with you? Me and you are partners . . . I'll see to it you get everything coming to you."

"Sure you will! The same as you've done every other poor son of a bitch who's ever sided with you? I'm wise to you, Mister J. T. *Tuck* Priest!" Macklinberg was trembling, his eyes wide and shiny, not much different than Joe Cherry's had been on the cocaine powder.

"Jesus, Mack!" Priest looked completely bewildered by Macklinberg's sudden change.

"Don't call me Mack, you sneaking bastard! I'm seeing you for what you are!" His hand closed around the pistol on his lap. "You're not going to do me in! Not without a fight!"

J. T. Priest flung himself from his saddle, seeing the cocked pistol come up from across Macklinberg's lap. As Macklinberg's pistol fired repeatedly, one shot grazing the knee of J. T. Priest's horse, Priest rolled across the ground, snatching up both pistols from his waist and firing as he rolled.

Simms jerked his horse back out of the way and jumped to the ground, pulling Kate McCorkle down with him. As shots exploded back and forth, Macklinberg came down from his saddle as well, a streak of blood across his shoulder, his hat spinning away from his head, his forehead bearing a bloody bullet crease.

With their faces against the hot sandy ground, Simms and Kate stared back and forth as the duel raged. Fighting at close range, both Priest and Macklinberg were as busy dodging bullets as they were at firing at one another. Bullets sliced the air like angry wasps. Then, in what seemed no longer than the breadth of a second, the fight was over. A total of fourteen shots had been spent before a bullet from one of J. T. Priest's pistols slammed solidly into Rance Macklinberg's chest. Macklinberg fell backward, but struggled up onto his knees, his pistol dangling loose on his trigger finger.

"Drop it, Mack!" Priest shouted, coming forward two steps, the pistol in his right hand out at arm's length.

"You . . . dirty . . . rotten—" As Macklinberg's strained words squeezed past his bloody lips, with all his waning strength he tried to raise the pistol.

One final fatal shot from J. T. Priest's pistol resounded across the empty Texas flatland, and Rance Macklinberg's head snapped backward, the force of it jerking the rest of his body to the ground. "Lord God almighty!" Priest said, stepping forward, looking down at Macklinberg's limp form in the dirt. "What got into him?"

"I don't know," Simms whispered as if in awe, getting to his feet, helping Kate up beside him.

Hearing Simms, J. T. Priest swung the pistol toward him, blood running down his wounded forearm, his hand, and dripping from the pistol butt. "Don't act innocent, you damned grifter! You caused this! I saw how you kept egging him on! For two cents I'd—"

"For two cents you'd kill him?" Kate stepped

quickly in front of Simms, cutting Priest off. "But for seven hundred thousand dollars, you *won't*!"

"Keep pushing, Simms, see if I don't reach a point I'll say to hell with the money." Priest gritted his teeth, checking himself down.

Simms pulled Kate from in front of himself, saying, "Come on, Priest! I didn't cause that! Sure I was playing the two of you against one another a little . . . but my God! He lost his mind!" Simms gestured toward Rance Macklinberg on the ground. "You can't blame me."

Priest stared cold and hard, then took a breath as if to keep from boiling over. "If there was any chance of me cutting you two in for part of that money, you just blew it, Simms."

"Yeah?" Simms responded. "Don't make threats now, J. T., there's just you here . . . no gang of outlaws to put between you and—"

"Shut up, both of you!" Kate McCorkle demanded. She shoved Simms back a step, then turned to J. T. Priest. "Look, you're bleeding all over. Sit down. I'll get a canteen and tear some rags for bandages. We'll get you patched up."

But Priest raised the pistol toward her. "You keep back from me, Kate. You made it clear where you stand. Bring a canteen and some bandages and pitch them over to me . . . but come any nearer and I'll kill you." He turned to Simms. "Bring that horse over here and toss me the reins. Don't neither of you get any ideas about making a run for it."

"Easy, J. T.," said Kate, backing toward a canteen hanging from a saddle horn, "I was only offering to help."

"Help?" Priest let a short insane chuckle. "You can

help by keeping your treacherous mouth shut." He looked at the blood on his wounded arm, shook his head and murmured to himself, "I've never been able to trust one damn living soul . . . bunch of back-stabbing, dirty-dealing trash is all I've ever met, my whole damned miserable life. . . ."

After pitching him a canteen and a couple of dusty bandannas—one of which she'd loosened from Rance Macklinberg's neck—Kate sat down on her haunches beside Simms in the dirt and watched Priest tend to his wounds from fifteen feet away. Priest murmured and growled and cursed to himself as he tore the bandannas with his teeth and fashioned a crude bandage for his upper arm, his shoulder and his forearm. All the while, he kept the reins to both Macklinberg's horse and the one Simms and Kate had been riding clamped to the ground beneath his boot. The wounded horse Priest had been riding walked in a wide circle, limping from the bullet graze on its leg.

"Priest," Simms called over to him, "let me drop that saddle and set that horse loose. He'll be all right in a couple of days. Let him hook up with some wild horses out here somewhere."

"To hell with him," said Priest.

"I'm going to do it anyway," Simms said with finality, rising slowly to his feet. "If you kill me for that, you don't deserve the money."

Priest raised the pistol toward Simms, watching him as he sidestepped over to the horse, then slowly turned and dropped the saddle from its back and the bit from its mouth. He slapped the wounded horse and watched it limp away at a stiff trot. "There now," Simms said, walking back to Kate McCorkle, "that didn't hurt you a bit, J. T."

"Damn a bunch of lame horses," Priest growled, turning his attention back to his wounds.

Kate whispered to Simms, "I hoped he'd let me close enough to him to do us some good." Her eyes flickered down toward the razor under her arm.

"No, Kate, we've gotten this far," Simms replied, "let's play it on out."

"But why?" She looked puzzled.

"Because I made Sullivan Hart a promise," Simms whispered. "I aim to keep it. I didn't intend for things to get so out of hand with Macklinberg a while ago," he added. "I just wanted to keep both of them on edge."

Kate stared at him for a moment, then said in a hushed voice, "I hate to break this to you . . . but it wasn't your antagonizing that caused Rance Macklinberg to go nuts on us."

"Sure it was, Kate, you saw how nervous and jumpy he was getting all day."

"Yeah, I saw," Kate agreed. "But it was because I took the leather bag from around Joe Cherry's neck when I killed him and then dumped it into Macklinberg's coffee cup."

Simms gave her a curious look. "You did that?"

"You're damn right I did," Kate hissed. "I don't know what kind of promise you made Sullivan Hart, but I made some promises of my own . . . to *myself*. Nobody drags me out into this furnace against my will, handcuffs me, makes me have to kill some poor dope-eating flunky like Joe Cherry." She raised her cuffed hands for emphasis. "The next time I get within cutting distance of J. T. Priest, he's mine, all mine."

Chapter 22

Twojack Roth lowered the telescope from his eye and handed it back to Sullivan Hart. "I say we ride down there right now and finish this thing," said Roth. "You know Simms must be worried, wondering why we haven't showed up already." A few feet to Roth's left, the prisoner, Leonard Hergo, sat on his horse with his hands cuffed, his head bowed beneath his hat brim.

"I know," said Hart, collapsing the telescope between his gloved hands, "but I want to see J. T. Priest standing beside that safe when he looks me in the eye. I only wish the door was open, with a ton of money falling out of it, when I step up to him and put him out of business."

Twojack Roth looked him up and down, then said, "For your father's sake?"

Sullivan Hart sat quiet for a moment, then let out a breath. "No, it's not for my father's sake anymore. It started out to be. But it's not anymore. After seeing the way J. T. Priest has done, the way he's spit in the law's face, broken every rule of decency, then managed to waltz away from justice, laughing about it—my father's death has nothing to do with it anymore. I'd kill Priest now, even if my father were still alive."

"I understand." Twojack Roth nodded and turned in his saddle and looked all around. "Think Simms has gotten this far and managed to never fire a shot the way he said he would?"

Sullivan Hart looked around with him. Their eyes went back toward the border through the wavering heat. "I wouldn't be surprised. Simms does have his ways."

Leonard Hergo spoke up from beneath his hat brim, barely lifting his face. "One thing's for certain, he hasn't been hard to track. All you had to do was watch for the buzzards and follow the bodies."

The deputies shared a thin, grim smile. "Come on," Roth said, stepping his horse to the left, reaching out with his hand and slapping Hergo's horse on the rump. "Let's make sure we're there waiting when they arrive." They both turned their horses toward the Burdine spread and gave them heel, swinging wide around a low butte and along a wide shallow creek bed to keep their dust down.

When they rode onto the Burdine spread, they kept to the far side of the front yard and rode along the fence to keep from leaving fresh hoofprints on the path to the empty house. At one point, the fence had been broken and pulled to one side; and where once cattle had grazed in the sparse pale grass along the endless stretch of flatland, now only the bodies of a few suckling calves lay dead where rustlers had shot them before driving the cattle out and off into the night.

"Cattle thieves wasted no time, did they?" Roth commented, looking out across the barren land.

"A good cattle thief can't *afford* to waste time,"

Leonard Hergo commented, raising his hat brim on his brow. "It's the kind of business where every minute counts. You have to get them beeves somewhere and get them cross-branded . . . then you got to get them somewhere to where nobody recog—" His words stopped short as he looked around and saw the way the two deputies sat staring at him.

He cleared his throat and said quickly, "Not that *I* ever stole any cattle *myself*, you understand. But I've heard lots of things along the way."

"Sure you have," said Hart as all three nudged their horses farther along the fence line.

"Well, it's the truth, I never stole any cattle," Leonard grumbled, once again lowering his hat brim.

"Of course not," said Roth. "Same as you had nothing to do with robbing that stage and killing the driver."

"Boy, if there was a Bible here, I'd slap my hand to it. I didn't hook up with Priest's bunch till *after* they robbed that stagecoach. Fact is I've been a law-abiding man my whole damned life." They rode on in silence until they passed the blown-up house and headed back along a narrow path toward a thin stand of cottonwood and mesquite brush. "I'll just be honest with yas," said Leonard Hergo, grudgingly. "I did do what you might call some *minor* thieving, back after the war . . . but only because there was no work to be had."

"Well, you'll be plenty busy for the next few years," said Sullivan Hart, "provided the judge doesn't hang you."

"Hang me, hell! I told you I never had nothing to do with it. Even if I did—which I didn't—where's there any proof?"

"There's a couple of cowboys who can identify anybody who was there," said Roth.

Leonard Hergo looked relieved. "I'm glad to hear that, because if they can say who was there, they can damn sure tell yas I wasn't. So, that'll just about save my bacon." He grinned. "I'll be free to pursue my career."

"Oh, what career is that?" Hart asked, the three of them stopping their horses and swinging down from their saddles.

"Promise not to laugh?" Hergo asked.

"We'll do our best," said Roth.

"I've been lately feeling drawn to law work, the same as you two boys. I just haven't found a way to get my foot in the door."

Sullivan Hart led his horse into the cover of brush and spun his reins around a short dry sapling. "Maybe you need to talk to the judge," he said wryly. "Parker's always looking for good men . . . even overlooks a few blemishes on a man's criminal record so long as it's not too bad."

"Is that a fact?" Hergo seemed interested.

"Yeah, but killing a stagecoach driver is a hard one to overlook," said Roth, lifting his pistol from its holster, checking it, then putting it away.

"But if I'm not charged? Or say if I'm found innocent? What do you suppose my chances would be?"

"Put it out of your mind, Hergo," said Hart. "Sit down and keep quiet until we get this thing finished."

"You're not really going to kill ole J. T. Priest in cold blood, are you?" Hergo asked. "Not that he ain't got it coming, you understand. But I can't rightly see how you can call yourselves lawmen, doing something like that. Somebody like me shooting him, I can understand . . . but not if I was wearing a badge, no-sir."

Sullivan Hart and Twojack Roth only looked at one another. Then Hart had to turn his face away and gaze out across the land. "Did you hear me tell you to keep quiet, Hergo?" he said.

While the deputies and their prisoner waited in the cover of brush behind the blown-out hull of a house, on the road out front J. T. Priest rode a few feet behind Simms and Kate McCorkle, keeping a wary eye on both sides of the narrow entrance trail leading up into the Burdine spread. "Hold it right there," he said, lifting one of the pistols from his lap.

As Simms drew the horse to a halt, he turned to face Priest, saying, "What's wrong, J. T.? We're here now. Let's go spin that baby and get it over with."

"Something feels wrong here, Simms. I feel like I'm walking into a trap."

"Oh? Well, that's the chance you have to take, J. T." Simms gave him a flat smile. "There could be law waiting anywhere up ahead. You'd rather stop here and forget all about it? Where's your sporting blood?"

Priest's eyes turned hard and determined. "Go on, Simms. Just remember I've got you in my gunsights. Anything goes wrong, you and Kate are the first to fall. I don't care if there's somebody waiting. There's already blood on that money, and a little more won't hurt a thing."

"Don't worry, J. T." Simms turned the horse and nudged it forward on the path toward the house. "Your biggest enemies here are the ghosts of all the men you killed." Simms nodded toward a scrap of cloth fluttering in the hot breeze, a sliver of bone shining through it in the blazing sunlight. They rode on slowly, Simms stepping his horse wide of the sun-dried remnants of hide and bone, of boot wells chewed through by coyotes, and of vertebrae picked clean by buzzards and ants. A sand lizard turned at their passing and crawled away from a white bone fist still clutching a pistol.

When they had passed the charred hull of the house and rode on toward the pile of brush Simms had used to cover the large safe, J. T. Priest moved his horse up beside Simms, with his pistol cocked and pointed at him. A few feet from the safe, Priest couldn't hold himself back any longer. He dropped down from his horse, letting the reins fall to the ground, and ran forward, shoving his pistol down in his waist, paying no regard to Simms and Kate for the moment.

"Come to *Daddy*!" Priest shouted, spreading his arms wide toward the pile of brush covering the glistening black steel. He began throwing brush aside, his breath rushing in his excitement. He shouted over his shoulder, "Come on, Simms! Get it spun! Let the big door open!"

"The poor fool," Kate McCorkle whispered to Simms, the two of them down from the horse now, watching J. T. Priest flap his arms and rave like a madman. "We could have rode away and left him standing there. He wouldn't have noticed."

"But they would have," Simms replied, letting out a breath of relief at the sight of Roth and Hart stepping out of the brush, ten feet to Priest's right.

Priest didn't even see the lawmen. He turned and looked at Simms, a wide grin on his face. "Come on, Simms! Get moving! Let's get this done and get out of here!"

"Don't you see anything wrong, J. T.?" Simms asked in a calm voice.

Priest looked puzzled, still not noticing Hart and Roth stepping closer, Roth moving away from Hart a few feet, giving him room.

"Wrong? What?" Priest looked at Simms, then at Kate, then back to the safe, kicking the last piece of brush away from the door. He froze for a second, staring at the safe. His shoulders began to shake.

"Now he sees it," Simms said sidelong to Kate McCorkle. To Priest's right, Sullivan Hart stopped and spread his feet a shoulder width apart, pulling his riding duster back behind his holster.

"Simms! You lying snake!" Priest bellowed, still staring at the safe. "You didn't open it before! It's still upside down . . . still stuck in the dirt!"

"I didn't open it because it won't open, you idiot," said Simms. "Don't you know what that safe is?"

Priest just stared, a string of saliva seeping down his lower lip.

"It's a dummy," said Simms. "The railroad had it built as a decoy! It's nothing but slabs of steel forged together. That's why the big government dynamite couldn't blow it! The dial is just for appearance! Burdine and Sergio never saw the inside of that safe . . . neither has anybody else."

Priest let out a shriek, his hand going to one of the pistols at his waist. "I'll kill you—"

His words stopped, as did his gunhand, at the sight of Sullivan Hart standing ten feet away, facing him.

"You've got the right idea, J. T. Priest," Hart said, nodding at Priest's hand on the pistol butt. "Now follow through."

Priest stood stone-still, seeing Hart's gunhand

poised and ready, seeing how the big Indian, Twojack Roth, had dropped over out of the way. Beside Roth stood Leonard Hergo in handcuffs. Priest clenched his teeth and swallowed a dry knot in his throat.

"Huh-uh, Hart, I'm not drawing on you. . . . Watch now, I'm going to take my hand away from this pistol real slow and easy. I'm giving up. . . . Everybody see that? Hergo? You see it, don't you?"

Leonard Hergo spit and wiped one of his cuffed hands across his mouth. "I ain't seeing nothing today, J. T. You sorry bastard. I just wish they could kill you more than once."

Priest stood still tensely. "It makes no difference," he called out, his eyes moving across Simms, across Kate, and settling back on Sullivan Hart. "I'm not resisting! I'm not drawing."

"Priest," Hart called out to him, "whether you draw or not, I'm going to kill you when I count to three. One!"

"You can't do it, Hart! You're a lawman!" Priest shouted.

"Two!" Hart stood poised, his eyes and expression resolute.

"No ssir! You've got to take me back; let a jury decide me! Hell, I haven't even broken a law—ask Hergo! Me and him wasn't even there when those boys robbed that stage. We only heard about it! Where's any witnesses? Anything I might have done was down in Mexico! You've got nothing on me, Hart, for God's sake!"

"Three!" Hart's hand streaked up, his pistol cocked.

"No!" Priest snatched his hand up away from his pistol and spread his fingers wide.

Hart hesitated, trying hard to force himself to drop

the hammer and put an end to J. T. Priest forever. His gun trembled in his hand, but he couldn't do it, not like this. "Draw, Priest! Damn you, draw!"

"Not today, Hart," said J. T. Priest. "Look at you . . . you thought you could, but, by God, you couldn't. I just beat you again, Hart! The next thing you know I'll be getting out free and clear, and the rest of—"

The first explosion beside Twojack Roth caught him completely by surprise. He'd felt something move at his holster, but as he'd reached a hand down to it, the sound of his pistol roared, and roared again as he spun and jumped away from the streak of fire. Roth flinched at the next shot, then the next, and the next, as Leonard Hergo stepped forward, Roth's pistol bucking in his cuffed hands, J. T. Priest dancing a wild broken dance in the dirt with each fall of the hammer, until the pistol only made a clicking sound.

"Don't shoot!" Hergo called out to Sullivan Hart, seeing Hart's pistol pointed at him. "I'm done, see?" He dropped Roth's pistol as if it were a rattler and spread his cuffed hands in front of his face. J. T. Priest lay dead in the dirt. Leonard Hergo nodded at Priest's body. "Stupid sonsabitch just got on my nerves. I wanted to kill him the last time we was here—acting like he knew so much." Hergo spat toward Priest's body, then stepped back and stood with his head bowed beneath his hat brim.

Simms, Kate McCorkle, Hart and Roth stood stunned into silence.

A hot breeze whipped in and licked at their collars, hat brims and duster tails. After a long pause, Twojack Roth was the first to make a move, reaching down, picking up his empty pistol and turning it back and forth in his hand. "Jesus," he whispered to himself, opening the cylinder and letting the spent shells drop to the ground.

Simms spoke next, looking down at Priest's bullet-riddled body, saying to Sullivan Hart, "I brought him here for you, Hart. . . . You still owe me one."

"I know," Hart said in a quiet voice.

Roth took six cartridges from his belt, reloaded his pistol, and spun it into his holster. He rounded a finger into his ringing ear, turned a harsh gaze to Leonard Hergo and said, "What you just did was murder."

"No it wasn't," said Hergo firmly, his face still lowered. "He went for that pistol—you all just wasn't paying attention."

Roth and Hart looked at each other as Simms and Kate McCorkle stepped in closer. "Did you see him go for the pistol?" Roth asked Sullivan Hart.

Hart didn't answer.

"Well, if none of you saw it," said Hergo, "it's a good thing I did. I saw it in his eyes . . . he was right on the verge."

Sullivan Hart lowered his pistol back into his holster, walked over and looked down at Priest, noting the bullet holes in a tight pattern on his bloody chest. "All I know is, J. T. Priest is dead. . . . Hergo never missed a shot."

"I never meant to miss a shot," Hergo said quietly. He seemed to consider something for a second as the others stood looking at him. Then he suddenly raised his face and pushed up his hat brim. "You all *did* hear him say I had nothing to do with that stagecoach, didn't yas?"

Hart walked from Priest's body. "We heard him say it, Hergo, but J. T. Priest's word wasn't worth much as the law goes."

"It's better than none." Hergo smiled. "Just remember he said it if anybody asks."

"Simms," said Hart, "didn't you tell us before that you didn't know this man?"

"That's right," Simms replied. "I never saw Hergo before in my life."

Hart turned to him. "Yet, you're the man who knows all the outlaws, aren't you?"

"Yes, but Hergo here is a new one on me." Simms shrugged.

"I already told you, I'm no outlaw, not really, although I admit I was coming pretty close, getting to throw in with *Los Pistoleros*. Like I told yas, I ran into hard times after the war, lost my place. My wife left me for a gamecock fighter—"

"Easy, Hergo, keep quiet for a minute," Hart said, raising a hand to shut him up. "We're trying to see if we can do you some good here."

"Yes, sir!" Hergo said, almost snapping to attention. "You go right on ahead, I won't interrupt yas."

As Simms, Hart and Roth drew to one side and huddled in a discussion, Kate McCorkle looked Leonard Hergo up and down. She gave him a skeptical look and said, "A gamecock fighter?"

Hergo shrugged, his cuffed hands folded before him. "So what can I tell you? You know how women are."

That night, when they had ridden a full twenty miles or more from the deserted Burdine spread and made camp alongside a stream reaching down from the north, Kate McCorkle bathed herself and lay soaking for nearly a full hour. She rubbed her chaffed wrists, stretched her arms out and gazed up at the darkening sky until Simms walked to the side of the stream and held a blanket out for her to wrap around herself. Simms smiled, watching her pat herself dry.

"So, what do you think is going on with Jake Coak by now?" she asked.

"Oh, by now him and that Pinkerton man are probably halfway to Fort Smith," said Quick Charlie Simms. "Why? Are you still thinking about him a lot?" He cocked his head. "Should I be jealous?"

She smiled. "A little jealousy would be nice—but no. I was just curious."

"Well, Coak turned out to be no less than I expected," said Simms. "He's no longer the *new* man. After this, he'll be one of us."

"Oh, isn't that big of you?" Kate said, playfully sarcastic. "And what about this Leonard Hergo? Is he going to be the *new* man now?"

Simms chuckled. "If Hart can help him out with Parker, yes, I believe he just might. It wouldn't be the first time Parker hired somebody with a checkered past. Look at me!"

"Yes, but Hergo?" Kate said. "He's lying faster than a cat can scratch its behind. If you ask me, he probably *was* in on the stage robbery. He might not have done anything, but he was there."

"But it wasn't actually a robbery," said Simms. "As far as him being there, we'll never know about that one. But then, we'll never know for sure if Priest was really going for his pistol or not. If he was, Hergo might have saved somebody's life."

"You know J. T. Priest wasn't going for his pistol, Charlie, and so do I."

"All I know is Parker always needs good lawmen. Maybe sometime you run into a man like Hergo, catch him before he turns to a full-blown life of crime, maybe it turns out good for everybody concerned." Simms shrugged and put his arms around her, dismissing it. "Did you enjoy your bath?"

"Yes, thank you." She nestled her face against his chest and asked in a gentle tone, "Charlie, why'd you make such a promise to Hart—telling him you'd bring J. T. Priest to him?"

Simms held her close, and looked off into the sky. He thought about it for a moment. "Well, I knew it would take some time to come find you"—he smiled to himself—"and I needed *something* to occupy my mind."

"Charlie, Charlie," said Kate, also smiling, "what am I going to do with you?"

They stood in silence beneath the wide starlit sky.

Epilogue

Another week would pass before Quick Charlie Simms, Kate McCorkle, Twojack Roth and Sullivan Hart had settled back into day-to-day life in Fort Smith, Arkansas. Upon returning, Hart, Roth and Simms had told Judge Parker all that had happened before sitting down to file their official report on it. When the three had finished, Parker only looked back and forth, studying each man's eyes in turn. He could tell things might not have happened exactly the way they said, but he was satisfied with their story.

It wasn't quite clear to Judge Parker how the deputies had come upon the new man, Leonard Hergo, or how in the mix of things Hergo had shot J. T. Priest—*six times!*—when Priest almost managed to get the drop on all three deputies. *All three . . .* ? That was hard to swallow, he thought.

"The main thing is, we're through with Priest and *Los Pistoleros* once and for all," said Parker, lessening the intensity of his gaze and sitting back in his chair. "Am I safe in saying so?"

The three deputies looked at one another as if deciding who should answer. Finally it was Simms who said, "Yes, Your Honor. We feel confident that once Jake Coak returns, *Los Pistoleros* will have been put out of business."

"*If* he returns," Parker put in. "I can't imagine what's kept him so long. You don't suppose he's . . . ?" Parker's words trailed off.

"No, sir, Your Honor," said Simms, "I'm confident he and the Pinkerton man are both just fine. . . . Probably coming back the long way, talking over old times."

"Yes, hopefully that's all it is," said Parker. "What are the odds of him running into a former student of his out there?"

"That's remarkable, all right." Simms nodded.

"Well, Coak has some good news awaiting him here," said Judge Parker. "Deputy Slater has informed me that there are rewards totaling six thousand dollars on four of the men he brought in before leaving town. That should make him a little happier about what a U.S. Deputy Marshal can make."

"Yes, sir, Your Honor," said Simms, "I'm certain it will."

"Well, gentlemen, if there's nothing further to discuss, I'll look forward to your written reports." As the three stood up to leave with their hats in their hands, Parker stood up with them and said, "Good work, men."

But five days passed and still there was not a sign of Jake Coak, nor had there been any word from him. Out front of the Red Bull Saloon, Simms stood chewing on a toothpick, watching Hart, Roth and Hergo walk toward him from the telegraph office. Since their return, Leonard Hergo had taken on a change of new clothes, complete with a pair of shiny black boots, a shave and a close-cropped haircut. He wore a battered tin star the judge had pinned on him the day before. As they drew near, Simms took the toothpick from between his teeth. "Still nothing?" he asked. Behind him stood Kate McCorkle in her new green satin dress and white lace gloves, a fashionable parasol propped over her shoulder.

Kate McCorkle looked concerned when Sullivan Hart shook his head in reply. "Not a word," said Hart. "You don't think he'd just up and quit, do you?"

"Naw," said Simms, "not without first collecting what's due to him. You heard the judge—six thousand dollars. Nobody turns down that kind of money . . . especially an ole bounty hunter like Coak."

"Yeah, you're right," said Roth. "He'll be back . . . after all, he's one of us now." But standing there, the four deputies all looked out across the western sky as if the answer to Jake Coak's whereabouts lay somewhere in the soft distant clouds above Mexico.

"I wouldn't be too sure," Kate McCorkle whispered to herself, twirling the parasol back and forth slowly. *Take care of yourself, Jake. . . .* She joined the deputies in their search of the wide blue heavens.

Jake Coak and Bob Herns sat stop their horses and watched R. Martin Swan ride down from the ridge and soon disappear along the winding trail toward the border. "That was quite a story he told, wasn't it?" said Herns. "About Priest giving him a gun with one bullet in it—said, invest it wisely."

"Yep, quite a story." Jake Coak's off-center gaze lingered on the low swirling dust standing in Swan's wake. "But Swan wasn't as scared or as pliable as Priest thought he was. Told me he'd made up his mind, once he got that powder out of his system, he was going to sober up and put that one bullet through J. T. Priest's head. Said that would be the best investment he could think of." Coak smiled wryly.

"Think he would have?" asked Bob Herns.

"We'll never know. . . . Neither will he, fortunately." Coak took a long deep breath and let it out slowly. "All I know is, Swan'll sure have something to tell his grandkids someday." He backed his big dapple-gray a step and turned it, saying, "Of course, he won't tell all of it, not the way it actually happened." Coak considered it for another second, then said, "Naw . . . come to think of it, he'll never mention it at all."

"That's what I figure." Bob Herns turned his horse in beside Coak and together they nudged the animals into a slow walk. They rode a few yards, then Herns said, "Are you sure about this, Jake?"

"I said I was, didn't I?" Jake Coak stared straight ahead. "Are *you* sure about it, Bob?"

"I can't say I was ever crazy about the cattle business, but yep, we can give it a try. I wouldn't quit Allen Pinkerton in the midst of a job . . . but now that it's over, I'm ready to go on to something else. I'd feel better if we had a little more start-up money. I can't believe the *federales* are going to send somebody over to claim the bounties."

"It's their country; they can do what they want to," said Coak.

"I've got no pay coming from Pinkerton's," said Herns. "Do you have anything coming from Parker?"

"I've got half a month's pay waiting in Fort Smith, but it's hardly worth the trip there. Don't worry though, we'll make out. Besides, I don't feel like facing Simms and the others. Nothing against them, but they're not my kind of folks, and law work ain't my kind of business. Don't know what it is about me, but ever since I left teaching school, seems like I do something for a while, then soon tire of it. Sounds crazy, I guess."

"Not to me it doesn't . . . I'm the same way," said Herns. They rode forward in the warm Mexican wind. "Cattle, huh? Think there's any real money in it?"

Coak replied, "I met an ole boy last year who came out from Kentucky after the war—said he'd lost money at everything he'd ever done, but he lost *less* money droving cattle than anything else."

"That must be the right business then." Herns grinned. They rode on, and at the turn in the trail, Herns asked, "It's not the woman, is it, the reason you don't want to go to Fort Smith and pick up your pay?"

A silence passed, then Coak stopped his horse, turned in his saddle and said down to the dog limping along behind them, "Get up here, Buster. Looks like you could use a ride." The dog came forward stiffly, a thick bandage wrapped around its ribs. On the dog's third attempt at bounding upward, Coak caught him by the nape of his neck and pulled him up across this lap. "You better take it easy, boy. The pace you live at, I worry about you sometimes." The dog lay across Coak's lap, looking up at him, cocking his head sideways as if trying to understand.

"Well, is it?" Herns asked again.

"What?" said Coak.

"The woman . . . is she the reason you don't want to go to Fort Smith?"

Coak nudged his dapple-gray forward, one hand on the dog's head, rubbing it with his gloved hand. He gazed east across the sky and smiled to himself. "What woman?" he said.

They followed the trail until it turned north up into the low foothills, then followed it north through the hills until the sun lay coppery red at about shoulder level.